I0668663

Freedom Lost.

By Richard Neave.

Published by New Generation Publishing in 2014

Copyright © Richard Neave 2014

First Edition

The author asserts the moral right under the Copyright,
Designs and Patents Act 1988 to be identified as the author
of this work.

All characters and events in the story "Freedom Lost" are
fictitious, and any resemblance to real persons living or dead
is purely coincidental.

All Rights reserved. No part of this publication may be
reproduced, stored in a retrieval system or transmitted, in any
form or by any means without the prior consent of the author,
nor be otherwise circulated in any form of binding or cover
other than that which it is published and without a similar
condition being imposed on the subsequent purchaser.

www.newgeneration-publishing.com

 **New Generation Publishing**

Chapter 1.

In the spring of 2008 during the Easter school holidays Edward Crowther thirty-eight, his wife Elizabeth thirty six both of whom were teachers, and their only daughter Susan aged thirteen from Norwich, Norfolk decided to spend a day out visiting Thetford Forest, which is the largest lowland pine forest in Britain and is located in south Norfolk and north Suffolk. They planned to take a walk through parts of the forest and visit the leisure centre as well as have a picnic in one of the many picnic areas. It was a sunny, mild day, and they set off looking forward to having an enjoyable day out.

When they arrived, they found that there were many people who had also decided to spend the day there, and the car parks were filling up fast. They managed to squeeze into a space between a small green van and camper van. They got out and carrying their picnic bags they set off to explore.

After walking along one of the many tracks through the trees and collecting a number of pine cones, they went in search of a place to picnic and having found one they sat down at one of the tables provided and took out their plates glasses and cutlery along with the foods that Elizabeth Crowther had prepared. It was then that they discovered that they had left the jar of salad dressing they needed in the car. Susan volunteered to go back to the car and fetch it. Her father gave her the keys to the car and off she went.

When Susan reached the car, she unlocked the boot and looked inside but could not see the jar, so she locked the boot then opened one of the rear doors of the car and reached in looking under the seats. When suddenly she was pushed down onto the rear seat of the car a hand grabbed her round her mouth, at the same time she felt a sharp jab in her left arm. She desperately began to struggle trying to break free of the weight that was holding her down but within seconds she became unconscious.

Her attacker, a tall, thickset man, lifted her up and carried her in through the side door of the camper van that was parked right next to the door she had opened. He then tied her hands and ankles tight with some bailing twine, before tying a cloth gag around her mouth to stop her calling out should she become conscious.

Once he had finished he drew the curtains on the windows of the camper van, stepped out, closed and locked the door. Then locked up the Crowther car and threw the keys to the car that Susan had had in her hand under the car.

He walked round to the front of the camper van looking around him as he did so to ensure no one had seen his actions. Satisfied no one had seen him he got in behind the wheel of the campers van started it up and backed out and drove off out of the car park on to the main road where he put his foot down and headed back to where he had come from.

After twenty minutes of waiting for, Susan to return with the jar of salad cream her father went to see why she had not returned.

On arriving back at the car and finding no sign of Susan, he searched the immediate area surrounding the car park to see if perhaps she had gone to the toilet or to the nearby leisure centre. Finding no sign of her, he returned to the picnic area only to discover that she had not returned in his absence. Worried he informed his wife that he had not seen any signs of Susan.

They hastily packed up the picnic things and returned to the car park, but there was still no sign of Susan, so they went to the leisure centre and looked around and having not found Susan went to see the manager to report that she was missing. The manager having asked a lot of questions as to whether it was possible that she might have wandered off somewhere else in the vicinity and having got negative answers said he would phone the police which he did.

When a police patrol car arrived some twenty minutes later, Edward and Elizabeth Crowther, who were becoming frantic with worry explained to the two police officers what they had done since arriving in the car park. One of the officers wrote down in his notebook everything that they told him. He then asked them if they had a recent photo of Susan with them, but as they hadn't he asked them to give him a description of what she looked like, her age and what she was wearing.

Once they had finished the two policemen along with Edward and Elizabeth went back to the car and looked all-round the car. One of the policemen looked under the car and spotted the car keys which he retrieved and handed to Edward Crowther saying that he needed to inform his boss at the police station.

This resulted in a police search of the area surrounding the car park as well as the woods and tracks within a given distance that it would have been possible for Susan to have reached within the time she went missing.

As there was still no signs of her and having talked to visitors to the car park and leisure centre as well as people who had been at the picnic area a nationwide search was launched through the media which failed to bring any positive results.

One year later during the October in the Knole Forrest, in seven oaks, Kent, Samantha Brooks aged thirteen who lived with her parents close to the forest was walking her dog along the side of the woods after school one evening when a man driving a camper van pulled up beside her and got out with a map saying he was lost and could she show him on his map whereabouts he was. He passed her the map which she took, and as she looked at the map he stood behind her looking over her shoulder at the map. Suddenly he grabbed her round her mouth and with his free hand he hit her on the side of her neck sending her unconscious. She dropped the map at the same time letting go of her dogs lead and sank into the man's arms.

The man then opened the side door of the camper van and carried her inside where he laid her down on one of the long seats took out some twine from one of his pockets and proceeded to tie her wrists together then her ankles. He then tied a gag around her mouth before reaching into a wall cabinet above the seat and took out a loaded syringe and injected her in one of her arms.

Once he had completed his tasks he got out and closed up the side door of the van. Picked up the map and got into the front of the camper van and drove off leaving Samantha's dog standing alone looking bewildered.

Ten minutes later a passing motorised stopped when he saw the dog walking along the side of the road trailing its lead behind it. The motorised got out of his car and caught hold of the lead and bending down saw that the dog had its name and address on a metal tag attached to its collar. Having read the address he put the dog in his car and went to the address to report to Samantha's mother he had found the dog wandering alone along the side of the road at the edge of the forest.

Samantha's mother went into panic and asked the motorist if he had seen a young girl anywhere near where he had found the dog. When he said he hadn't she asked him to stay while she phoned the police? The motorist agreed willingly to stay and inform the police where he had found the dog.

The police carried out an extensive search of the area, but the only clues that they found were a man's footprints along with Samantha's on the soft ground alongside the road.

As in the case of Susan Crowther a nationwide appeal was launched with the media but without any results.

Six months late in mid-April of 2010 on the Ashbridge Estate in Birkhampstead in Hertfordshire in the forest on the estate eight year old Adrian Prentice disappeared, and two months after that a Jamie Simonds aged fifteen also went missing whilst in the forest there. The only clues found were the youngster's footprints as well as a man's footprints.

During the summer months of 2011 in Windsor Great Park Julian Peters aged six along with his sister, Celia aged fourteen were reported as having gone missing whilst walking through the woods in the park. The only clues found were torn threads from each of their clothes along with their footprints and a man's footprints.

Then on a cold Sunday morning in January 2012, Sixteen year old Joy Manders, could have continued to lay asleep in her warm bed for another hour, but she woke up at her usual time of seven got out of bed, and showered before putting on her riding breeches thick woollen socks a T shirt over which she put on a thick woollen jumper. She then quietly tiptoed downstairs not wanted to disturb her parents who were still sleeping. She went into the kitchen and made herself a bowl of instant porridge and a cup of hot milky chocolate which she consumed whilst putting on her riding boots and thick padded waist length jacket.

Once she had finished she picked up and put on her gloves and riding hat from a cabinet near the kitchen door. She then unlocked the door and went out into a large square concrete covered yard that had stables on three sides. Walking over to one of the stables, she unlocked the door and went in and there in front of her stood her new pony a Christmas gift from her parents. He was a tall neatly groomed chestnut colour who was happily eating from a large bucket. Joy smiling patted the nose of the pony saying.

"Morning Zephyr, time to go for some exercise"

The pony snorted letting out hot vapour from its nostrils as it lifted its head as if in agreement.

Joy lifted down a saddle and set of reins from a shelf and put them on Zephyr while he continued to munch his food.

When Joy had kitted up Zephyr she led him out of the stable and climbed up onto his back then patting his neck said.

"Lead on we will go into the forest today"

Zephyr moved forward slowly walking out of the stable yard through a wide open gate that led onto a narrow quite Essex country lane. Joy steered him to the right where he continued to walk keeping close to the side of the lane passing low hedges behind which were open meadows. On the other side of the lane, there was Epping Forest with its continuous line of mixed pollard leafless trees. Between the gaps of the trees, Joy watched the cold early morning mist as it rose up from the wet leafed covered floor of the forest and drifted in amongst the trees. The sky above was a mixture of light and dark grey, and there was a cold, damp chill in the air.

They continued to walk for ten minutes before Joy lightly pulling the reins steered Zephyr across the lane into an opening between the trees where before them was a long straight narrow leaf laden track surrounded on either side by trees. Joy dug her heels into Zephyr's side gripped the reins saying.

"Come on Zephyr lets go"

The pony immediately broke into a steady gallop, and Joy leaned forward holding the reins tightly as they flashed past the trees. Pigeons rose high into the air squawking from the branches of the nearby trees. They continued to gallop until they came to the end of the track where Joy pulled in the reins, and Zephyr came to a sudden stop hot breath blowing from his nostrils. At the end of the track, there was a wide open space of meadow grass surrounded on three sides by trees. Joy steered Zephyr into the middle of the open space and turned him to the left where he proceeded to walk at a steady pace heading towards a hardcore track that crossed at the end of the open space.

Parked directly in front of them in the middle of the track there was a large white van that had its rear doors open. A tall, stocky built man with thick dark brown curly hair who was dressed in a dark navy blue donkey jacket, dark brown trousers and wellington boots was busy loading large back plastic bags into the back of the van. As Joy steered Zephyr onto the track and rode towards the van, the man turned and seeing Joy smiled and waved a greeting before turning back to loading the bags. Joy waved back continuing towards the van with the intention of going round it.

Then just as she got close to the back of the van the man suddenly turned round and stared at Joy with an evil smile on his unshaven face. In his hands, he held a loaded crossbow which was pointing directly at Joy.

Joy gasped; her expression changed to a look of shock and fear.

"Stop! Get down off your pony or I will shoot you" the man said.

Joy hastily looked all around her, but there was no one else around, there was no escape, it was just her Zephyr and the man. Seeing the crossbow pointing at her chest and knowing that she wasn't close enough to make Zephyr rein up and knock the man down without either her or zephyr being hit by a bolt from the crossbow she instantly pulled in the reins saying to Zephyr.

"Wow boy stop"

"I said get off your pony" the man repeated.

Joy gingerly climbed down off Zephyrs back and stood at his side not taking her eyes off the man as he walked towards her.

"Right get in the back of the van and be quick about it or I will shoot either you or your pony" the man said looking her straight in her eyes.

Joy let go of the reins and slowly walked towards the back of the van. She could feel her knees starting to shake. The man circled round behind her and took hold of Zephyrs reins pulling him to the left with one hand while still pointing the crossbow straight at her, he then gave zephyr a heavy slap on his rump. Zephyr shot forward and galloped off across the open space into the trees leaving Joy and the man on their own. Joy stopped and watched in fear as Zephyr disappeared from view. Then turning towards the man she asked with a shaky voice.

"Who are you and why are you doing this, what is it you want from me?"

"Shut up and get in the back of the van, you will find out soon enough" the man replied.

Joy continued walking and, on reaching the back of the van, she crawled on her hands and knees into the back having to climb over the black bags from which blood was seeping onto the floor; the interior of the van smelt of fresh meat and cigar smoke.

The man quickly followed Joy into the back of the van pushing her forward with one hand while continuing to point the crossbow at her in his other hand. He then straightened his free hand and hit her hard on one side of her neck. Joy instantly fell down in a heap unconscious. The man then carefully laid down the crossbow and took some thick string and a short length of cloth from his jacket pocket and proceeded to gag her before binding her hands and feet. Satisfied that she could not move or shout out he backed out of the van closed and locked the doors, before getting into the front of the van behind the steering wheel starting the engine and driving off.

When Zephyr was discovered two hours later wandering aimlessly around amongst the trees by a neighbour who had taken his dog for an early morning run in the forest. The neighbour managed to get hold of Zephyr's reins and searched around calling out Joys name, but there was no response or sign of her, so he took Zephyr back to Joy's parents who hearing that Zephyr had been found without Joy immediately phoned the local police who came and took statements then organised a search of the forest for Joy, but she wasn't to be found. A nationwide appeal was launched with full media coverage to try and find Joy but brought no positive results.

Seven months later the lives of Rose and Sam Cooper were about to change. Rose aged fifteen was tall; slim with shoulder length straight black hair and brown eyes. Her brother Sam aged eleven was of medium build and height with short brown wavy hair and grey eyes.

They had driven up from Exeter in Devon on the Sunday with their parents John and Mary Cooper to stay for a week with their great Uncle Walter and great Aunt Nancy in their Tudor cottage, in the village of Takely in Essex. Whilst their parents were due to spend a week attending business meetings at their company's offices in Hong Kong. Leaving the two youngsters in the care of Walter and Nancy until they returned the next Saturday.

John and Mary set off early Monday morning to catch their flight from Heathrow to Hong Kong after saying goodbye to their two children and Walter and Nancy. Rose and Sam spent the rest of the Monday both inside the cottage playing on their laptops as well as out in the garden with Walter and Nancy where they played clock golf on the pitch that Walter had set up on one of the lawns the previous summer, when they had all spent a week with them.

After breakfast on, Tuesday Rose and Sam spent the morning in the garden. They began by playing shuttle cock until Sam became bored having lost every game and decided to go on the swings. Rose reluctantly joined Sam on the swings and suggested they have a competition to see who could swing the highest. They both rose higher and higher until Rose seeing that if they continued one or both of them was likely to go over the cross bar and possibly break their necks, so she slowed down to a stop and yelled at Sam saying.

"Enough! Now stop ok"

Sam laughed out loud until he saw the look of pain on Roses face, so he slowed down until he too came to a stop saying.

"Wow that was exciting and a bit scary; I've never been so high on a swing before"

"Yes it was exciting, but don't ever do it again it's dangerous you could end up breaking your neck"

"Yea whatever you say, but I was enjoying that. So what shall we do now?"

"I fancy going out and exploring"

"Exploring Where?" Sam asked.

"Oh, I don't know let's go anywhere; there is not much to do here. I will get bored if I have to stay in the cottage or garden all afternoon"

"It's almost lunch time; we could go out after lunch"

"I'll ask great Aunt Nancy if she will make us a picnic lunch to take out with us, I'm sure she will. I'll tell her we want to go for a walk around the village"

"Cool that sounds like a good idea. Go on then go and ask her"

Rose got off the swing and ran down the garden path and into the kitchen. Ten minutes later she came running back smiling as she carried with her two small backpacks.

"Here we are great Aunt Nancy has packed us some sandwiches and a bottle of lemonade each. She said it's alright for us to go out, as long as we are back by six o'clock for dinner"

"Great come on then let's go. You still haven't said where we are going"

"I told you we will go anywhere"

"Yea but where is anywhere?"

Rose sighed then smiling replied.

"You will see, come on hurry up".

They both ran across the lawn and through a set of double metal gates that led out onto the lane.

"Which way left or right?" Sam asked with a slight frown.

"Well go right"

They walked side by side along the quiet narrow lane that weaved its way through the village. Passing rows of detached cottages that stood back from the road with neat front gardens. Most of the cottages were similar to Walter and Nancy's cottage dating back to the Tutor age with whitewashed walls and thatched roofs. There were very few people to be seen in the gardens of the cottages, and no one else appeared to be walking or driving along the lane.

"It's so peaceful here; I have only seen a few people in their gardens. Where do you suppose they all go to?" asked Sam.

"I expect a lot of them are working in either the nearby towns or London. I reckon that some of the cottages are empty during the week and only used as weekend cottages by people who live and work in London during the week"

"Well I haven't seen anybody of our ages; goodness knows where they go to"

"Goodness knows Sam where they go. I wouldn't want to live here all the time; I would be bored; there are no interesting shops, cinemas, cafes. Besides I would soon miss not seeing my friends"

"Yea me too"

They continued walking for about ten minutes in silence lost in their own thoughts before coming to a cross roads where they stopped.

"OK now which way are we going?" Sam asked.

"Just follow me, you will soon see"

Rose replied with a smile as she turned and began to walk briskly up the lane to the left, where there were no more cottages to be seen, just fields and meadows on either side of the lane that had low hedges. In some of the meadows cows were busy grazing. The fields contained either vegetables or nearly ripe corn and barley. The air was still the only sounds to be heard were Rose and Sam's footsteps, accompanied by birds tweeting in the hedges and cows munching and puffing close to the hedges as they chewed at the grass not paying much attention to the two youngsters passing by.

Having continued to walk along the lane for about a quarter of a mile Rose suddenly pointed to her right and said.

"There that's where we are going into the forest"

"What! You're crazy you know mum and dad made us promise that we wouldn't go there without them" Sam replied frowning and looking worried.

"I know; I know, but it will be all right, we just won't tell anyone that we have been there. Let's face it, it's the only interesting place to go to round here apart from getting on a bus and going into town, and I don't fancy doing that today. We can do that tomorrow if you like".

"Ok but you had better hope that dad and mum don't find out we went into the forest on our own"

"I shan't tell them. As you know, there are lots of things to see in this forest. I like to walk round the large lake where there is the old café that is covered with exotic seashells that once belonged to a famous family before the forest became owned by the forestry commission. But today we will go into the thick of the forest and look for some Deer"

"If you had told me that you were planning to come to the forest I would have asked great Uncle Walter if I could have borrowed his fishing rod, and told him that we were going fishing in the lake"

"Don't be daft Sam you know he wouldn't have allowed us to come here on our own, besides even if he had you don't have a permit to fish in the lake. No today we will go exploring instead"

"We have never explored all of the forest. I remember I was only three years old when I first came here with mum and dad. They always like coming to the forest whenever we all stay with great Uncle Walter and Aunt Nancy"

"That's because they like to see all the different trees and look for all the different wild animals like rabbits, squirrels, Badgers and even Deer"

"We've never seen any Deer or Badgers in the forest. I don't believe there are any".

"Of course, there are Deer in the forest, and I expect there are Badgers too, we might be lucky and see some. We will need to be very quiet if we go into the thick of the forest because if there are any Deer about they will be able to hear the slightest sounds, which will scare them off"

"Right so we will go in search of some Deer, but I bet we won't see any. Did you bring your mobile phone so that you can take photos if we do see any?"

"Of course I always have my mobile phone with me so that I can keep in touch with my friends"

"Yea that's right you are always chatting to your friends on your phone. Can we eat our sandwiches first before we go searching for Deer?"

"Yes of course, look there's the entrance gate with the main track and sign post pointing to the different walkways through the forest".

They crossed the road and went through a wide open gate passed two men who stood collecting parking fees for vehicles coming into the forest. They turned left and walked across to a large oak tree that stood in the middle of a spacious grass area that bordered the edge of the forest and sat down on the grass under the tree. Opposite to where they sat a large number of cars were parked up in rows on the grass on the other side of the main track.

They opened up their back packs and took out their sandwiches and lemonade and sat busily eating whilst watching some of the adults and children who had also come to visit the forest. Some were walking off along the different tracks, while others were either playing ball games or like them were sitting enjoying the summer sunshine whilst picnicking on the large grass area in front of the trees.

"How big do you reckon this forest is Rose?"

"I don't know I just know that it spreads in all different directions for many miles and was once used by Henry the eighth when hunting for Deer"

"I will have to ask Great Uncle Walter he will know seeing as he was the head forest ranger before he retired last year"

"Yes you should. Just think Nancy and Walter have lived in this area all of their lives. Walter and his brother Joseph, our grandfather on dad's side of the family were born in the cottage where great Uncle Walter and Nancy live. Nancy was born and grew up in a cottage further down the village and met Walter and grandfather when they were both children, and went to the same schools".

"But granddad moved away from the village years later to live in Devon and met grandmother and they got married"

"That's right and dad like us was born in Devon, not in Essex".

"I wonder why Granddad decided to move from Essex to go and live in Devon."

"I have no idea; your guess is as good as mine. Have you finished your sandwiches?"

"Yes"

"Good come on then let's go and see if we can find some Deer"

They stood up and put away what was left of their lemonade in their backpacks and walked across the grass and onto one of the tarmac tracks that led into the forest.

As they walked along the track they were not alone as other people were busy walking some with dogs others pushing young children in pushchairs, everyone seemed to be relaxed chatting and looking to their left and right into the forest at the trees which for the most part were evenly spread out. There were oak, beech, lime and silver birch trees. Between the trees, there was a mixture of many smaller trees and bushes which included holly, rhododendrons, thorn and rosebushes, as well as rabbit tracks and manmade footpaths. Dry leaves from the previous winter littered the forest floor. The older trees especially the oaks had large thick, gnarled trunks and heavy branches, whereas the younger trees had thinner trunks and branches. As they slowly strolled along looking at the trees, Rose suddenly said.

"Right come on Sam, let's get off this track and go in amongst the trees, we can follow one of the small man-made footpaths."

"Ok, which way left or right?"

"We will go in here on the left"

Rose stepped off the track in amongst the trees closely followed by Sam. They found a narrow man-made track and began to follow it as it weaved its way through the trees. They each walked in silence looking all around as they went. After about half an hour Rose stopped and turning round to Sam said.

"Wow we seem to be deep in the forest now far from the main tracks; I can't see or hear any people about and the only animals that I have seen are the occasional rabbit"

"I too I have only seen one or two rabbits, there doesn't appear to be any other animals about. I saw a number of different dogs, and their owners wandering about amongst the trees earlier but now we are so deep into the forest I haven't seen any more people or dogs. I've seen loads of sparrows and pigeons and one or two finches, and two thrushes"

"Yes but now that we are deep in the forest we stand a better chance of possibly seeing some deer, we need to be really very quiet from now on and keep our eyes and ears alert"

"Well I hope you remember how to find our way back to the main track for when we need to return to the cottage. Mind you it's only three o'clock so we still have some time left before we have to go back"

"I'm sure it won't be hard to find our way back to the track, as you say we still have some time left before we have to head back to the cottage. If we keep going in a straight line we are bound to come upon one of the main tracks sooner or later"

"Ok, well let's try to keep in as a straight line".

"Quiet! Listen do you hear that, it sounds like water I think there is a stream just over there" Rose said pointing to her right.

"I hear it, come on let's go and take a look, we might be lucky enough to see some deer drinking from the stream as well as other animals. Walk slowly and try and keep as quiet as possible" He whispered.

"Ok follow me"

Rose whispered back as they slowly and carefully made their way towards the sound of the running water.

They suddenly came to the side of the tree line and stopped behind a thick oak tree where peering round they saw a fast flowing narrow stream that was weaving its way through the forest.

Directly in front of them in the middle of the stream there was a dip where a small waterfall had been created by fallen twigs, leaves and branches that had drifted down the stream and become clogged up.

The water pushed its way through creating a noisy splashing sound. But there were no signs of any animals at the side of the water either to the left or right. They slowly and quietly came out from behind the tree and walked to the side of the stream stopping by the small waterfall where they both stooped down and peered into the water, each looking to see if there were any small fish or frogs in the water, but there were none to be seen.

"Let's follow the stream we might see some animals further along" Sam whispered.

"Ok, let's keep to this side of the stream" Rose whispered back.

They quietly stood up and began to walk along the side of the stream keeping a sharp look out for any signs of Deer. After about ten minutes Rose, who was leading the way, stopped suddenly and bobbed down, turning at the same time and looking up at Sam she waved her right hand downwards indicating for Sam to bob down while, with her other hand, she pointed along the stream.

Sam quickly bobbed down and looked to where Rose was pointing. His eyes widened in amazement as he caught sight of a giant stag that had wide antlers. It was standing at the water's edge twenty yards away on the opposite side drinking from the stream. They both stared at the beast completely transfixed, smiling as they watched the Stag who had yet to see them as it drank from the stream.

Rose reached into her jean's pocket pulled out her mobile phone and having pressed for the camera, she focused, and zoomed in to get a close up picture of the stag; she pressed the button several times then checked to see she had got some good photos. Satisfied she pressed to use the camera once more.

When all of a sudden the stag raised its head from the stream its ears pricked up water dripping from it open mouth. Rose took a deep breath fearing that she had disturbed the stag, but it was not looking in the direction of Rose and Sam instead its eyes were focused directly to its front at the trees on the opposite side of the stream.

In those same split seconds, there came a "Whoosh" sound. Instantly the giant stag reared up on its hind legs, its eyes glaring, its body twisted into a contorted half turn, a loud ear piercing screech along with water and blood frothed and sprayed from its wide open mouth, then it buckled and crashed to the ground landing on its side, its long legs kicking in all directions, its head and neck twisted upwards pointing to the sky before it let out one final gasp and its head fell to the ground.

A short arrow could be seen sticking in the stags exposed chest.

Rose and Sam gasped and froze their jaws dropping as they stared wide eyed at the scene before them.

Suddenly from behind a tall, thick holly bush directly across the stream opposite to where the stag lay dead, and on the same side of the stream that Rose and Same were squatting down a tall, thick set middle aged man appeared.

He had an unshaven face, thick dark brown curly hair. He carried a crossbow slung over his left shoulder and on his back there was a large back pack with a quiver full of arrows sticking from the top. He wore a short sleeved dark blue and red checked open necked shirt and dark blue jeans with a thick leather belt around the waist that had a long scabbard to hold a hunting knife. On his feet, he had a pair of ankle high brown leather boots.

The man quickly stepped forward crossing the stream in one large stride and knelt down beside the stag. Taking off his back pack and the crossbow he laid them down beside him, before drawing out a large hunting knife.

He looked all around him before with one skilful slice with the knife he cut open the stag from head to tail along its front. The innards of the stag slopped out onto the ground before him. He put down the knife and scooped up the innards in both his hands and threw them into the tall grass at the base of a birch tree close to where he was knelt.

Having cleaned out all of the innards from the stag he extracted the arrow and wiped it clean along with his hands on the grass before he returned the arrow to the quiver. He then proceeded to skin the animal.

Rose and Sam still squatting down watched in amazement and disbelief at what the man was doing. Then Rose turned and looked at Sam, who had tears in his eyes, beckoned for him to make for the trees behind them. Sam seeing her gestures nodded.

Slowly and quietly they both stood up; Sam took hold of one Rose's hands as they turned and made a dash back towards the trees behind them. There was a sudden loud cracking sound as Sam's left foot went down on an old branch which instantly snapped.

The man on the other side of the stream instantly looked up and seeing Rose and Sam running towards the trees leapt up grabbed his backpack and crossbow with his free hand and still holding his knife in his other hand he leaped back across the stream and began to chase after them.

Rose and Sam seeing that the man was following them frantically began zigzagging between the bushes and trees. Rose shouted out.

"Sam for goodness sake try and keep in line with me, we have got to find our way back onto the main track before that man catches us".

"I'm trying to, do you remember the way back to the main track" Sam gasped.

"Just keep running we will find a way out. Once we get onto the track, there are bound to be people about whom we can turn to for help. He won't dare to follow us if he sees us talking with other people"

"Look out Rose! He's catching us up"

"Run faster Sam"

They continued to run as fast as they could, zigzagging through brambles and bushes that tore at their clothes and skin leaving tears cuts and scratches. The man also quickened his pace following them oblivious to the bushes tearing at his clothes; he was determined to stop their escape no matter what.

Suddenly Sam's foot caught in an upturned tree root he fell forward sprawling heavily on the ground crying out in pain.

Rose hearing and seeing Sam cry out and fall down on the ground quickly ran across to help him back up on his feet. But Sam had already quickly picked himself up and was trying to run again but finding it difficult called out.

"Ah! Rose I think I have sprained my ankle."

Rose knelt down to look at his ankle, and out of the corner of her eye she saw a man coming up fast behind them. She instinctively grabbed one of Sam's arms putting it round her shoulder then proceeded to drag him along as fast as she could, but too late within seconds she felt one of the man's rough hands grab her right shoulder, and he pulled her to the ground dragging

Sam with her. Rose let out a scream; the man went down on his knees and punched Rose in the face sending her spinning into unconsciousness.

Sam glared at the man and kicked him in the stomach as hard as he could with his unhurt foot. The man winded let out a yell from the blow then struck back punching Sam in the face sending him also spinning into unconsciousness.

When Rose became conscious she found herself sitting propped up against a rough brick wall and the floor beneath her was concrete. A glaring bright single bulb hanging from wires in a low ceiling lit up what appeared to be a cellar. Immediately in front of her in the centre of the room there was a large solid pine table. Between the legs of the table, she saw Sam lying in a heap on the floor against the opposite wall, and he wasn't moving. Like her had been gagged, and tied hand and foot with thick course string; the tight gag of torn cloth restricted her from opening her mouth. The left side of her face and jaw hurt like mad; with her swollen tongue she could feel that one of her teeth to the left side of her mouth felt loose.

Looking around the cellar, she could see that to the left of Sam there was a large ceramic square sink that stood on casts iron legs, a single tap protruded from the wall above the sink. Butted up to the sink there was a row of metal cupboards that went along the wall finishing up against the right hand side wall, a continuous stainless steel worktop covered the cupboards. In the centre of the right hand side wall just below the grey plastered ceiling, there was a narrow blacked out window that was covered with a cast iron grill to prevent it from opening. In the middle of the left hand side wall, a set of steep narrow stone steps led up to a solid metal door. On all the rough brick walls around the room, there were large sharp metal hooks that had been evenly spaced out and positioned at a height of about five feet. On the floor below each of the hooks, there were dark stains that looked like dry blood.

Rose lifted her arms and looked at her watch and saw that it was half past eight. A wave of panic swept through her as she knew that her Great Uncle and aunt would be worrying as to why she and Sam had not contacted them to let them know why they had not returned for dinner at six.

She reached up and began pulling at the gag and after a few minutes of twisting and contorting her face which caused her to let out muffled cries from the pain that it was causing her she managed to get the gag from her mouth. She then felt for her mobile phone in her jean's pocket, but it had gone as had their backpacks, she cursed to herself as she quickly crawled across the room passing under the table and knelt down beside Sam and shook his shoulders saying.

"Sam it's me Rose wake up, come on please wake up"

At first he didn't respond, Rose shook him harder then suddenly his eyes opened and seeing Rose his eyes widened with a look of surprise. He tried to speak but couldn't due to the gag in his mouth. He shook his head trying to clear his mind as he eased himself up into a sitting position on the floor, at the same time he took in his surroundings and saw that like Rose his hands, and feet were tied.

Rose reached forward and began pulling at the gag in his mouth saying.

"Let me help you we need to talk. You are going to be ok I'm here to help you"

Sam's face contorted with pain as Rose managed to get the gag free after about a two minutes struggle.

"Ach! Thanks Rose my face hurts. I think I have a broken tooth. Your face is swollen up are you ok? Where are we and what time it is?"

"I'm ok apart from having a loose tooth. I haven't been conscious long; we appear to be in the cellar of a house, and its quarter to nine, I don't know if it is morning or night. My mobile phone has gone and so have our backpacks. Great Uncle Walter and Aunt Nancy will be worried sick wondering why we've not returned."

"Gosh! We've been unconscious for ages. You say your mobile phones gone, great so we can't call for help. Yes, Walter and Nancy will be frantic with worry. I said we should never have gone into the forest this is all your fault".

"I'm sorry Sam, I didn't expect us to be chased and assaulted by that horrible man and end up tied up here did I".

"We need to find a way out of here and fast. I don't know why we have been brought to this place wherever it is? After that man knocked you out I kicked him in the stomach and winded him, then he punched me and I don't remember any more until you shook me awake"

"We can't get out of here until we get our hands and feet free of these bonds. Let me help you untie your hands then you can untie mine"

"Ok well be quick"

Rose began to pull at the knot of the string that bound Sam's hands, when suddenly they heard a key turning in the lock of the door at the top of the steps. Rose raised her head, and looked into Sam's eyes before they both turned to look up towards the door.

A light shone briefly from behind the now open door as the man from the forest appeared at the top of the steps. He closed the door behind him before descending down the steps grinning on his face as he looked at Rose and Sam. On reaching the bottom of the steps, he walked over saying.

"Ah, you are both conscious trying to untie yourselves. I can cut you both free there's no need to keep you tied up, not that either of you are going anywhere"

"Who are you; where are we and why have you brought us to this place. You had no right to chase us, knock us out, bring us here and tie us up. You're crazy to do such a thing. We've done you no harm. I suppose it's because we saw you kill a Deer, and you didn't want us to give your description to the police" Rose mumbled.

"Ha, ha that's right I couldn't let you get away and give my description to the police and telling them that you had seen me killing the Deer. It's illegal to kill the Deer in the forest. But it's a hobby of mine from which I earn good money from the Deer that I kill. People pay a nice price for venison, and there are those who want the Deer skins for making things. As for stags heads that have a full set of antlers some people will pay large amounts just so they can display them on the walls in their homes"

"So what do you intend to do with us, you can't keep us here forever; you will have to let us go sooner or later. The police will soon be searching for us and if they discover that you have held us prisoner then you will be in real serious trouble" Sam shouted.

"I can keep you here as long as I want too. There is no way that you can get away from here; you can shout as loud as you like, but no one will hear you because this house is in a secluded place far from the road, and far from the forest with no neighbours".

"You still haven't said what you intend to do with us" Rose replied with a look of pain on her face.

"Did you go into the forest on your own or did you go there with your parents?"

"We went on our own" Sam replied.

"So you didn't come to the forest with your parents or with your great uncle Walter and great aunt Nancy"

"How do you know about our great uncle and aunt?"

"Because Rose I found your mobile phone on which you have listed along with all yours friends names and phone numbers your parents' names, address and phone numbers along with your great uncle and aunts names and address and phone numbers".

"So what are you planning to do phone them and demand money for our return?" Rose asked.

"You will just have to wait and see. When I come back I will let you know what I intend to do with you both until then you will stay down here"

The man then turned and ran back up the steps and through the door locking it behind him.

"Wait come back" shouted Rose.

But there came no reply.

"I'm scared and cold Rose I wonder how long he intends to keep us down here without any food and drink. We could end up dead; we've got to get out of here somehow"

"I don't know, like you I'm scared and cold Sam, but we mustn't give up or show him that we are scared. We can't plan anything until we get ourselves free of these bonds"

Rose took hold of the string around Sam's wrists and began again to try and untie the knots.

"I bet he will have noted the numbers in your contact list before getting rid of your mobile phone, he's bound to know that if he keeps the phone it can be traced to where ever it is".

"Yes I expect so. I'm really sorry Sam for getting us into this mess. This knot tying your wrist is really hard to get undone"

"Why don't you look in one of those cabinets by the sink there might be something sharp in there to cut the string?"

"Good thinking I'll have a look"

Rose stood up and hopped across to the cabinets and turned all the handles on the doors, but they were all securely locked.

"He thought of that didn't he? Oh, well I will just have to keep trying because we can't do anything until we get our hands and feet free" Rose replied as she hopped back and sat down next to Sam and started once again to try and untie the knot.

"Come on Rose for goodness sake try harder, I am busting for a pee now"

"You will just have to wait, and anyway where are you going to pee there's no toilet in here"

"I will pee in that sink of course"

"Yea right ok. Ah I've got it hang on the knot is finally coming lose"

Rose pulled at the knot, and it came undone. Sam wriggled and pulled his wrists apart, and the string dropped in his lap.

"Thank goodness, hang on a minute then I will try and untie your wrists"

Sam stood up and hopped and limped across to the sink and turned on the tap which let out a stream of cold water into the sink. Pulling the zip down on his jeans, he turned to Rose and said.

"Ok turn your head away I don't need you to watch me having a pee"

Rose laughed and turned her head away as Sam relieved himself in the sink. Once he had finished he put his face to the running water and rinsed out his mouth and as he did so he could feel the loose tooth in his mouth which he pushed back into place with his tongue letting out a gasp as the pain shot through him. He then turned off the tap and pulled up his zip half dried his hands down the front of his jeans before hopping and limping back and sitting down next to Rose where he took hold of her wrist and began to try and untie the knot.

"Better now. Well at least we have water. How many of your teeth are loose?"

"Only one at the back of my mouth, I was lucky. How about you, how many of your teeth are loose?"

"Just one on the left hand side of my face, I will rinse my mouth once my hands are free. How is your ankle?"

"Painful I'm sure I have sprained it, look it's swollen and having my ankles tied up doesn't help"

"Once we have got ourselves free then you had better use your handkerchief to make a cold compress, which should ease the swelling"

"Hopefully, I'm hungry Rose aren't you?"

"Yes but I can last out for now without eating. We can drink water which will help"

"Ah there you go you're lucky I have got the knot undone, it can't have been tied as tight as mine"

"Great thanks now we can undo the strings round our ankles"

Rose flexed her wrists and the string fell to the floor. She and Sam sat with their knees up and began to try and undo the knots holding the string round their ankles. Quarter of an hour later they had finally managed to free themselves.

"Sam give me your handkerchief and I will soak it and put it round your ankle"

Sam fished in his pocket and pulled out his screwed up handkerchief and passed it to Rose, who went over and turned on the tap and having first soaked the handkerchief she then rinsed out her mouth and let out a shout as she pushed her loose tooth back into place.

Once she had finished, she returned to where Sam was sitting and lifted the trouser leg covering his swollen ankle and wrapped the damp handkerchief around the ankle then covered it with his sock to keep it in place. Sam winced as the coldness touched his swollen ankle.

"There that should ease the pain. I wonder when that man will return, and what his next move will be. We need to think of a way of getting out of here and fast"

"I agree but there is no way that we can tackle him he is too strong for us"

"We shall just have to await the right opportunity. With two of us tackling him we stand a better chance"

They both sat in silence thinking about ideas of what to do. Then Rose suddenly stood up and said laughing.

"Look the other way Sam I need to go for a pee now"

Sam burst out laughing and replied.

"Go on then, I can see that if we are going to live on just water we are going to be doing a lot of peeing in that sink"

"Ha, ha look the other way"

Sam turned his head looking up to the door at the top of the steps while Rose went over to the sink undid her jeans and pulled them down along with her pants to her knees before turning and lifting herself up onto the top of the sink.

She was in mid flow when suddenly the door opened, and the man reappeared. Rose turned and looked at the man with an expression of surprise and embarrassment. Seeing what she was doing the man ran down the steps glaring at Rose and shouted.

"Hey! What do you think you are doing I can't have you pissing in that sink"

Rose having finished leaped down from the sink and turned her back away from both Sam and the man as she pulled up her pants and jean's, and as she did so she shouted back.

"What do you expect us to do seeing as you're keeping us locked up down here? We need toilet facilities and food to eat; we also need some medicine, because thanks to you we both have loose teeth. What do you expect us to sleep on, the hard floor without blankets, it's cold and damp in here" Rose said as she walked back and sat down next to Sam.

"You will get all of those things"

"You won't get away with holding us for ransom, the police will track you down and find you," Rose said with a faint grin.

"I'm not going to hold you for ransom I have other plans for you both. You're not the only youngsters that I have snatched"

"Ha! Really so what did you do with them?" Sam asked.

"They work for me as my sex slaves and you two are going to work for me as sex slaves. There are people out there who will pay good money for you both. Especially you Rose pretty girl that you are with a nice figure, you're just right to earn me money as a prostitute and Sam will earn me good money from paedophiles."

"What! No way you're sick and perverted, you can't sell me into prostitution, and I won't let you sell off my brother to sick perverted paedophiles" Rose shouted glaring at the man.

"Ha! You can't stop me".

"Ah, come on please no you can't do that to us let us go" Rose shouted.

"No way not now you are going to earn your keep"

The man laughed as once more he turned and ran back up the steps and disappeared through the door locking it behind him.

As soon as the man had gone Sam turned to Rose and asked.

"What does he mean he's going to use us as sex slaves, what are sex slaves?"

"I will explain to you what it means, you remember when dad bought us each a computer and how he spent time setting up the programmes on them, well he put a block on what he didn't want us to see on the internet. As you know, he is always checking to see which sites we have tapped into. That's because he doesn't want us to see the naughty sites that are available on the internet".

"What naughty sites, you mean sites with extreme violence?"

"Yes and also sites that contain what is known as porn, they are sites that some adults use for watching films of people having sex"

"That's disgusting. So are the people who let themselves be filmed having sex, sex slaves? I didn't know there were such sites"

"I agree it's disgusting, and no they are not all sex slaves they make those film for money. Sex slaves are people who are forced into making porn films as well as being forced into having sex with adults. A lot of them are youngsters like you and me who have been kidnapped or bought. There are adults who like having sex with young people of your and my age and even younger which is illegal? Those people are called paedophiles".

"What! You mean adults have sex with children?"

"Yes and some friends of mine at school who use Facebook have been asked for friend requests by other people who were shown to be of their age and having accepted them as their friends and got chatting with them were invited to meet them, and it was always in either parks or areas that they weren't familiar with. But they innocently went to meet whom they thought were their new friends only to find out that they were really adult males who had pretended to be youngsters. When they realised the truth the adults threatened them with violence and on some occasions dragged them into their cars or vans where they attempted to sexually assault them"

"They did what, no that's crazy"

"It's true I'm telling you, fortunately those friends of mine who had that experience managed to get away without getting seriously hurt. They never told the police or their parents because they were scared of what might happen, because the men who attacked them might do so again. But I have heard about some cases where other youngsters haven't managed to get away and the adult males have taken them away and sold them to people known as pimps who have kept them prisoner fed them with drugs and used them for prostitution, and in some cases they have even ended up being murdered"

"No! Really I've never heard of that, what's a pimp, I have heard some of the senior boys call others senior's pimps but never knew what it meant, and what does a prostitute do?"

"You mean you don't know, I'm surprised at you Sam I didn't know you were so naïve, and you've never heard about the fake friend's scams on Facebook?"

"Never the only friends I have on my Facebook are my friends in school. I have had people requesting to be my friend that I don't know but I have always rejected their request"

"Well that's safe. I do the same. Now for your education a pimp is someone who sells girls or women for sex to men. A prostitute is a girl or woman who allows men to have sex with her providing the man pays her money. The price varies and depends on how good a prostitute she is"

"Oh, that's disgusting, so where do these pimps do the selling?"

"In the streets, bars, betting shops and cafes, anywhere"

"So this man who has snatched us is a pimp and wants to try and sell us as prostitutes, but I'm a boy, not a girl like you, why would a male be interested in wanting sex with me?"

"Oh, dear Sam, because there are men who prefer to have sex with boys and other men and also like to take photos of their bums and penises. Like in porn magazines where woman show off all their bits, that's why they have porn channels on the internet, and that's why dad has blocked us from seeing such things"

"You seem to know a lot about these things, how come?"

"I know because my friends have told me about these things. Their parents unlike our parents have warned them about such things"

"I'm scared Rose I don't want that man using us as sex slaves, I would rather die first"

"I too, I won't let him. We have to escape, but it won't be easy. We will just have to wait for the right opportunity. If you see chances to get away before me go for it and head for the nearest police station and let them know who you are and where you have been held prisoner I will do the same ok"

"Ok but it's better if we escape together. I don't want to leave you behind because there's no telling what that man might do to you"

"Look if we can both escape at the same time all well and good but if we can't then better that one of us gets away to inform the police. I bet great Uncle Walter has already contacted the police and they will be looking for us"

"Gosh! Look at the time Rose it's midnight Great Uncle Walter and Nancy will definitely have contacted the police. They will be worrying themselves sick. Do you think they will have phoned mum and dad?"

"I don't know Sam, but I know that if we get away from this place wherever it is and get back to Great Uncle Walters we are going to be in really big trouble especially when he finds out and lets mum and dad know that we went into the forest"

"Yes true, but I would rather face that than being abused or murdered. The police won't be very happy either seeing as they will have had to spend time looking for us"

"Well we never expected that we would get into this situation, we only went for a walk in the forest. I'm never going into that forest again without mum and dad"

"I neither I can't believe this has happened to us it's a nightmare. I only wish that it was only a bad dream, but it's not. I'm so tired, cold and hungry and need to sleep isn't you tired and hungry?"

"Yes I am it's been a long day and I'm scared and cold"

"Me to lets cuddle up Rose and try and sleep"

Rose wrapped her arm around Sam's waist, and he put his head on her shoulder and like Rose he closed his eyes and within a few minutes they both fell asleep.

They hadn't been asleep long before they were awoken abruptly by the sound of the door opening at the top of the steps. The man appeared and came running down the steps and seeing them huddled together asleep laughed out loud saying.

"Time to move, you first Rose come along"

He grabbed one of Roses arms and pulled her up and lifted her over his shoulder and ran back across the room and up the steps through the door before Rose had time to come to her full senses and call out.

Sam having woken and seen what was happening jumped up and ran after the man but only got half way up the steps before the door closed, and he heard the key turn in the lock. He shouted out.

"Rose, Rose"

But there was no answer. He stood for a moment staring at the door before turning and slowly walking back down the steps his head down on his chest, a look of total despair on his face, as he went and sat back down where he and Rose had sat asleep. Tears welled up in his eyes, and he began to sob loudly knowing that he was now completely on his own without the company of his sister to give him support, and he was more afraid than he had ever been before in his short life.

Rose having become fully awake began to scream, struggle, and kick the man's back but he took no notice as he quickly carried her along a narrow semi lit passage that led into a large hallway where there were doors to the left and right and a solid front door to the front. The man turned right and ran up a set of wide red carpeted stairs onto a large landing where there were doors on three sides and another set of stairs to the right. Crossing the landing he went through a door which led into a long narrow passage where there were more doors both left and right. Half way along he stopped and opened the door on the left and went in and threw Rose, who was still kicking and screaming down onto a single bed.

"This will be your room for now. You will see that the windows have been securely boarded up from the inside so you won't be able to get out, and even if you did you would have a long drop which would break your legs if you attempted to jump. Like the cellar, no one will hear you if you scream and shout. So make the most of your room. I will be back at around seven. Bye"

The man turned and went out of the door locking it behind him. Rose sat up on the bed and shouted out.

"No please I need to go to the toilet"

The man called back as he was locking the door.

"There's a pot under the bed"

Rose heard him go back along the passage.

She sat and looked around her. The bed she lay on which was against the left hand side wall and on the same side as the door had clean pale yellow sheets and two pillows with matching yellow covers, and there was a lightweight quilt also in pale yellow. A small white table with a glass of water and some tablets on it stood beside the bed, on the opposite wall to the bed there was a white single wardrobe. To her right on the wall there was just a narrow, tall window that had been covered with sheet metal that had been securely fastened to the wall. The walls were all painted white, and the floor was covered with a faded plain green fitted carpet. A single light bulb hung in a yellow plastic shade from the dirty white ceiling. Rose got off the bed and went and opened the wardrobe and found that it was completely empty. She checked the metal sheets at the window then checked the door which had also been covered with metal sheet that had been painted white.

She then went back over and sat on the bed and took off her lightweight jacket, shoes, jeans and shirt and laid them on the floor beside the bed before lifting the quilt and getting into the bed. She picked up the glass of water and smelt it, then looked at the tablets, but not knowing what they were she left them as well as the water and laid down worrying about what might happen to Sam would he be left down in the cellar or would he to be brought and put into a room on his own like her.

She felt completely and utterly terrified of the situation that both she and Sam were in. At least in the cellar she had Sam for company but now she was on her own and dreading what might lie ahead. Tears rolled down her cheeks, and she sobbed loudly calling out for her mum before finally drifting off to sleep.

Having locked Rose up the man returned to the cellar and grabbed hold of Sam, who was sat crying. Like he had with Rose he lifted him up over his shoulder and ran up the steps through the cellar door along the passage and back up the stairs, crossed the landing and went through the same door as before then along the passage past the room containing Rose, and opened one of the doors further along on the right hand side. On entering the room, he threw Sam down onto a single bed before promptly leaving and locking the door without saying a word.

Sam had also kicked and screamed, but it was pointless as no one came to help him. Once the man had gone he sat up and looking around him saw that he was in a narrow room where all the walls were painted pale blue, and the ceiling was a dirty white colour with one single light hanging down in a plastic white shade. Like in Rose's room there was a single white painted wardrobe and bedside table on which there were a glass of water and some tablets. The single window again like the door had been covered over with sheet metal that had been firmly secured. The bed had two pillows clean sheets and quilt all in pale blue that matched the colour of the walls.

Sam sheepishly took off his clothes leaving them where they lay on the floor and crept under the quilt, lay down without bothering with the water and tablets. Like Rose, he sobbed himself to sleep.

Once he had locked Sam up, the man returned back along the passage and went out onto the landing, and up the short flight of stairs to the next landing where there were more doors. He opened one of the doors and went into a large bedroom. Not bothering to switch on the light, he yawned as he got undressed and threw his clothes on to a large wing chair before getting into a king sized bed, where he laid on his back thinking about the day ahead before he fell asleep.

The only sound to be heard from inside the house was the sound of a grandfather clock in the hall that chimed out the hour of two in the morning. From the outside of the house, an owl could be heard hooting in a tree close by.

Two hours later the man woke up got out of bed took a bunch of keys from the pocket of his trousers on the chair grabbed his dressing gown from the back of the door then quietly left the room and went back to the room that Rose was in and quietly unlocked and opened the door and tiptoed over to the bedside table unlocked the drawer and took out a loaded syringe and proceeded to inject Rose in one of her arms.

Rose stirred and winced in her sleep but did not wake as the man withdrew the needle from her arm and returned it to the drawer of the bedside table and locked it. He then tiptoed out of the room and relocked the door, and went and carried out the same procedure with Sam, who fast asleep showed no signs of resistance to receiving the injection.

Having completed his task, the man returned to his room got back into his bed and went back to sleep.

Chapter 2.

When Rose and Sam failed to return at six o' clock for their dinner Great Aunt Nancy, who was aged 66 of medium height and build with shoulder length fair hair that had hints of grey, had not been unduly alarmed because she understood that youngsters could not be relied on to turn up on time, and when they did turn up late and were asked the question "Where have you been until this time" the usual answer was a shrug of the shoulders with a reply of "Oh nowhere really".

So Nancy and Walter went into the kitchen, and Nancy served up dinner, when they had both finished Nancy washed up their plates and put Rose and Sam's ham salad in the fridge for them to eat when they eventually returned. While she did that Walter, who was also aged 66, tall and of stocky build with short brown straight hair with hints of grey went into the living room sat down and began to work on solving the crossword puzzle in his daily newspaper. He was soon joined by Nancy, who went and sat in her favourite comfortable chair and continued to read the book that she had begun to read during the afternoon. As the time, went by she kept looking at the clock on the living room wall. Walter also kept looking at the clock not able to concentrate on completing his puzzle.

At eight thirty Nancy suddenly closed her book got up out of her chair and went into the hall. Returning ten minutes later, she stood in the living room doorway and said to Walter.

"I've just tried phoning Rose on her mobile phone, but her line is dead, she has either lost her phone or switched it off for some reason. I can't think why she hasn't phoned us or returned by now Walter she must know we will be worrying. It's not like her and Sam to stay out so late. Where would they go, they don't know anybody apart from us in the village?"

"I don't know any more than you do as to where they have got to, I agree Rose should have at least have phoned us to let us know why she and Sam were still out and where they were"

"They might have gone into town on the bus to have a look around, and then gone to the cinema which would explain why Rose switched off her mobile phone"

"True but she should have phoned us to let us know that she and Sam had decided to go to into town. If having looked around the town they decided to go to the cinema, it's likely that they won't be back until at least eleven thirty. We shall just have to wait, and see if Rose phones us after they come out of the cinema".

"As you say she should have phoned, well we shall just have to wait. I will go and make us each a mug of tea"

"Good idea"

Walter continued to work on his crossword puzzle, while Nancy went into the kitchen to make tea. Ten minutes later Nancy returned with two large mugs of tea.

"If they are not back by eleven thirty I will phone our old friend Chief Superintendent Charley Humphreys and give him their description and ask him to get the local patrols to look out for them and when they find them to bring them straight back here"

"Good idea you do that if they haven't returned by then. Now drink your tea" Nancy said with a smile.

Walter took his tea and continued to work on his crossword puzzle. Nancy sat down and went back to reading her book. By, nine o'clock, they had both dozed off.

The clock above the fireplace struck midnight, and Nancy woke up with a start and looked up at the clock and seeing the time she quickly stood up and went over and shook Walters arm saying.

"Walter wake up it's past midnight and there's still no signs of Rose and Sam"

Walter opened his eyes and looking up at Nancy standing over him replied in a sleepy voice

"Hell is that the time I must have dozed off"

"We both did, you had better phone Charley because if Rose and Sam did go into town and to the cinema they should have been home by now. I'm not happy with Rose Walter she should have at least phoned us"

"Yes she should have I will phone Charley right away"

Walter eased himself up from his chair stretched and went out of the living room and picked up the phone off the hall table and dialled Charley Humphreys number, there came a short ringing tone before Charley's voice at the other end said.

"Chief Superintendent Humphreys who's calling and how can I help you?"

"Charley its Walter Cooper, look I'm sorry to phone you at this late hour but I have a problem. Rose and Sam who are staying with us for a week while John and Mary are on a business trip to Hong Kong went out with a packed lunch earlier today and have not returned or phoned us to let us know where they are. It's possible that they may have gone into town, but they should have been back by now. Could I ask you to ask your patrols in town to have a look for them?"

"Hello Walter yes I understand it's very late as you say for them not to have returned. I'm surprised that they didn't phone you it's not like them not to do so. The last bus back to your area will have gone and returned by now. They might have got a taxi, but I'll notify the patrols and give them their descriptions and ask them to look out for them, and if they come across them to bring them straight back to you. Let me know if they turn up ok"

"Thanks Charley I'll get my car out and drive in towards town because if they did miss the last bus and not take a taxi they might have decided to walk back I'm bound to see them. I will phone you on my mobile if I find them. Likewise, you can phone me back with any news on my mobile you have my number. Sorry to put you to this trouble at this late hour, speak to you soon bye"

"No problem Walter I'm on night duty tonight anyway. Speak to you soon, bye"

Walter put down the phone and took his jacket down off its peg in the hall and as he began to put it on Nancy came out of the living room saying.

"Did you speak to Charley?"

"Yes he is going to get his patrols to look for them and if they see them they will bring them straight back here. I'm going to drive in towards town because if they did miss the last bus they may have decided to walk home, and I'm bound to spot them. Now where did I put my mobile?"

"It's on your desk I'll get it for you, have you got your car keys?"

"Yes they are in my pocket"

Nancy hurried back into the living room picked up Walters's mobile off his desk and brought it out saying.

"Phone me as soon as you hear or see anything ok, now hurry"

"Will do and phone me if they turn up, bye"

Walter gave Nancy a quick peck on the cheek as he opened the front door and went out. Netty stood watching him as he got in his car that was parked on the driveway and backed out down the drive and out through the open gates. Once he had gone she closed the front door and returned to the living room and sat down in her chair just as the clock struck a quarter to one. She gave a deep sigh, and tears began to roll down her cheeks.

Out on the road Walter drove at a steady pace through the village looking out for any signs of Rose and Sam. When he reached the crossroads where Rose and Sam had turned to head for the forest earlier that day Walter turned right in the direction of the nearby town of Bishops Stortford and passing the village bus stop he saw no sign of them. He continued on his way and within a very short time he arrived in the town where he could see that the streets were for the most part deserted of both traffic and people. He passed the bus station where they would have caught the bus but again no sign of them. All the buses were locked away in the stations garage for the night, and all the staff had gone home. Walter drove round to the main Taxi office which was still open, he pulled up and got out of the car and went into the office where a grey-haired, thickset man wearing glasses sat behind a desk reading a newspaper. The man looked up and asked.

"Evening or more precisely Morning you want a taxi?"

"Thank you no, can I ask have you been on duty all night?"

"Yep and I'm due to finish very soon, why do you ask?"

Walter took out his mobile phone switched it on and pressed the file that contained his collection of photos and flicked through the photos until he found one of the photos he had taken the previous day of Rose and Sam posing in the garden at the cottage with Nancy. Passing across the phone so the man could see the photo he said.

"Can you remember if these two youngsters came in here this evening to order a taxi?"

The man looked at the photo raising his eyebrows and let out a sigh, then shook his head saying.

"Police are you, what they been up to then?"

"No, I'm not from the police, they are relatives of mine I have reason to belief that they may have come into town earlier today and then gone to the cinema this evening. They should have returned by now"

"I see well I'm sorry to disappoint you, but no I haven't seen them. You sure they came into town?"

"I can only assume that they came into town. My wife and I live in Takely. Trouble is they haven't phoned us to let us know where they had gone. They left our cottage just before lunch with some sandwiches and bottles of lemonade that my wife prepared for them. Said they wanted to go out for the day"

"I see well yes they should have at least phoned you, youngsters there's no telling these days what they get up to, they stay out till goodness knows what hours of the day and night. You should phone the police"

"I already have. Thanks for your help sorry to have troubled you, bye"

"No trouble I hope you find them ok, take care bye"

Walter dashed out of the office and got back in his car and headed for the police station. As he drove he toyed as to whether he should phone Nancy and let her know that he had not found them. But if he couldn't be sure how she would react especially as she was on her own. She would get herself all in a state. Better to wait until he had seen Charley. He parked up in front of the police station got out of the car and ran up the steps and through the doors up to the reception desk where a sergeant was sat busy filling in a duty log. The sergeant looked up and said.

"Steady sir, what seems to be the problem?"

"I need to see Detective Chief Superintendent Humphreys I phoned him earlier. My name is Walter Cooper"

"Just a second sir and I will let him know that you are here"

The Sergeant picked up his phone and pressed two numbers and on hearing a reply said into the phone.

"I have a Mr Walter Cooper here who wishes to see you sir. Right very good sir I will get one of the constables to bring him up"

The Sergeant put down the phone then turning and opening a door behind him called out.

"Constable Daly would you come out here now"

A young fresh faced constable appeared and asked.

"You called sergeant"

"Yes would you kindly take Mr Cooper here up to Chief Superintendent Humphreys office, the chief is expecting him"

"Very good Sergeant, Mr Cooper would you follow me please"

"Certainly"

The Constable led Walter through a door into a corridor that had offices either side; they walked past the offices to the end of the corridor where there was a lift. Seeing that the lift was vacant the Constable opened the door, and they both got in. The Constable pressed the button for the fourth floor. Once they arrived the Constable opened the lift door, and they both stepped out into another corridor which again had offices either side. They walked past several offices before the Constable stopped outside one of the offices and knocked on the door which had the name Detective Chief Superintendent C Humphreys written on a sign on the door. From within a man's voice called out.

"Come in"

The Constable opened the door ushering Walter to go in to the office. Walter stepped in and there behind a large desk that was neatly set out stood his old friend Charley Humphreys, who was of medium build with short brown hair neatly parted in the middle that was going grey, he had dark brown eyes and a swarthy complexion. He wore a dark grey neatly pressed suit. Sat at a smaller desk opposite Charley's desk there was a thick set man with fair wavy hair pale complexion and grey eyes, like Charley he was dressed in a suit. Seeing Walter, they both smiled, and Charley said.

"Come and sit yourself down Walter, thank you Constable Daly you can go, oh but first Walter would you like some coffee I know it's late but it will help keep you alert"

As Walter walked across the room and shook Charley's hand and sat on a chair in front of his desk he smiled and replied.

"Thank you yes I could do with a cup of coffee"

"Good Constable Daly rustle us up three coffees would you, I'm sure my colleague Detective inspector Roberts here would also like a cup of coffee wouldn't you?"

Inspector Roberts smiled at his chief replying.

"Thank you that will be very welcome"

"Ok, off you go Constable Daly"

The Constable went out closing the door behind him.

"Well Walter I'm really so sorry to hear about Rose and Sam. I still have no news for you. Have you heard from Nancy as to whether Rose and Sam have turned up?"

"No, not a word, I'm really worried Charley it's just not like Rose and Sam to disappear and not contact us. I was going to phone Nancy to let her know that I was coming in to see you, she will be worrying herself sick I just know it, but I didn't know what to tell her"

"I understand, now Walter I need to ask you some questions in the hope that we can find some clues to Rose and Sam's whereabouts"

"Of course where do you want me to start?"

"You said on the phone that Rose and Sam are staying with you for the week while John and Mary are on business in Hong Kong"

"That's right they arrived late last Sunday night; John and Mary brought them in the car up from Devon. John and Mary stayed overnight then left early in the morning to go to Heathrow to catch a plane to Hong Kong. They are due to return midday on Saturday"

"Did Rose and Sam go out anywhere on Monday?"

"No they spent the day in the cottage and in the garden; I took photos of them which I have on my phone"

"You said that they went out earlier today Tuesday, well yesterday now. What time did they go out? Did they mention that they might be coming into Bishops Stortford?"

"No, they had spent the morning in the garden playing on the swings, then just before lunch Rose ran into the kitchen and asked Nancy if she, and Sam could have a picnic lunch as Rose said she and Sam wanted to take a walk around the village and picnic on the village green. Nancy agreed and made up some sandwiches for each of them and gave them each a bottle of lemonade which she put in their small backpacks. She told Rose to be sure that they were home by six for dinner. Rose promised that they would be. Then she took the packs and ran down the garden collected Sam and they both went off out onto the lane, and we have not seen or heard from them since"

"You said that they hadn't phoned did they each have a mobile phone with them?"

"No only Rose has a mobile phone and she has our numbers on her phone as well as John and Mary's numbers"

"Do they know anybody else in the village that they may have gone to visit, friends they had made on previous visits to you and Nancy?"

"No, not that I know of, whenever they come to stay they always stay within the grounds of the cottage apart from when they go to the village shop or catch a bus into town. Other times when they go out they're always with both Nancy and me or John and Mary. Nancy and I don't have any surviving relatives living in the village for them to go and visit. However we both know a lot of people in the village but they don't know Rose and Sam well enough to invite them into their homes"

"How often have they been into Bishops Stortford before on their own?"

"Many times, they always used to go with John and Mary up until a few years ago when John said that they were old enough to go on their own into the town on the bus"

"When was the last time that they went into Stortford on their own?"

"Last Christmas when they came to stay, they went on the bus into Stortford to buy presents. Whenever they went into town they always came back on time"

"Do you know if they had a lot of money with them this time when they arrived?"

" No, they didn't have a lot; John and Mary gave them twenty pounds each to last them for a week, so that they could buy ice creams, or if they went into town they would have bus fares and money for the cinema and to buy snacks. Nancy and I usually give them some money but we hadn't got around to it this time"

"Is it possible that they might have gone to one of the other nearby towns like Dunmow for instance?"

"No there is nothing of interest in Dunmow for them; as you know it's only a small town not like Bishops Stortford"

There was a knock on the door "Come in" called out the chief.

The door opened and in walked Constable Daly with a tray on which there were three cups of hot coffee.

"Ah, thank you Constable, good timing" the chief said with a smile.

Smiling back, Constable Daly walked over and put two of the cups down on the chiefs desk before turning and walking over and putting the other cup down on Inspector Roberts desk where he was busy writing down the notes in shorthand from the discussion that was in progress between Walter and the chief. He smiled at the Constable and nodded a thank you. Constable Daly smiled back then left the room.

"Here you are Walter drink your coffee while we continue" the chief said as he passed Walter a cup.

"Thank you Charley"

"Now where were we, ah yes I remember that they liked going into the forest in the village, how many times has Rose and Sam visited the forest?"

"Oh many times they either went there with John and Mary or they went with Nancy and I, sometimes we all used to go there together"

"Had they ever been there on their own?"

"Never John and Mary made them swear that they would never go there on their own until they were both adults. Nancy and I stuck by that agreement and never allowed them to go there on their own"

"When was the last time that they went to the forest?"

"Last summer, we all went there for a day out and had a picnic before walking along some of the tracks"

"When you say all you mean Mary, John you and Nancy?"

"That's right"

"Did you or Nancy or John and Mary ever take them off the tracks and into the depths of the forest?"

"Never, we always kept to the tracks. As you know the forest is very dense and unless you know your way around as well as I do it would be easy to get lost"

"But Rose and Sam must know the forest quite well from all their visits?"

"They only know their way around the area close to the village, that's the area we always used to go to. They haven't been to the areas further afield"

"Walter you know the forest better than anyone, having spent all your working life in the forest until you retired last year as head Ranger. I remember from my many visits to see you there that there are map boards up in different parts of the forest showing the different routes"

"Yes that's right there are and each of the maps has a red mark that shows you where you are in the forest. The forest as you know is spread over a large area and is divided up by roads, some of which are country lanes others main roads which interconnect with the different villages. In the forest, there are hardcore tracks as well as grass tracks which have been there for many years. Visitors use both the hard core and grass tracks, either walking, horse riding or driving their cars. The forest gets a lot of visitors all year round. There is always work going on in the forest to keep it in good order and shape"

"So Rose and Sam would know about the map boards"

"Yes they would"

"Do you not suspect that as it was a hot day that they might just have decided as youngsters do to disobey their parents and ventured into the forest?"

"No,I never gave it a thought because they are very well behaved youngsters. You have known them since they were born Charley and know how strictly John and Mary have brought them up"

"Yes I know, but sadly Walter these days even the best behaved youngsters can be tempted to go where they know that they shouldn't it's all part of growing up"

"Yes but come on Charley I'm sure that they wouldn't disobey John and Mary or me. No, I can't think that they would go on their own into the forest. Anything could happen to them; they could easily get lost if they ventured off the tracks into the depths of the forest, one of them could have an accident, and they could end up stranded. They know how dangerous it can be"

"Well we have had no signs of them having visited the town, if they had gone into town they would certainly have returned by now even if they had decided to walk back to your place. Do you think they might have got on a train and gone into London?"

"No way, neither of them knows their way around London"

"Might they have gone somewhere else in the area?"

"I wouldn't have thought so; they only know the village and Stortford. Besides they didn't have a lot of money to go far away"

"Well Walter I need to check to find out if they went into the forest. If they did it's more than likely that they went through the main gates passed the parking attendants on duty at the gate. I will give George Armstrong a call and ask him to check with the gate attendants to see if they remember seeing Sam and Rose come through the gates. Not that he will be able to do that until he gets into his office later this morning"

"Excuse me sir who is George Armstrong?" Inspector Roberts asked looking up from the notes he was taking of the discussion.

"George Armstrong is now the head ranger of the forest, he took over from Walter when Walter retired as head ranger at the end of last year. Like Walter, he has worked in the forest all his working life. I have known George for years as I have Walter isn't that right Walter?"

"Certainly is. Are you going to phone George at this time of the morning Charley he will be fast asleep?"

"Yes I have to because if his attendants confirm that they remember seeing Rose and Sam come through the gates I will have no option but to organise a search of the forest. I will probably do that anyway, and will contact the other police stations in the area emailing a photo of Sam and Rose to them asking them to be on the lookout for them. I will also organise house to house questioning in Takely to find out if anyone in the village saw them yesterday"

"Right you had better use the photos of them that I have on my mobile" Walter replied looking pale as he took out his mobile phone and flicked on to the photos section and having found the photos of Rose and Sam he passed the phone to Charley.

"Thank you Walter, now just bear with me while I make some calls"

Charley picked up his phone and pressed out two numbers, and a voice answered.

"Detective Sergeant Phillips, how can I help you sir?"

"Would you come up to my office straight away I have some photos that need to be copied off a mobile phone and emailed to the surrounding police stations as well as to George Armstrong the head ranger of the local forest"

"Right away sir"

Charley cleared the line then dialled out a number and waited. Presently a sleepy voice answered saying.

"Hello George Armstrong here who's calling?"

"George its Charley Humphreys, sorry to wake you at this hour of the morning but I need your support"

"Christ Charley do you know what time it is? Can it not wait until I get into my office?"

"No George sorry, listen I have Walter Cooper with me who has reported that Rose and Sam Cooper have gone missing. You remember them, well it's possible that they might have gone into the forest and got themselves lost. I'm going to email you their photos and need you to show the photos to the attendants who were on the gates yesterday to see if they remember seeing them come through the gates yesterday"

"Goodness Charley that's serious. If you have reason to believe that Rose and Sam have gone missing in the forest, we will need to carry out a search. Naturally you will have my full support. So email me Rose and Sam's photos, I will ask the attendants if they saw them come through the gates. Then I will phone you back as soon as I have spoken to the attendants".

"Thanks George, sorry to wake you at this hour, I will speak to you later, bye"

"That's ok Charley I understand, phone you back later, bye"

Charley put down his phone, just as there was a knock on his door.

"Come in" Charley called out.

Detective Sergeant Phillips walked in and said.

"You wanted to see me sir"

"Yes I want you to print off copies of the photos of these youngsters Rose and Sam Cooper on Mr Cooper's phone, and send five Constables over to Takely at eight o'clock each with copies of the photos to carry out door to door enquiries to find out if anyone saw these youngsters yesterday in and around the village. Also distribute copies to all the morning shift patrols in the town, and get them to go to the shops, bus station, bowling alley and all the other venues that youngsters use in the town to check if these youngsters were seen at those places yesterday. I also want you to email copies to George Armstrong the head ranger of Hatfield Forest in Takely, and to the senior officers at all the surrounding police stations and requesting them to ask their officers to be on the lookout for these youngsters and notify me if they have reports of seeing them. Contact Stansted airport police and sent them copies as well just in case; these two youngsters went there. This is urgent as these youngsters have gone missing"

"Right sir I will do that straight away, oh and I will make some extra copies for the media"

Charley handed the Sergeant Walters phone, as Walter fished in his pocket and took out his phone charger cable and passed it to the Sergeant saying.

"You will need this to connect the phone to your computer"

"Thank you sir yes, I will need it" the sergeant replied taking the cable and was about to leave when Charley said.

"Just a minute sergeant"

Then looking at Walter he said.

"Walter it's three in the morning, there is not much more that we can do until we hear from George. You need to go back home and try and get some sleep. I will phone you as soon as I have heard back from George"

"That time already yes I need to get back to make sure Nancy is all right and let her know that you are doing everything you can to find Rose and Sam. I will want to be with you when you carry out the search of the forest though"

"Yes of course Walter I will pick you up on my way to the forest. Now get yourself home. Sergeant would you show Mr Cooper the way out"

"Certainly sir, Mr Cooper would you come with me please"

"Right I'm coming. Thank you Charley I appreciate your help, sorry to burden you. I will see you later."

"It's no burden Walter, be assured I will do all I can to find Rose and Sam, but please don't phone John and Mary yet, let's see what happens first ok"

"Ok, I'll wait and see what the search brings, see you later bye".

Sergeant Phillips and Walter left Charley's office and when they had gone Inspector Roberts looked across at his boss and said.

"It doesn't look good does it Sir, we haven't had any youngsters reported as missing for ages"

"No, not in Stortford, but remember six months ago Joy Manders went missing in Epping Forest, which is only 26.5 KM from Takely Forest, and as of yet she has not been found. I have a nasty suspicion that Rose and Sam did go into the forest, and there's no telling what might have happened to them. Of course if they did it's possible that they got lost and then spent all the daylight time trying unsuccessfully to find their way out onto one of the tracks. Then when it got too dark they settled down to sleep until they could start again in the morning to find their way out"

"But surely if they did go into the forest and got themselves lost they would phone for help unless of course they didn't want Mr and Mrs Cooper to know that they had gone into the forest"

"You may well be right they wouldn't phone to say they had got lost because they would know that they would be in serious trouble. Then again they might have lost their phone so weren't able to call for help. One of them might have had an accident whilst trying to find a way back to one of the tracks again they might have decided to stay put until the morning to seek help. No, if one of them had had an accident they would have definitely phoned for help, regardless of the fact that they would get a severe telling off for going into the forest on their own".

"But if they didn't go into the forest and didn't come into town then there is no telling where they might have gone. From what Mr Cooper said they didn't have a lot of money with them so they wouldn't have been able to return to their home in Devon should they have chosen to do so? However they would have had enough to have caught a train into London, and if they did then goodness knows where they might end up"

"No, they wouldn't have gone back home and they wouldn't have gone to London. I bet they went into the forest. I just hope that if they did we find them safe very soon, because if we don't and I have to contact the parents there will be hell to play because knowing the parents they will stop at nothing until we find them. I can assure you that the father John has a great deal of influence in high places so you can imagine what's likely to happen, we will have the Chief Constable on our backs chasing us until we find them, as well as all the national media swamping us"

"You seem to have known the Cooper's for long time"

"Yes I have known them for years from way back when I used to patrol the village of Takely. I used to visit Walter at his office in the forest when he was head Ranger of the forest. I remember first seeing Rose shortly after she was born when John and Mary brought her to visit Walter and Nancy. The same when Sam was born".

"How old are the youngsters now?"

"Rose is fifteen and Sam is eleven. I last saw them when they came with John and Mary to stay at Walters last Christmas"

"Are they bright kids?"

"Yes and they are well behaved. Rose easily gets bored though and is always looking for new things to do, that's why I won't be surprised if we discover that they went into the forest, she will have wanted to go exploring even though she knows that she has been told not to go there without her parents or Walter"

"There's no telling with youngsters these days, unlike us when we were their age we didn't have computers where we could find all sorts of information, and we didn't have mobile phones to phone all our friends day and night. We had to go and use the local or school library to help with our homework"

"True and they have more interests available to them. I used to play football and rugby or go fishing. Walter Cooper and I used to go fishing together in the lake in the forest, but we haven't done that for some time now".

"Is there good fishing to be had in the lake there"

"Yes we caught some good sized fish I caught a very large pike there once"

"I used to fish as well years ago I should take it up again might even be able to persuade my kids to take it up if I can get them away from their computers" Inspector Roberts replied with a smile as he switched on his computer to word process his report.

Charley smiled back and replied as he began to prepared plans for the search of the forest. "Well I hope you have better luck with your kids, mine like yours are always too busy on their computers"

Chapter 3.

At eight thirty, that morning the Wednesday the phone on Chief Superintendent Charley Humphrey's desk rang. He picked it up, and a voice said.

"Good morning sir I have Mr Armstrong the head ranger of Takely forest on the line who wishes to speak to you"

"Morning Sergeant Phillips thank you put him through would you"

There was a click then a voice said.

"Morning Charley I received the photos you had emailed across of Rose and Sam Cooper and showed them to the gate attendants that were on duty yesterday and yes they remember seeing them come through the gates at lunchtime yesterday. They don't remember seeing them go back out, but that's not unusual for walkers because they often leave through other exits which are not manned"

"Morning George it is just as I thought they did go into the forest. I have arranged to carry out a search of the area. I shall be bringing some of my officers and tracker dogs, and I have more officers and trackers coming over from some of the neighbouring police stations. I also have two divers who will check the lake"

"Very good well I have closed all the exits and the main gates to stop visitors and informed my staff that you are coming to do a search. Can you spare some officers to be on duty at the different exits? I have also instructed some of my staff that I want them to go with your search teams seeing as they know all the areas of the forest"

"Thanks George yes you can have some of my officers for each of the exits. I should be with you at about nine forty five ok"

"Ok I will see you soon then bye"

"Bye"

Inspector Roberts who sitting at his desk had heard the conversation said.

"So you were right sir they did go into the forest"

"Yep, so let's go and see if we can find them. You take your car and I will go in mine I need to pick up Walter Cooper on the way so can you lead the team over to George's office once we get to Takely and wait for me"

"Yes no problems, have you got the maps of the forest?"

"Yes here you are, and George will have looked some out as well"

Charley and Inspector Roberts left the office and went down to the police car park where there were two minivans full of police officers and a plain white van in which there were tracker dogs parked up waiting to go. Charley and the Inspector walked over to their cars. Charley got in his dark green Range Rover, and the Inspector got in his pale blue BMW. Charley then led the way out through the gates in the direction of Takely.

When they arrived in Takely Charley turned off into the lane to go to Walter while Inspector Roberts and the others continued towards the entrance to the forest.

Charley pulled up outside the cottage and got out and walked up the drive where Walter and Nancy were already waiting at the front door.

"Morning Charley any news" Walter asked looking worried.

"Morning Walter, Nancy yes George phoned and confirmed that both Rose and Sam were seen going through the main gates into the forest yesterday. I have some of my officers along with some officers from some of the surrounding police stations on their way to the forest now, and we will begin a search".

"Dam! How could they, they know that they are forbidden to go on their own into the forest. Right well I'm ready to come with you so let's go Charley"

"I just hope you find them safe. They are really very naughty fancy them doing that. I'm so sorry Charley to have caused you all this extra work" Nancy said rubbing her hands together with a worried expression on her face.

"Well as I said youngsters will do these things. Come on Walter let's go and try and find them. I'm sure that they must have got lost and having not been able to find their way onto the track before it got dark settled down to sleep in the forest. Thankfully it was a warm, dry night. I'm sure we will find them safe Nancy I'll let you know as soon as we find them"

"Thank you Charley see you later; Woe betides them when I see them, no more going out for them this week that's for sure" Nancy replied as she turned and went back inside the cottage.

Charley and Walter went down the drive and got into Charley's car and drove off towards the entrance to the forest, and as they drove Charley said to Walter.

"I spoke to the Chief Constable first thing this morning and let him know the situation naturally he is concerned and hopes that we find Rose and Sam and that they will be all right. I'm to keep him informed and let him know of anything that I need, and he will ensure that I get full support. Oh by the way before I forget here is your mobile"

"Thank you Charley I appreciate everything that you are doing, I'm just sorry that I have had to burden you. I find it hard to belief that Rose and Sam disobeyed

John's instructions about going to the forest, Nancy and I would have been happy to have taken them for a day out in the forest".

"Well there's no telling with youngsters, they sometimes go where they have been told not to go too. I'm sure you must have been the same when you were a youngster, I know I went to places where I was told not to go, and it's the curiosity factor that all youngsters have "

"Yes I suppose so; I must admit that I used to go into the forest when I was a youngster even though my father said that I was never to go there without an adult".

"There you are you see we are all as bad at that age. As I said it's more than likely that they went into the depths of the forest and having got lost and not being able to find their way out by the time, it had got dark they stayed put in the hope that you may have guessed that they had gone into the forest and would come looking for them in the morning. Which is exactly what you're doing"

"Well I hope your right. Rose must have lost her mobile phone or the battery was flat because I'm sure that she would have phoned me even knowing that she would get a telling off for disobeying John and Mary?"

"I'm sure she would have".

"Have you got many men involved in the search?"

"Yes I have a dozen men plus tracker dogs and their handlers going from my station, plus more officers from the surrounding police stations who will meet us outside George's office to join in the search. George is getting some of his men together as well to help".

"Oh dear, oh dear I just hope that when we find Rose and Sam they will realize what an inconvenience they have caused"

"It is never an inconvenience Walter it's all part of the job and we like to think that we do everything we can to help. Ah here we are"

Charley swung the Range Rover off the road and in through the entrance gate into the forest where there were two police Constables stood by the gate. He briefly stopped and spoke to the Constables who recognised him and said.

"Good morning Constable Walker and Constable Jones, can you insure that you don't allow any visitors in past these gates, the only people allowed in are police officers and forestry staff"

The two Constables returned his greeting and said they would make sure that his orders were obeyed. Charley then speed along the track to the left before pulling up alongside six police mini buses and four small plain white vans which were parked outside a large one story building that was the visitor centre where visitors could go to learn about the forest. Charley and Walter got out of the Range Rover and went into the building and made their way to George's office and went inside. George was stood behind his desk along with Inspector Roberts and three police Inspectors as well as three men who wore green forestry jackets. They were busy looking at a large map of the forest that was on the wall behind George's desk. George stopped talking to the group, and they all turned to see who had come in. Seeing Walter and Charley George came round from behind his desk saying.

"Morning Walter, Charley, you are just in time I was showing the Inspectors here the map of the forest and where I propose we should start to search. I'm sorry to hear what's happened Walter and hope that we find Rose and Sam safe and sound"

"Morning George, Sidney and John, I'm sorry to have burdened you with this situation. This is the first time we have had to go searching the forest for missing people for ages." Walter replied shaking hands with George and the two gatemen who he already knew.

Charley shook George's hand greeting him with a smile then shook hands with Sidney, John and the three Inspectors whom he knew had come from the different surrounding police stations. Then Charley said.

"Right George I will let you begin your briefing. All the entrances into the forest should now be sealed off and have officers manning them"

"Thank you Charley"

George turned and pointing to the map said.

"Now I suggest that we split up into teams and that each team combs through the different sectors closest to where we are now, we will start from this point here and work our way through in a line calling out for Rose and Sam as we go. If any of us hear one of them call out in reply then we will alert the leaders of the other teams straight away. The team nearest to them will then move forward until they come across them. Should we not come across them having combed our way through each of these sectors then we will all meet up at this point here where we will move to the next sector areas and start the searches there. If having combed all the sectors in this area and we haven't come across them then we will have to move to the next sectors which start on the other side of the main road here. Should we have to do that then we will need to bring in more men for the search because those sectors are bigger. But,I think that it is more than likely that we will find them before having to move to the larger sectors, because I don't think that they will have had time to travel that far. We will of course if we need to stop for snack breaks during the day. My estimate is that given the time that they first arrived yesterday and entered the forest they won't have been able to have got much further than this area here on the map because it would have become dark by the time they reached that area. Has anyone got any questions they wish to ask?"

"George I take it that you will have at least one of your men with each team of searchers?" Charley asked.

"Yes there will be one of my men in each team along with a police Inspector. My men will each have short wave radio so that they can contact me back here in the office. My men will need to have their radios tuned into the police officers radios that are involved in the search and the police officers will need to be able to contact me here as well"

"Thank you George yes that shouldn't be a problem just let the Inspectors here know your radio frequency and they will make sure that all the officers have it, likewise the Inspectors will let you have the frequency that they will be using"

"You said you had brought two divers with you I will get one of my men to take them over to the lake so that they can search there. So shall we get the teams organized and let's make a start" George said looking around at the group assembled in the office. Everyone nodded, and they all went outside where all the police officers that had been in the mini buses were assembled and chatting in groups. The dogs had been taken out of the vans and were eagerly pulling on the leeches that were being firmly held by their handlers.

"I would like to go with one of the teams George," Walter said.

"No better that you stay here at base with George, myself, and Inspector Roberts" Charley said.

"Ok, if you say so, but I feel that I should go"

"No Charley is right it's best you stay with us" George replied.

Within a quarter of an hour the teams each of which consisted of one of George's men, an Inspector, twelve

Constables, two dogs and their handlers moved off to start the search. The two divers went over to the lake and began the task of searching underwater the full length and depth of the lake while Charley, George, Walter went back into George's office. Inspector Roberts stood outside and took written statements from Sidney and John the two gatekeepers who had said they had seen Rose and Sam come through the gates the day before. Once the statements were finished Inspector Roberts went back into the office, and Sidney and John went off to join the search teams. George had made some coffee, and everyone sat down and waited for any news.

By lunch time, there were no positive results, each of the teams had radioed in to say that they had combed through most of the area that they had been allocated to but there was still no sign of Rose and Sam. The divers had checked the full length and breadth of the lake and found nothing.

Then at two in the afternoon Inspector Farthing who was leading one of the teams radioed in and speaking to George said.

"We have just come across the remains of a half skinned stag by a narrow stream and it looks as if it has been shot with a bolt from a crossbow. Your man says he thinks that the stag was more than likely killed yesterday and it looks like you have a poacher back again"

"Ok, really well thank you Inspector, any other news?"

"No not at the moment, we are still looking"

"Okay bye"

The Inspector rang off, and Walter asked George.

"Are you having problems with Deer poachers again?"

"Regretfully yes over the last two weeks we have found stag carcasses in various parts of the forest, the poacher is targeting stags and its always the same, whoever it is cuts the heads off the stags, skins them and expertly cuts the beasts up for their meat leaving very little left apart from the legs and rib cages"

"Interesting Chief Superintendent Humphreys was telling me last night that you had similar problems with Deer poaching some years ago. You should have informed us so that we can help you find the poacher" Inspector Roberts said.

"I was going to contact you but didn't want to trouble you. We have increased our patrols to try and find the poacher ourselves and then bring him in for you to sort out." George replied.

"The Inspectors right George you should have let Charley know. You know we had this same problem some years ago, and we and Charley spent considerable time trying to find the poacher, but never did because whoever he was he was too smart for us. Once he found out we were looking for him he suddenly stopped poaching" Walter said.

"I have just had a thought I wonder if......"

Before the Inspector, could finish the radio phone on George's desk buzzed again. George picked up the radio phone saying.

"Hello yes"

"George its Inspector Farthing again let me speak to Chief Superintendent Humphreys we might be on to something"

George passed the radio phone across to Charley who said.

"Hello Inspector Farthing what's up?"

"Well sir I think we are onto something. We need a forensic team out here now because after we found the remains of the stag by a stream the tracker dogs suddenly became very agitated and kept sniffing at the ground and jumping up and down they must have picked up a scent because they pulled their handlers across the stream and through the trees zigzagging first left then right. Having followed them we have come across a number of footprints which look like youngster's footprints as well as a man's footprints. The man's footprints appear to match those that we found next to the remains of the stag. We have also found some torn clothing threads on some of the bushes, which consist of blue, red, light grey and green threads. We then found a small area where the leaves on the ground have been disturbed, the ferns have been crushed, and there are more youngsters' footprints as well as the man's footprints there. It looks as if there must have been some sort of struggle. The dogs continued through the trees following the man's footprints and brought us out onto one of the grass tracks where we found tire tracks that look to be from a van. The dogs settled down when we got to the tire tracks as if they had lost the scent"

"Right ok, just a second"

Charley covered the mouth piece of the radio phone and looked at Walter, and asked.

"What colour clothes were Rose and Sam wearing?"

"Oh, they were both wearing light blue jeans, Rose was wearing a pale Yellow T-shirt and Sam was wearing a green T-shirt, and they both wore lightweight, light grey bomber style jackets why?"

Charley put a finger to his lip then uncovering the mouthpiece of the radiophone said.

"Hello Inspector, yes that sounds like a possibility because they were wearing clothes with those colours. What else can you tell me?"

"Well sir we back tracked from the grass track where we found the tire marks following the threads right back to the stream and measuring the distance we found it to be six hundred yards. We searched all-around the immediate area close to where the tire tracks are located, but there are no further signs of youngsters footprints, only the man's footprints. It looks as if the man must have carried the youngsters through the trees from the area where we found signs of a disturbance to a parked vehicle on the track"

"I see and did you follow the direction of the tire tracks?"

"Yes sir the vehicle had continued along the track then turned left onto an open grass area where it continued in a straight line until it came to a hard core track. The hard core track leads onto a country lane where if you turn right you go in the direction of Stortford and if you turn left you could pick up one of the main roads going towards London. If the vehicle had gone in the opposite direction along the hard core track it would have joined the track that goes out through the main Takely entrance to the forest"

"Did you find a mobile phone anywhere in the area?"

"No sir we didn't"

"Right Inspector Farthing I want the whole route from where you found the tire marks on the grass track back through the forest to the stream taped off; I will get a forensic team out as soon as possible. What is the map reference for the location?"

"Will do sir, the map references are"

Inspector Farthing looked at the map he had with him and with the help of a forester who was with him he read out the references.

"Excellent thank you. Now I want you to leave two officers at the scene and bring the rest of the team back here, and please notify the other team leaders that they and their teams can now return back here. I will see you soon, bye"

Charley passed the radiophone back to George then turning to Walter he said.

"Walter as you will have heard Inspector Farthing and his team have found clothing threads on bushes that match in colour with the clothes that Rose and Sam were wearing. They have also found youngster's footprints as well as one adult's footprints. It would appear that there has been some sort of a struggle. They have also found tire marks on a grass track close to the scene. I'm very sorry Walter, but it looks very probable that the youngster's footprints could be those of Rose and Sam. We shall have to wait until forensics has gathered all the clues. If we find that the youngster's footprints match with Rose and Sam's sized shoes then, it's very probable that they have been snatched and that the person who snatched them is the poacher. They didn't find a mobile phone"

"Oh! My God! You're saying that the poacher has snatched them"

"I'm very sorry Walter but it looks that way. Inspector Roberts phone through to base and get a forensics team out here straight away"

"Will do"

"I must phone John and Mary as well as Nancy and let them know what's happened. This is turning into one hell of a nightmare" Walter said with a pained expression on his face.

"No Walter I don't want you to phone them yet not until the forensics team have done their job. If the results are positive then of course John and Mary will have to be informed"

"So what am I supposed to do just sit and wait?"

"I'm sorry Walter but that's all we can do for now" George who looked ashen said.

"I'm so sorry Walter, Charley is right we have to wait. However, what we can do is start checking all the registration numbers of vehicles that came through the gates yesterday. I have the lists here. What is the map references Charley were Inspector Farthing's team found the tire marks?"

Charley stood up and went behind George's desk and looking and pointing at the map on the wall said.

"They found the tire tracks on this track here. So it's possible that the vehicle did come in through the main gates went along this hard track here before turning onto the grass track, then left by continuing along the grass track that leads out into this open area here before heading out through this opening onto the road. The vehicle would then have either gone towards Stortford or the other way towards London. On those vehicle registration lists, George do the gatekeepers say what type of vehicle the registration number belongs to?"

"Yes they do, and the gatekeepers check and mark of on the sheets when the vehicles return through the main gates. Looking at yesterday's lists, it appears that there were four vans that came through the gates yesterday, and only three of them left through the main gates. Here I have circled their registration numbers for you. The one that didn't leave by the main gate is this one which I have put a cross beside the registration number. If that van left through that opening onto the road that you mention, the driver would have had to remove a metal barrier that seals the entrance. That barrier is normally secured with chains and padlocks"

"Right thank you George, just a second"

Charley picked up the radio phone and pressed two numbers, and Inspector Farthing answered saying.

"Hello sir"

"Inspector did you check the barrier at the exit onto the road?"

"I'm just walking towards the barrier now to check it why?"

"Because it is supposed to be secured with chains and padlocks"

"Right just a minute, ah yes I'm there now and it appears that the padlocks have been cut from the chains. Forensics will need to check for fingerprints"

"Yes they will, just a second"

Charley covered the mouthpiece of the radiophone and looking across at Inspector Roberts asked.

"Have you spoken to forensics?"

"Yes sir they are on their way as we speak"

Charley uncovered the mouthpiece and said.

"Inspector Farthing forensics should be with you very shortly, post one of your men by the barrier and instruct him not to tamper with the locks or chains ok"

"Very good I will do sir"

Charley switched off the radiophone and said.

"George do me a favour and make us all some coffee, Inspector Roberts I need to speak to you outside"

"Good idea I will make us some coffee I have a bottle of Brandy in my drawer I think we could all do with a shot of that in our coffee" George replied standing up and passing the vehicle lists to Charley.

Charley took the lists, and he, and Inspector Roberts went out of the office and made their way outside of the building where they stood by the front door. Charley fished in his pocket and brought out a packet of cigarette's and took one then offered one to the Inspector who taking a cigarette said.

"Thanks I thought you had given up smoking sir"

"I had the only time I start smoking is when I have a difficult situation on my hands. Christ those poor kids what a bloody nightmare"

"Yes I'm sorry this can't be easy seeing as you know these kids so well"

"What was this idea you have that you were about to mention when Inspector Farthing rung?"

"I was about to say I wonder if Epping Forest had been having a problem with Deer poaching at the time that Joy Manders disappeared whilst riding her pony in the forest back in January of this year and if so could it be that the poacher snatched Joy Manders"

"Bloody hell, Epping Forest of course the Joy Manders case. You could be on to something. Get back to the office and pull down all the information on the Joy Manders case and check if there had been reported incidences of poaching at that time. Oh and check who owns that van that was listed as having not gone back through the main gates here yesterday. We are going to catch this bastard whoever it is and fast"

"Right will do, if forensics comes up with a positive ID of those two youngsters, the parents will have to be contacted. Do you want me to do it?"

"No, I will have to contact them, but before I do that I need to speak to the Chief Constable first. We are going to crack this case, but we need to move and fast; I just hope that we find those youngsters alive because when John and Mary hear what's happened to their kids, you can bet that John will demand that we get a positive result or we will both be out of our jobs. Like me he will stop at nothing until he's found and caught whoever took them"

"We will find whoever it is I know we will. I will see you later back at base"

"Ok, good luck, see you later"

Detective Inspector Roberts turned and got in his car and swiftly drove out of the forest grounds and headed back to Bishops Stortford. Charley stubbed out his cigarette and returned to George's office where he found Walter pacing the office floor looking both nervous and impatient. George was trying to console him by saying that he was sure that the police would find Rose and Sam and that they would be all right.

"Walter I will get one of my officers to take you home, you need to be with Nancy. As soon as forensics has been and taken casts of the footprints I will get one of the forensic team to come over to yours to check to see if the prints match. If they do which I have reason to belief that they will then, I will contact John and Mary and explain to them what's happened. Inspector Roberts has gone back to Stortford where he is going to continue making enquiries. I believe from what he has told me that we might have some very strong leads to finding whoever may have snatched Rose and Sam"

Walter stopped in his tracks and looked Charley in his eyes saying.

"You really think you're on to something already, can you be sure, and can you guarantee that you will find Rose and Sam safe and sound?"

"Like I said Walter I believe we might have some hot leads. As soon as I am sure I will keep you John and Mary informed ok".

There came a knock on the office door and in walked a tall slim built man who, looked to be in his forties with neat fair hair. He was dressed in light grey slacks and an opened necked light blue shirt and black shoes.

"Good afternoon gentlemen can you give me directions to where in the forest you want me and my team to go to carry out the forensics?"

Charley turned and looking at the man said.

"Hello Jack thanks for coming over so promptly. This is Walter Cooper, who is a relative of the missing youngsters, and this is George Armstrong the head ranger of the forest. George, Walter, this is Jack Cotton he's the head of our forensics department. George would you give Jack directions on how to get to the site?"

George and Walter nodded at Jack, and then George replied by saying.

"Yes of course, if you care to look at the map on the wall I will show you how to get there"

Jack stepped forward and looked at the map on the wall behind George's desk while George showed him the directions. Once finished Jack turned and just before he left the office he said.

"Once my team and I have examined the site and collected all the clues I will come back here Chief Superintendent to report our findings. See you later bye"

"Thanks Jack sees you later" Charley, said.

No sooner had Jack left the office when there was another knock on the door and in walked one of the Inspectors who had been involved in the search.

"Chief Superintendent I and my team are back; what would you like us to do now?"

"Thank you Inspector Riley I'm grateful to you and your officers for giving up your valuable time to come and support us. As you will have heard I have called off the search because we have found what looks to be positive signs of the youngsters whom we believe have been snatched. You can send you're men back to your police station. I need to ask you one more favour could you take Mr Cooper who is a relative of the two missing youngsters back to his home?"

"Certainly sir I have my car outside. Mr Cooper would you care to come with me please"

Walter said as he walked out of the office with the Inspector.

"Thank you George, Charley, and Inspector for your support. I just hope you find Rose and Sam very soon and that they are safe. See you later Charley"

"I hope so to, speak to you later, bye".

"Yes take care Walter; I'm sure Charley will find them safe soon. Bye" George said.

Once Walter and the Inspector had gone George sat down at his desk and looking at Charley said.

"This is terrible news for all of us those poor kids. You said you were on to something, do you really think you might find whoever is responsible?"

"Oh, you bet I will. I'll find whoever is responsible George be sure of that. Now can you give me more details about the other Deer that were recently found and show me on the map where they were found?"

"Yes in this forest we have a mixture of Deer but the majority are either Red Deer or Fallow Deer. The poacher has been killing Red Deer stags. We found Red Deer stag remains in this place here, and another was found in this spot here, and the one found today as you know was found here. As you can see there is some distance between where each of them was found"

George said pointing to the map.

"Yes I see, so whoever the poacher is he appears to know his way around the forest very well, and he always kills Red Deer stags, and all the Deer were killed and cut up in the same way"

"Yes that's right they were. Whoever it is that is killing these animals not only knows his way around the forest but could be a trained butcher judging by the way the animals have been cut up so neatly"

"Yes and he also knows his way round all the other forests, which suggests to me that he could be someone who has worked in those forests as a ranger and been a butcher at some time. Have any of your rangers worked in any of the other forests and been a butcher in the past George?"

"All my rangers have worked in this forest continuously since they were in their late teens. Walter and I have known each of them most of our lives; a number of us were at school together. Walter and I were at school together, as you know he's ten years older than me. We are the longest serving rangers; Walter with over forty years' service was head ranger for years. I as you know have been here for over thirty years so when he retired last year I took over from him".

"Wow! That's some record"

"It runs in the families and has done so for generations. I'm the exception because my father never worked in the forest; he was a tenant farmer of Copley farm just the other side of Takely. Walter was the one who got me interested in working for the forest when we were youngsters. Walters's brother Joseph worked in the forest but only for a few years, before he suddenly left and went to live in Devon"

"Yes I remember your saying that you never wanted to work for your father, and Walter telling me years ago that his brother left the village when he was a young man. He never talks about his brother and has never told me why Joseph left to go to live in Devon"

"Ha, well that's Walter for you, he never talks about it"

"Do you know why Joseph left?"

"Yes I know I'm the only person who he has told"

"How come it's such a secret?"

"Well seeing as we have all known each other for years I will tell you, but don't let Walter know that I told you"

"OK, go on tell me," Charley said with a faint smile.

George related the story and had just finished when there was a knock on the door and Jack walked in saying.

"We have finished carefully examining the site and have taken casts of all of the footprints; tire tracks, and collected all the fabric fibres. We managed to get fingerprints from the padlocks and chains on the barrier leading out onto the road. I need to take fingerprints of the person who locked the barrier because there are bound to be a different set of prints"

"Good work Jack, George do you know who would have been the last person to lock the barrier?"

"Yes, Peter Thorn was working up there on Monday so he would have gone through the barrier. I will give him a call he should be working near the lake today"

"Thanks, so Jack what do you think having examined the site?"

"We found a man's footprints by the stream next to the carcase of the Deer and also found the same prints directly opposite the stream. There were youngsters footprints further back along the stream on that side. The man's prints then come back across the stream going towards where we found the youngsters footprints. Then all the footprints go off into the trees. We found a zigzag pattern of footprints on the ground going through the trees; the ground is still quite moist even though it's hot weather, so the prints are well defined. The youngsters and man's footprints going through the forest are the same as those by the stream. The youngster's size footprints differ in size indicating that there were two of them. We found snapped branches on bushes as well as different coloured threads from what appears to be the youngster's clothing. In addition, we found small pieces of cloth with red and blue check markings on a number of bushes where there were the same man's prints. The youngster's footprints come to a stop in the area where there are definite signs of some sort of fracas. The ferns have been flattened in such a way as to look like two young people have fallen and ended up lying down. The leaves on the ground there have been scattered about and there are the same youngsters and man's footprints there"

"I see and what of the tire markings?"

"Looking at the tire markings I would say they are from a large van. I also found white flakes of metal close to the tire marks that appear to be from the van. There are the same man's footprints in between the tire tracks as well as around where the van would have been parked which appear to be deeper suggesting that the man was carrying something. But there were no youngster's footprints near the van. We have casts and photos of those prints"

"Are you saying that he could have carried the two youngsters' to the van?"

"It is possible yes"

"Right I need you to go out to the cottage where we believe the youngsters came from to check to see if the youngster's footprints match with other shoes they will have at the cottage"

"Will do"

Turning to George Charley asked.

"Did you manage to speak to Peter Thorn?"

"Yes he's on his way here now"

"Good now George I need to know how long do you keep the lists of vehicle registration numbers that come in through the main, gates?"

"We keep the lists for three years that way we can keep a check on regular visitors. After that, the lists are sent to head office. I don't know how long they keep them for"

"Good I need you to dig out all the last three years lists"

"Not a problem we enter each year's lists on the computer and at the end of the year save the lists on to pen drive. So I can let you have that pen drive with the lists for the last two years and the file with this year's list. I will get them for you, you have yesterday's list already"

George stood up and went and opened a filing cabinet and took out a pen drive and a thick folder and brought them over and put them on his desk.

There was another knock on the door and in walked Peter Thorn saying.

"You needed to see me George"

"Yes Peter this is Detective Chief Superintendent Humphreys and Jack Cotton from Stortford police station. Jack needs to take your fingerprints so that he can distinguish your prints from other prints found on the padlocks and chains of the barrier you closed on Monday"

Peter looked at Charley, and Jack in surprise then said.

"Right no problem, this to do with the search for them two youngster's what have gone missing"

"Yes Peter it is" Charley replied with a smile.

Jack took a flat tin from a small bag he was carrying along with a sheet of paper and then guided Peter over to the other desk to take his prints.

Once Jack had finished and got the prints he thanked Peter and told him he was free to go. Peter said his goodbyes and left. Jack then said.

"Right sir I will now to go to the Coopers cottage to see if the shoe prints match"

"Ok good, well I have finished here for now. Did you see Inspector Farthing and his team?"

"Yes sir and having completed all I needed to at the site I informed him that there was no longer any need for his men to stay at the scene. They have all gone back to Stortford, and I saw the other teams driving off through the gates"

"Good, so George thanks' for everything, sorry to have messed up your day, you can open the forest up to visitors again. I expect you will have the local press coming to want to know everything the same as they will when they come and see me. I will return these files and pen drive to you within a few days, bye for now"

"No trouble Charley good luck I hope you catch this bugger and quick and find Rose and Sam safe, see you soon, bye and bye Jack"

Charley and Jack left the office and went out of the building. Once outside Charley asked.

"Have you got your car Jack or did you come in your van with your team?"

"No I came in the van it's parked just over there"

"Good ok, so off you go to the cottage and get those prints; I need to get back to the office. Give me a call if those youngsters' prints match"

"Will do, see you later, bye"

Charley got in his Range Rover and headed off along the track and out onto the road in the direction of Stortford, looking at his watch he saw it had gone six fifteen in the evening. He felt exhausted and hungry.

On arriving back in his office, Charley found Inspector Roberts busily printing off files that he had downloaded on his computer. Seeing his boss come in, he said.

"Ah, good your back sir, how did Forensics get on?"

"They have taken casts of the footprints found and managed to get some finger prints from the barrier locks and chains. They have gone to take prints of the youngster's shoes at the cottage. How about you, what have you found?"

"I checked the registration number of the vehicle that didn't return back through the main entrance to the forest yesterday. The owner is a John Mitchell a self-employed builder who lives in Enfield. I notified Enfield Police, who went to see Mr Mitchell. Trouble is he had a van with that registration number stolen from his yard two weeks ago. He had reported it as being stolen, and when the policemen turned up he thought they had come to say they had found his vehicle. I also ran a check on the other vans that came into the forest yesterday, but they all checked out as being ok"

"Damn, so the only thing we have is the finger prints, let's hope we find something when we run those through the computer. What have you found out about the Joy Manders case, were there reported incidents of Deer poaching in Epping Forest at the time she went missing"

"Yes there were and the poacher having killed the Deer carried out the same butchering technics as found in Takely Forest. I also checked up to see if other forests in and around the London area had been having Deer poaching problems"

"What did you discover?"

"I found out that, at other forests in and around the London area over the last five years there have been incidents of Deer poaching all of which match with Takely and Epping Forest. Also while the poaching was being carried out in each of the forests there were reports of youngsters having gone missing from the forests".

"Really and have any of the youngsters been found?"

"No"

"So, didn't the local police in those areas find any useful clues as to who may have been responsible for snatching the youngsters?"

"Like today they found both a man's footprints as well as the missing youngsters footprints and torn strips of fabric off the youngsters clothing, but nothing else"

"Have you seen each of the case files for the missing youngsters?"

"Yes I have downloaded and printed off each of the case files and there are photos of each youngster as well as photos of the casts made of the footprints found. I have all the details about the individual investigations. In each case, there were no witnesses who saw anything suspicious at the time the youngsters went missing".

"So in which forests have there been reports of poaching and child snatching?"

"The forests concerned include Epping as you know where Joy Manders aged sixteen went missing in January of this year. At Knole Forest in Seven Oaks Kent, in 2009, a girl Samantha Brooks went missing she was thirteen at the time. A month after she went missing a boy Adrian Prentice then aged eight went missing from the same forest. In 2010, a boy Jamie Simonds aged fifteen at the time went missing in Ashbridge Forest, Birkhampstead. In 2011, a girl Celia Peters then aged fourteen and her brother Julian then aged six went missing in Windsor Great Park. I also found that a girl Susan Crowther went missing from Thetford Forest in Norfolk in 2008; she was thirteen at the time. I have spoken to the senior officers who were in charge of the different investigations and let them know about what has happened in Takely Forest. I let them know that we had found a set of fingerprint and that we would contact them if we get a match".

"Right ok, well that's a good start let's just hope those fingerprints prove positive. We need to check if anyone in the London area has been convicted of being in possession of an illegal crossbow, also if any Butchers have been convicted of selling illegal Venison in the London area over the last five years. It's interesting that with the exception of Thetford all poaching and missing youngsters have taken place in the London area, which leads me to think whoever is responsible could live in or around one of the areas. I wonder why there has never been any ransom demands for any of the youngsters? What does he do with them; I can't think that whoever has snatched these youngsters goes to all that trouble just to kill them, and bury them somewhere".

"I was wondering that, and then I thought what if they were snatched to be used for child sex trafficking. There has been a significant increase in child sex trafficking over the last few years"

"Child sex trafficking, yes it's a possibility. If they are being used in the sex slave business then you can bet there are heavy drugs involved. Which could mean we might also be dealing with a large drug dealer? Who may also be making and distributing of black market hardcore underage porn videos? So, we need to check for known paedophiles, large scale drug dealers, as well as those involved in the selling of black market under age porn videos"

"We need to get a professional team together to check all of that out. Have you spoken to the Chief Constable again?"

"Yes I spoke to him on my mobile on the way back to let him know what we have found. There could have been another problem because Takely is in Essex, so any crimes come under the responsibility of the Essex police. We are Hertfordshire police. However the Chief

Constable being aware of that has spoken to the Chief Constable of the Essex police who is happy for us to handle this case work and has agreed to give full cooperation, which is a relief."

"We will need more specialised officers, because we don't have enough here for this case?"

"That's what I told the Chief Constable who has asked me to head up this case which we will call 'Poacher'. He wants you as the most senior Inspector here to be my second in command. He has agreed to send us some senior specialist officers from headquarters; they are Detective Inspector Franks, who has a lot of experience in the hunting down drug dealers. Detective Inspector Bryant experienced in catching paedophiles, and Detective Inspector Munro who has had considerable experience of working on large vice cases. He is also sending us some detective sergeants, as well. They are on their way over as we speak. We will use incident room four for this case"

"That's good so do you want me to get some of our detectives together for the initial briefing and set up the room?"

"Yes call the team together and we will get the room set up. I will get Sergeant Braxton to make copies of all the information you have printed off the computer as well as photos of Rose and Sam enlarged to go on the board in the room along with the photos of the others who have gone missing. What's the time now, ah it's seven fifteen, we will have a briefing at eight thirty, when the briefing is over, and the team has been given the information that we have, and assigned to their areas of responsibility you and I need to get our heads down for some sleep. I don't know about you but I'm exhausted and starving hungry"

"Yes I am we haven't slept or eaten for what seems like ages. As you say once the team has the information on the case we can leave them to get on with enquiries then join them later"

" Oh, and do me a favour phone Jack and chase him up we need all the Forensic info that he has got from today, inform him about who is in the team and where to bring the information, remind him to leave copies on each of our desks"

"Will do, here are all the files that I printed off that you need to get copied"

Charley picked up all the files and promptly left the room to find Sergeant Braxton and give him his instructions before returning to help set up the room to be used for the investigation. Inspector Roberts picked up his phone and phoned Jack, and after he had spoken to him he went and gathered together the other Detectives that he wanted to work on the case.

By half past eight,, the room had been set up, and the team had been brought together. The detectives from headquarters in Welwyn garden city had arrived along with Jack, who brought with him copies of his Forensic reports, and confirmed with Charley that the youngster's footprints that had been found in the forest matched with the other shoes of Rose and Sam found in the cottage of Walter and Netty.

After the introduction of the officers from headquarters and Charley had delivered a detailed briefing for operation 'Poacher' he and Inspector Roberts left saying that they needed to get some sleep as they had been on duty for over twenty four hours and would meet up again in the morning.

Chapter 4.

On the Wednesday, the day that the search of the forest was being carried out Rose was awoken by the sound of the key turning in the lock of her door. Raising her head from the pillow rubbing her eyes she tried to focus but everything before her appeared blurred and the inside of her head felt numb, she tried to call out but the sounds that came from her mouth were slurred. She felt a sudden cold as the man pulled back the duvet, grabbed one of her arms lifted her almost naked body up over his shoulder and carried her out along to the end of the passage through another door into a large bathroom.

Inside the bathroom, he laid her face down on the white rug in the centre of a highly polished grey and white marble tiled floor. He then pulled off her knickers, bra and socks before lifting her back up and standing her inside a wide shower cubicle. He then turned on the shower and closed the shower doors.

Rose gasped as she felt the hot jets of water hit her body. She felt dizzy unable to stand her legs gave way, and she slid down the side of the shower into a crumpled heap. The hot jets of water continued to spray down on her back, but she felt powerless to be able to stand up and gasped for breath. She lifted her head directly away from the spray, and through blurred eyes she saw a sponge, and a plastic bottle of liquid soap. She reached out, and grabbed them, and having managed to pour some of the liquid soap into the sponge, she proceeded to wash her hair, and body. She then tried to stand, but her legs gave way once more, and she ended up in a sitting position against the right side wall of the shower. Her head hung down the hot spray continuing to beat down on her. She felt powerless to move or speak.

Suddenly, the shower doors opened, and the man reached in turned off the shower then scooped Rose up in his arms lifting her out of the enclosure, and sat her down on the rug, and threw her a large white towel saying.

"Be quick, and get dried you have work to do"

Rose slowly began to dry herself with great effort as the man leaned with his back against a basin staring at her with an upturned grin on his pox marked unshaven face. She tried to say something, but the words came out in a slur. She was only half dry when the man stepped forward grabbed the towel from her with one hand throwing it across the room. He grabbed her arm, and pulled her up and put her over his shoulder, and carried her out back along the passage, and through the door at the other end where he crossed the landing, and opened another door, and carried her into a circular room where the walls and ceiling were all painted white.

In the middle of the room, there was a large circular bed that was covered with a white silk sheet and a large black fur rug.

He threw her down on to the bed and she landed flat on her back her legs and arms spread-eagled. Her hair all matted up. She lifted her head and with blurred vision she saw looking around her that there were spotlights on stands to one side of the bed in the middle of the spotlights there were two cameras on tripods one had an extended lens the other was a video camera. Again she tried to speak and to get up but couldn't.

The man went and stood behind the cameras and from his trouser pocket he took out a small remote control box pressed a button and the bed began to turn in a circular movement. He pressed another button and the spotlights came on pointing their lights onto Rose and the bed. He pressed one of the buttons again, and the bed came to a stop. Rose was directly in front of the cameras.

"I am going to take some photos of you both still photos and video. I want you to lie back as you are; do not move until I tell you to". He said.

He then switched on the video camera adjusting the lens, so it zoomed in on Rose. He smiled as he zoomed in on her face then slowly moved the camera, so it followed down her body hovering over her naked firm breasts then down over her stomach to between her open legs where he zoomed in for a closeup view.

Rose, seeing what he was doing she put one arm across her breasts, and closed her legs before rolling over onto her stomach, where she tried to crawl off the other side of the bed.

"That's a nice bum now keep crawling and wriggling your bum as you go. No stop now and turn back over, and crawl towards the camera, smile come on. No stop trying to get off the bed"

He switched off the video camera went over and grabbed Rose pulling her back, and turned her over so that she lay on her back once again. He then pulled her legs wide apart.

"Now stay like that until I tell you to move. If you don't you will be sorry so just do as I say"

Rose tried to shout but again the words wouldn't come out. She tried to get up, but she found she had no energy or strength to do so. She lay back tears began to roll down her face. Seeing the tears the man took out a handkerchief from his other trouser pocket and wiped her face saying.

"Pack it in and do as I say the quicker you do, the quicker you will get fed. If you don't then you will starve, simple as that"

He then went back behind the camera and switched it back on and continued to film her. When he seemed satisfied he then took some still shots with the other camera again zooming in on her sensual parts.

Rose continued to lie as he had left her, her body and voice had ceased to function with what her brain was telling her she needed to do.

After three quarters of an hour, the man switched off the glaring spotlights and ceased taking photos. He walked over to the door and took a white dressing robe off the hook and came back and lifting Rose up put it on her and tied the belt tightly round her waist. He then picked her up and carried her on his shoulder out of the room and down the stairs along the hall passage and into the kitchen where he sat her down on a wooden chair at a round table.

Rose fell forward banging her head down on the table. She winced as the numb feeling inside her head made it difficult for her to focus and think coherently.

The man went over to the stove and reheated up some porridge that he had made earlier. Once it was hot he scooped some of it out of the saucepan into a plastic bowl added some milk that he took from the fridge then went over and sat down at the table next to Rose. He lifted her back so that she was leaning back in the chair. Then spoon fed her the porridge spoonful by spoonful until she had swallowed it all. Then made her drink a glass of milk before he once again picked her up and carried her on his shoulder back to her room where he threw her down on the bed. He then took another loaded syringe from the bedside drawer and injected her in the arm. Once finished he put away the syringe and left her, locking her up once more.

The man then went and carried out the same procedure with Sam that he had made with Rose. Sam had woken up in the same state as Rose finding that he could not get his brain and body to function in coordination along with his speech he felt powerless to resist as he was almost comatose.

Once the man had completed the video, and photos, he carried Sam to the kitchen where he spoon fed him porridge and gave him a glass of milk. He then carried him back to his room where he gave him another injection before locking him back up.

The man having locked up Sam then went into another of the rooms in the passageway, which like in Rose and Sam's rooms there was a single bed, wardrobe and a window that was covered with sheet metal. In the bed, there lay a sixteen year old girl who was tall of medium build with long blond hair and blue eyes.

On seeing the man approach the bed, she opened her eyes and shuddered as he pulled back the duvet exposing her naked bruised body. He slapped her backside saying.

"Get up Samantha you lazy bitch you're leaving this morning you're going off to Brazil in South America, I have finished with you, someone else needs your services"

"No, please, please don't send me to South America" Samantha replied as she sat bolt upright shaking and starting to sob.

"You'll go where I send you, now get up"

The man grabbed one of her arms and pulled her off the bed onto the floor, then started kicking her backside saying.

"Come on move you need to shower and get dressed, I haven't got all-day"

Samantha cowering yelled out in pain as she struggled to get up off the floor, and having stood up and shaking with fear the man grabbed her by the back of her neck dragged her out of the room and along the passageway to the bathroom and pushed her through the door and into the shower enclosure where he turned on the shower and closed the shower doors.

Trembling Samantha reached for the soap and sponge and began to wash herself tears rolling down her face. After two minutes, the shower doors suddenly opened and the man reached in turned off the shower and pulled her out with one hand and pushed a towel in her face with his other hand saying.

"You got one minute to get dried, hurry up"

Samantha still sobbing began to dry herself as fast as she could.

The bathroom door suddenly opened and in walked a tall slim woman who had olive skin and long black shoulder length hair and brown eyes. She was dressed in skin tight white trousers and a white short sleeved low cut blouse that showed the tops of her olive skinned plump breasts.

"Wayne go and see to the others I'll take care of Samantha" The woman said with a Spanish accent.

Turning and seeing the woman he smiled and replied.

"Celine thanks darling, I didn't know you were up, I thought you were having a lay in"

"No time, we have too much to do today. Have you sorted out the two new ones?"

"Yes and I took some photos and video of each of them, they are back in their rooms locked up. I need to talk to you about them later"

"Ok, well off you go. Now come on Samantha you bitch stop crying and hurry up" the woman said as she came forward and shook Samantha.

The man Wayne left the bathroom and unlocked another room in the passage where in a single bed there lay a seventeen year old girl of medium height and slim build with brown wavy shoulder length hair and green eyes. On seeing Wayne come in she raised her head saying.

"Leave me alone, I need to sleep. I was working from early yesterday morning until midnight and didn't get brought back till gone one this morning"

"That's what you're paid to do so get up Susan you lazy cow, go and get showered, you're making videos today"

Wayne pulled back the duvet exposing her naked body grabbed one of her ankles and pulled her off the bed onto the floor and kicked her backside. Susan yelled out and quickly stood up and ran out of the room shaking, not saying anything as she ran down the passage to the bathroom.

Wayne followed her out and unlocked the next bedroom and went in, where in two single beds two slim Chinese girls both aged seventeen were laying asleep. He pulled back the duvets exposing their naked bruised bodies and said.

"Cui-Fen and Hai get up and go and get showered and dressed, move yourselves, the van will be here in half an hour"

The two Chinese girls shuddered as they slowly got off their beds without daring to say anything as they left and hurried down to the bathroom.

Wayne then went into the next room where again in two single beds there lay two skinny Romanian girls one was sixteen the other was fifteen. Again pulling back the duvets he said.

"Alina and Cosmina get up get showered and dressed the van will be here in half an hour"

Like the two Chinese girls, they hurriedly got up and ran out to the bathroom cowering and not saying anything as they went.

Wayne unlocked the next room where a seventeen year old lad who was sniffing and shaking sat naked at the end of the bed.

"Jamie you're making videos today, so hurry up because Mike will be arriving soon to start the filming. When you're dressed get your breakfast and go straight to the studio room"

Jamie looked at Wayne with half open eyes and said sniffing.

"I need my tablets and injection man; I can't do anything till I have them"

Wayne unlocked a metal cabinet on the wall and took out a syringe and a small bottle of liquid and having filled the syringe he proceeded to inject Jamie in one of his arms. He then passed him two different pills from the cabinet and a glass of water from the bedside table. Jamie flexed his arm took the tablets and swallowed them down then said sniffing.

"I'll be there"

Wayne put away the syringe locked the cabinet and left without saying anything. He opened another door and went into a room where there were two twin beds in each of which lay two young boys; one was aged seven and the other was aged ten both were slim with long fair hair and grey eyes.

On seeing Wayne enter they both sleepily sat up in their beds shaking with fear as, they rubbed the sleep from their eyes.

"You're making videos with Jamie, Susan, Celia and Joy. So hurry up put your dressing gowns on get washed and go to the studio room"

The two youngsters turned and looked at Wayne with dazed expressions as they wearily dragged themselves off the beds and grabbed their dressing gowns and hurried out towards the bathroom without saying anything.

Wayne followed them out of the room and saw the two Romanian girls and the Chinese girls coming back along the passage not talking as they went towards their rooms.

"You can't have all had your showers you dirty bitches get back to the bathroom" Wayne called out.

"Please Mr Wayne Susan is still in the shower we had to have a strip wash in the bath" one of the Chinese girls replied.

"I said get back and shower, and tell Susan to hurry up; you know the van will be here soon"

The four girls turned and ran back to the bathroom not saying anything. The two boys followed the girls.

Wayne opened the door to another room and went in, where there were two twin beds. In one of the beds there was a girl of fifteen who was thin with long blond hair and grey eyes, and in the other bed there was a girl of sixteen who was also thin with short brown hair and green eyes. Both sat up and threw back the duvets on their beds staring at Wayne with expressionless faces. They were naked and had bruises on their arms and legs.

"Celia, Joy move yourselves and go get showered and dressed, Mikes coming over to make videos you will be doing it with Jamie today"

"Please Mr Wayne not more videos" Celia the fifteen year old said looking peevish.

"You will do as you are fucking told, do you want a beating, get a move on I haven't got all fucking day"

"Come on Celia we don't want another beating from this bastard" Joy whispered to Celia as she got off the bed and stretched.

On hearing what Joy had whispered Wayne rushed over and smacked Joy across the face then punched her in the side yelling.

"Move you fucking bitch"

Joy yelled out in pain and doubled up rolling onto the floor sobbing. Celia stepped forward and helped Joy up saying.

"Quick come on Joy do as he says"

The two girls grabbed their dressing gowns and ran out down the passage to the bathroom. Wayne followed them into the bathroom where the two Romanians were drying themselves. One of the Chinese girls was in the shower, and the other Chinese girl was in a large circular bath washing. The two young boys were also in the bath washing and were looking at all the naked girls around them with coy smiles on their faces. Jamie stood in front of one of a row of washbasins having a strip wash not paying any attention to the girls.

"Come on move yourselves you lazy fuckers. I want you out of here and dressed; you've got ten minutes, or else you'll all get a beating". Wayne said.

Taking a quick look around the crowded bathroom, before he went out and made his way down the passage and out onto the landing and up the other short flight of stairs on to the landing, where he walked along to the end of the corridor and into a large room where there were three single beds facing the door. On the first bed on the left, a medium height slim Somali girl aged sixteen sat naked combing her short hair. In the next two beds two Polish girls aged fifteen lifted their heads from their pillows still half asleep.

"Ah, Amaka you're awake, hurry up and get showered and dressed. Ania, Beata, come on get out of bed you lazy bitches and go with Amaka and have your showers" Wayne shouted.

Amaka put down her comb got up off the bed and walked towards the door to get her dressing gown and as she passed Wayne he grabbed her round her waist with one arm and fondled her breasts with his other hand saying.

"You've got such a nice body and tits I'm going to have to have you soon"

Amaka turned and with a half-smile replied.

"You want me now?"

Wayne smiled as his hand went down between her legs and fondled her crotch before letting her go saying.

"Later when you come back perhaps"

Amaka took down her dressing gown from the back of the door, and as she went out she turned and replied with a cheeky smile.

"It will cost you"

Wayne laughed replying.

"That's a good girl your learning"

Then turning to look at the two Polish girls who had got out of their beds he said.

"Don't stand staring get a move on I haven't got all day to waste chasing you up"

The girls hastily grabbed their dressing gowns and followed Amaka out and down the corridor. Wayne followed them down onto the landing then turned and went down the main staircase into the hall and opened the front door and went out and stood on the gravel driveway.

He looked around the spacious front garden. In front of him on the other side of the gravel driveway, there was a long wide immaculately trimmed lawn. Behind the lawn, there was a small lake surrounded by different trees. To the left and right hand side of the garden there were flower beds in front of high stone block walls that went around the property. In the middle of the left hand side wall, there was the only entrance that had tall black wrought iron gates with a video security camera mounted on top of one of the pillars. He walked round the front of the house to the right turned the corner and followed a narrow gravel pathway that led to the back of the three story

Edwardian house, where there was a wide raised stone flagged terrace that went the full width of the house.

He walked up the steps onto the terrace and sat down on a white wrought iron chair behind a matching wrought iron table. He took a cigar from the top pocket of his shirt and lit it blowing out smoke as he stared out across two wide sweeping lawns on one of which there was a tennis court. In the middle of the other lawn, there was a large circular swimming pool. A flag stoned pathway separated the two lawns. At the far end of the lawns, the stone block wall continued around the grounds, again with flower beds full of flowers of differing sort in front of the walls. The sky above was a clear light blue, and the hot July sun shone down.

It was going to be another of those rarely real hot summer days. He felt good knowing that he was due to receive a nice cash payment from the Brazilian having sold him Samantha and that he was also going to get a large shipment of drugs from him. Drugs that he knew Terry Parker one of his partners had already got buyers for. He continued smoking his cigar thinking about which of the other girls he would soon sell and what he planned to do with Rose and Sam. Once finished he stubbed his cigar out in a large ashtray on the table then got up and walked over and opened one of a set of large French windows and went inside into a large living room that was finely furnished with antique furniture and white silk covered sofas. He crossed the room and went through the door that led into a study that was lined on all walls with bookshelves containing leather bound books. In the middle of the room, there was a large antique desk and leather chair that sat on a large hand sewn Persian silk rug. He sat down at the desk and unlocked a drawer and took out a thick ledger and having opened it up he scanned through several pages before closing up the book and locking it back up in the desk drawer.

He stood up just as the door opened and in walked Celine who said.

"There you are Wayne darling Samantha is dressed and locked back in her room. Did you get the others up because it's time we got ready that fat Brazilian Carlos is due here soon?" she smiled.

"Yes I'm coming now darling; I have got the others up the lazy fuckers. Mike should be here soon, has Vince arrived with the van?"

"No not yet, he and Mike are both late this morning"

Wayne walked across and putting his arm around Celine's waist and kissing her on the neck whispered.

"Oomph you look and smell great come on let's go and get some coffee I need to talk to you about those two new ones I brought in yesterday"

"Ok, so what do you want to tell me, they are not going to be troublesome are they" she replied as they left the room entered the hall and walked towards the kitchen.

"No but I found out something amazing about them, which could bring us a nice fat earner"

"Really go on what you find out"

"I found out that they are my brother's kids, he is a millionaire businessman"

Celine stopped dead in her tracks and looked Wayne in the eyes and said.

"What! You are kidding me; you never told me that you have a brother?"

"Well I have and we have two options as to what we can do with those two kids. It will be sweet revenge"

"Tell me about this brother of yours and what you have got in mind?"

"Remember I told you that I was taken from my mother and put into care at birth. Well it was only a few years ago that I found out who my parents were, and I have been waiting for an opportunity to get my own back on the family that didn't want to know me. So this is what I have got in mind"

"Go on I bet it will be good"

Later having drunk his coffee and revealed his plans to Celine he went back out of the front door just as a white transit van followed by a blue BMW car drove in through the gates and pulled up in front of him. Out of the van stepped a tall, thick set muscular bald headed man who was dressed in faded blue jeans, a yellow T-shirt and a pair of dark brown trainers.

"Morning Wayne, are them fucking bitches ready, I'm late because the fucking traffic is murder this morning?"

"Morning Vince, yes they are ready Celine will be bringing them down any minute now. No worries mate go and get a coffee I've just made a fresh pot it's in the kitchen"

"Thanks I need a coffee after that trek across London. Hi Mike, did you get stuck in that fucking traffic out of London as well?" Vince said as Mike a tall thin man got out of the BMW and walked over to join them"

"Morning Vince, Wayne, yea I did the traffic on the M25 is fucking murder this morning"

"Morning Mike go with Vince and get a cup of coffee. When you have had your coffee go up to the studio everything is set up. Oh and I have left a couple of new videos for you up there that I took earlier of two new youngsters that I brought in yesterday, the videos need packaging"

"Ah ok great two new ones, are they any good"

"A sixteen year old girl with a nice body and her brother eleven, snatched them whilst poaching in Takely forest"

"Nice one, you're getting shot of Samantha today then?"

"Yea Carlos is due to pick her up this morning, taking her back to Brazil with him. He's welcome to her lazy fucker that she is. Oh and he's bringing in another shipment of drugs which I will need you Vince to take to Terry's place when you bring the bitches back tonight alright"

"Yea no problems, come on Mike let's go get that coffee"

Vince and Mike went into the house. Wayne took out and lit another cigar and walked across the lawn to the lake to watch some ducks that were swimming around when Celine called from the front door saying.

"Wayne what are you doing, the bitches are here ready to go into the van, where's Vince?"

Wayne raised his eyebrows and turning round replied.

"I'm watching the ducks all right. Vince and Mike are getting some coffee so put the bitches in the back of the van and make sure ,you lock the doors. Have they had their shots?"

"Yea they've had their shots so won't give Vince any trouble, they are all half asleep"

Wayne turned back with a smile on his face, and continued watching the ducks as Celine brought the girls out and loaded them into the back of the van and once they were all in she locked the doors and then walked over to join Wayne saying.

"Carlos should be here very soon, have you got his money ready?"

"Yea it's in the study, I deducted the price of Samantha from what is due for the drugs so he won't be expecting a lot of cash this time"

"Does he know?"

"Yea of course he knows that was the deal I arranged with him"

"Pity he couldn't take some more with him"

"No I have a buyer for the two Chinese girls, and a German guy has taken a fancy to that Joy Manders so I might be able to get a good price for all three of them"

"Really that's cool if you get rid of them we will need to get some more fresh stock. The Somali girl should fetch a good price if you can get a buyer for her. Have you talked to your Arab friends?"

"Yea but they want me to get some Filipino or Tai girls, because they can use them as domestics as well as sex slaves"

"Well that shouldn't be too difficult you can get them through your overseas recruitment agency when recruiting for care workers and domestics"

"I know I'm just waiting to hear back from my agents in Manila and Bangkok"

"Good because they always fetch good prices especially with the rich Arab and African clients we get visiting our clubs and the brothel in London"

"Hey! I'm off now thanks for the coffee. Will I see you late this evening when I bring the bitches back?" Vince called out as he came out of the house and got back into the van.

Celine and Wayne turned round, and Wayne called back.

"Yea we will be here. See you later, bye"

"Ok bye see you"

Vince started up the van turned it round and headed off out of the gate into a long tree lined driveway that led up to the main road.

Wayne having finished his cigar threw the remains into the lake then taking hold of Celine's hand he led her back across the lawn and into the house saying.

"Right we had better get ready to greet Carlos; he's bound to be hungry when he gets here. Did you prepare him some food?"

"Yea I set the table in the dining room and the foods already"

"Good what did you prepare?"

"Come and have a look, it's one of your favourites"

They walked back into the house and they went into the dining room where a large table was all set out with a fine linen tablecloth, fine bone china, gold cutlery and crystal glasses. On the ornate antique sideboard, there were solid silver platters that had solid silver lids. Wayne walked over and lifted the lids of the platters and smiling said.

"Ah great fresh lobster and crab"

"Yea and there's fresh Russian caviar and I prepared a salad, as well. I had everything sent up from Harrods"

"Good I will go and select some wines from the back cellar and put them on ice"

"Go on then while I go and slip into something cool it's already baking hot again"

"Yea it's good I will get showered and changed when I have brought the wine up. See you in a moment"

They left the dining room and Celine went to change while Wayne went to the back cellar to get some bottles of vintage wine.

An hour later a gold coloured Bentley drove in through the gates and parked up outside the front door and out stepped a short, stocky bald headed man who was dressed in a cream silk suit with a crisp white shirt and gold silk tie. He walked in through the open front door and called out.

"Wayne, Celine are you there?"

"Ah! Carlos at last you have arrived, good to see you my friend"

Replied Wayne as he stepped out of the living room into the hall followed by Celine.

"Ah, my friends you are both looking well, business good is it?"

"Couldn't be better, how about you?"

"Ha I'm always doing well. Have you got my package ready, and is she looking as good as ever?"

"Yes she is ready for you, but first Celine has prepared us an exceptional lunch which I know you will enjoy"

"Ah, great Celine always prepares the best. Lead me to the table I'm starving hungry as always"

"Come step into the dining room, you won't be disappointed"

They all walked into the dining room and sat down to enjoy their lunch.

After they had finished eating and entertaining Carlos they exchanged Samantha, for a large supply of drugs, and a briefcase full of cash. Celine had given Samantha a parting injection to ensure that she would not be any trouble to Carlos, and had handed over her passport with a new name that she had had prepared through one of Wayne's contacts. Carlos had previously sorted out the required visa and paperwork so that it would be easy enough for him to get Samantha out of the country to Brazil where he had valuable contacts in the immigration department who were accustomed to him bringing in foreign girls from time to time. Contacts that, were prepared to turn a blind eye as they were well rewarded financially by Carlos.

Once Carlos had gone Wayne and Celine went and changed into swimming costumes. Celine put on a

well high and thanks to the pills you gave him, he is up for anything, he doesn't know morning from night he just does as he is told to do"

"Ah, well at least you got some good videos. I'm getting rid of Susan as you say; she's fucking useless the lazy bitch. Now the two new ones did you look at the videos I made of them?"

"Yea the girls got a good body on her we should get her and Jamie together, what do you reckon?"

"Good idea yeah, we could do that now if that ok with you?"

"Yea no problems"

"I will take the young boys and the girls and get them showered and fed. Come on you buggers, get up come on" Celine said as she went over and dragged them all off the bed kicking them.

The two boys who were half asleep along with the girls all cowered as they left the room with Celine.

Wayne followed Celine out, and they all made their way across the landing into the passageway. Celine pushed and shoved the two boys and the girls along the passage to the bathroom while Wayne went and unlocked the door of the room where Rose was laying in her bed still semi-conscious. He went over and pulled back the duvet and grabbed one of her arms pulling her up off the bed saying,

"Come on get with it you've had all day to sleep now you're going back to work"

Rose looked at Wayne with a glazed expression and tried to say something but as earlier she couldn't get the words out coherently they came out as gibberish not making any sense. Wayne dragged her out of the room back along the passageway across the landing into the studio where Mike was gathering together the videos he had made that day.

Jamie was sitting up on the bed naked with a glazed expression on his face; his penis still as stiff as a stick of rock due to the Viagra tablets he had been given during the day.

"Here we are come on Jamie here's a fresh one for you to do what you like with she's yours to play with" Wayne said taking the dressing gown off Rose and throwing her down naked on the bed in front of Jamie.

Rose through blurred vision took in the bright lights of the studio and cameras and on seeing Jamie sitting there with an erect penis she became all too aware even in her semi-conscious state what was about to happen. She managed to lift herself up and started to crawl off the bed, but Jamie like a wild animal grabbed her by her hair and pulled her backwards so that she lay before him. Rose suddenly finding her voice began to scream out loud as she struggled to get up. But Jamie with a smirk on his face grabbed her and rolled on top of her pinning her down with her arms outstretched. Still screaming and frantically trying to get free Rose closed her legs tight together Jamie wriggling on top of her forcing one of his knees in between her legs pushing her legs apart. He then pushed his erect penis as hard as he could into her and began going up and down as fast as he could. Rose twisted and turned screaming at the top of her voice, but it was no use Jamie was to strong and heavy. Then Jamie suddenly let out a cry and lifted himself up off of her his penis covered in blood and dripping.

"Ha, you see that Mike she's a virgin" Wayne called out as he began laughing.

"Yea nice one I wish I had caught that on video, never mind we can get her and Jamie cleaned up and get Jamie to do her again"

Rose still screaming closed back her now bruised legs turned on her side curling up into a foetus position and began sobbing out loud.

"Go on Jamie go and get a shower you're sweating like a pig," Wayne said still laughing.

Jamie slowly crawled off the bed without saying a word and staggered out, of the room and went off to get showered.

"Come on Rose get up and stop that blubbing you haven't finished yet," Wayne said as he grabbed hold of one of Roses arms and dragged her off the bed and pushed her out of the room towards the bathroom.

Wayne made her shower then gave her another injection along with some pills which he forced her to swallow. The results of which left her unable to stop Jamie, who had also showered and received more pills and a further injection carrying out various sexual perversions with her.

Three hours later Wayne and Mike having completed three more videos called it a day. Celine having got the girls, and two young boys showered and fed returned and seeing Rose and Jamie lying flat out half unconscious on the bed said.

"I heard the screaming earlier did you manage to get them to make videos then?"

"Yes and guess what she was a virgin, but she isn't now" Wayne said laughing.

"Oh well ok, Mike you must be hungry I've made some dinner so come and join us I'll take these two and put them back in their rooms"

"Ah, thanks Celine yea all that work has made me hungry. Are you going to open a bottle of wine Wayne?" Mike said smiling.

"Yea why not let's go downstairs, bring the videos with you"

They left Celine to sort out Rose and Jamie while they went downstairs and sat in the dining room. Where they found that Celine had prepared and set out some more salad, lobsters and crabs as well as some bottles of white wine in ice buckets. They helped themselves to some wine and the food and began eating.

Half an hour later Celine came in and sat down saying.

"I put them in their rooms and have given all of them some food and drink. That brother of Rose is in a state those injections you gave him have left him in a bad way I could hardly get him awake to eat"

"We will have to keep an eye on him, he's too valuable" Wayne replied.

"It's like I said before if you're planning to sell more of them youngsters off then you will need to get some more" Celine said.

"Well we have done all right so far, getting them has proved easy. It's earned us a lot of money using them for the porn videos, as well as prostitution. Once they are so doped up and can't live without the dope that's the time to get shot of them. Look at Jamie he's definitely heading that way, but we won't be able to sell him; we shall just have to dump him on the streets somewhere once we have found a replacement for him".

"Can't you bring some teenage boys in from Asia," Mike asked.

"Yea we should be able to get those who want to come and work as domestics and care workers"

"What about immigrants coming in from Eastern Europe, I heard that the government is planning to bring more Romanians in next year, we could snatch some of them. You managed to snatch two of them Romanian girls and nobody paid much notice to them going missing, same with the two Chinese girls they had come here as tourists and we grabbed them off the street in London one night remember" Mike said.

"Yea it was easy getting them but we can only use them in the West End brothel we can't risk putting them in one of the parlours. We have to watch out that we don't have the Triads after us" Wayne replied.

"Yea the brothel up the West End is still attracting all the rich perverts?"

"Yea not half, you've seen the list of clients that come there, we've got MPs, businessmen from leading companies, high ranking members of different religious groups, high ranking coppers plus of course our friends from the middle eastern countries"

"Well I reckon we are doing all right the videos are selling well both here and abroad to them that like them. Bloody hell look at the time it's three in the morning. I had better be getting back to London. Thanks for the meal and wine I'll give you a call sometime tomorrow ok. I'll get copies of the videos done and sent to all our outlets"

"Ok, Mike you can stay over if you want but if you need to go back you had better go. Thanks mate for your hard work today. I'll speak with you later, take care on the way back ok," Wayne replied smiling as they all stood up and walked out of the dining room into the hall.

The sound of the van pulling up outside was heard as Wayne opened the front door to let Mike out.

"Vince is back then, see you soon bye" Mike said as he stepped out of the door.

"Bye" Wayne and Celine said in unison.

"You still here Mike," Vince said yawning as he got out of the van.

"Just off, see you mate bye"

"Vince you all right how did it go today any bother from the bitches?" Wayne asked.

"No problems they're all knackered now though" Vince said laughing.

"I'll give you a hand Vince to get them in and up to their rooms," Celine said.

"Cheers" Vince replied unlocking the back doors of the van.

Wayne went back into the dining room and sat down to finish drinking what was left of the wine.

By four, o'clock, all the girls had been given their injections and locked up in their rooms. Vince having helped Celine said goodnight to Wayne, who was half asleep, sat at the dining table then said good night to Celine before getting back in the van to return to London. When he had left, Celine went into the dining room and looking at Wayne sat half asleep at the table said.

"Come on my darling wake up it's time we went to bed. I will get one of the girls to tidy up this mess in the morning"

"Ugh yea right ok, come on then let's go" Wayne slurred.

As he stood up half asleep taking hold of Celine's hand he staggered out of the room, and they slowly made their way up the stairs to their bedroom.

Chapter 5.

At eight thirty Thursday morning, Detective Chief Superintendent Humphreys and Detective Inspector Roberts walked into the incident room. They had had a good night's rest, shaved, showered, changed and eaten a good breakfast.

"Good morning everyone, how is it going has anyone got any good news?" Charley called out as he looked around the room where phones were ringing and being answered by several Detectives that had been called in to work with the other three senior Detectives working on the case. Everyone appeared to be working sifting through information on their desks or talking on the phones.

"Good morning sir. We have begun house to house enquiries in Takely as well as making enquiries in Stortford to find out if anyone had seen Rose and Sam on Tuesday, and it would appear that they didn't come into the town. A couple in Takely said that they had seen them walking past their house in the direction of the lane that leads to the forest on Tuesday at around about twelve thirty lunch time. We enquired to see if they had been into the local shops, but they hadn't. We also checked to see if anyone had seen a white van acting suspiciously in the village, but nothing so far" One of the Detective Sergeants replied.

"Have the media been informed about Rose and Sam's disappearance and given photos of the two youngsters?"

"Yes sir we emailed the story to the local and national press and television companies so we can expect a visit this morning from the media wanting a full statement. An announcement about their disappearance went out on this morning's television news" Detective Inspector Bryant said.

"Have the customs and port authorities been notified to keep a look out for Rose and Sam in case the snatcher tries to take them out of the country?"

"Yes sir they have all been made aware" Detective Sergeant Morrison replied.

"What about the fingerprints found on the padlocks and chains, has anyone run a check on the fingerprints found?" Charley asked.

"Yes sir I'm still checking the central records on my computer to see if I can find a match" Detective Inspector Munro replied just as the phone on his desk rang.

Picking up the phone, he said.

"Detective Inspector Munro speaking, very good sir, yes he's here now, just a second"

Munro passed the phone to Charley saying.

"The Chief Constable wishes to speak to you sir"

Charley took the phone and said.

"Good morning sir, yes sir thank you sir. I see yes well I said that he would expect us to move heaven and earth to find them. He's already on his way back from Hong Kong; that doesn't surprise me. I understand so what time do you want me to come over; very good I will be there. Yes, sir I will hopefully have some positive news for you by then my team are following up all the leads. Thank you sir, I will see you at seven this evening in your office. Bye"

Charley raised his eyebrows and let out a deep sigh as he put the phone down.

"Right listen in everyone. That was the Chief Constable as expected Mr and Mrs Cooper the parents of Rose and Sam are on their way back from Hong Kong. They are meeting with the Chief Constable at seven this evening. I have got to be there, so woe betides us if we haven't got some positive leads by the time I have to go to the meeting. I hope you are all working contacting your informants to see if they have heard anything on the grapevine about these missing youngsters" Charley said so everyone could hear.

There was unanimous nodding, and confirmation around the room, and one of the Sergeants said.

"I ran a check to find out if any of the butchers in and around the London area had been convicted of selling illegal venison, but there have been no reported cases"

"Yes and I have run a check of all convictions for people being caught in possession of crossbows in and around the area, and there have been six cases which I'm following up. Constable Wilkins has run checks on people convicted of poaching and there have been numerous cases but none has been convicted of poaching Deer" Constable Brazier said.

"Good well let me, or Inspector Roberts know if you find anything positive. Inspectors Franks, Munro and Bryant out of all those people whom you have arrested in the past do you have you any suspicions as to if any of them might be responsible for the snatchings of these youngsters?"

"I don't think that any of the ones that I have arrested would have carried out the snatchings, they have all been convicted of being in possession of child porn videos and downloading child porn on their computers, one or two have been convicted of flashing in children's play areas, and one was convicted for showing porn magazines to a young boy of six in toilets in the town centre. Whoever this person is he must have imprisoned the youngsters he has snatched somewhere, which means he must have a large place to keep them if he has them all together in one place. It's possible of course that having snatched them he sells them on.

However, my officers and I are questioning all of them including those still serving sentences to see if they are prepared to say who might be behind the snatchings" Detective Bryant replied.

"Yes the Inspector could be right, I and my officers are questioning all those whom we have convicted of selling drugs on the streets, bars, and clubs to see if they are prepared to name names. I think we will need to offer substantial bribes if we are going to get anyone to come forward with any positive names" Detective Franks replied.

"Ok, you could both be right, well we can offer a substantial bribe if that's what it takes to find this person. However we won't pay out unless we get hard firm evidence that leads to a conviction is that clear to everyone" Charley said.

Inspector Munro suddenly leaped up out of his chair clapping his hands and called out

"Geronimo! I have a fingerprint match. Quick sirs look at this"

Charley and Inspector Roberts turned and looked at Inspector Munro's computer that was giving off a buzzing sound. To one side of the screen there was a copy of the prints found by Jack the day before and on the other side of the screen there was a sheet showing a man's criminal record which include his name, photo and a copy of his fingerprints above which there was a name.

"Great! Quick print off the file Inspector," Charley said with a look of excitement.

"It's printing now sir"

When the file had printed out Charley snatched it up and hastily read through it then said to Inspector Munro.

"Right find and print off the record for Nancy Ellison born 1946 in Bishops Stortford.

The Inspector turned back to his computer and typed in the name. Presently the file came up on the screen, and he printed it off and handed it to Charley who read through it and as he did, so the colour started to drain from his face.

Inspector Roberts watched as his boss turn very pale and asked.

"Are you ok sir?"

Charley coughed then regaining his composure smiled and nodded at Inspector Roberts before straightening up saying so that everyone in the room could hear him.

"Right pay attention everyone we have a positive match of the fingerprints they belong to

Wayne Smith.

He was born on the 16th September 1965 in Holloway Prison, in London.

Father: Not known.

Mother: Nancy Ellison, who was born on the 5th May 1946 in Bishops Stortford hospital. Address unknown.

Wayne Smith was taken into social care at birth and put into a care home. His mother had been convicted and was serving four years imprisonment at the time of his birth.

Wayne was registered with the surname Smith by social services.

In 1976, Wayne Smith then aged eleven ran away from the care home that, he was in and was arrested and tried for Burglary and shoplifting, for which he was sent to Borstal for two years.

In 1982, he was convicted for being in possession of and dealing in drugs whilst working as an apprentice Butcher. He was given a five year sentence.

In 1988, he was fined £150.00 for possessing a .22 rifle without a licence.

In 1989, he was fined £500.00 for poaching and unlawful killing of a Deer in the New Forest.

In 1990, was convicted for assault whilst serving as a bouncer at a strip club in Soho. He was sentenced to six months in prison.

In 1992, was convicted of Pimping and served twelve months in prison.

In 1994, was convicted for being in possession of and selling illegal under age porn videos. He was sentenced to two years in prison.

In 1996, was convicted of selling hard drugs, and sentenced to ten years in prison.

Present address unknown, last known address Flat 4, Kimberly Street, Soho. London.

Having read out the file there were gasps from around the room. Charley looked at Munro and said.

"Right everybody start making enquiries, someone is bound to know this Wayne Smith and where he can be found. He might also be known as Wayne Ellison. Inspector Munro I want you to question all your known porn dealers and night club owners. Hound your known Pimps, prostitutes and threaten them that if they don't talk and fast we will pull them all in. The same applies to you Inspectors Franks and Bryant question all your known Drug dealers and Paedophiles. I want this Wayne Smith found and brought in within the next twenty four hours".

"Right away sir will do" both the Inspectors replied.

"Sergeant Morrison contact the central customs office and send them copies of Wayne Smith's photo he is not to leave the country. Smith must be detained if he shows up at any of the airports of ports"

"Will do sir"

"Sergeant Baker I need you to get in touch with the officers who last arrested Smith and find out what they can tell us about him"

"On it" The Sergeant replied.

"Inspector Roberts we need to talk, come up to the office," Charley said still holding the two files in his hands. Inspector Roberts frowned and followed Charley as he hastily left the incident room not saying anything and went up to the office.

Once inside Inspector Roberts asked with a puzzled look on his face.

"Is everything all right you looked shocked when you saw who Wayne Smith's mother is or was?"

"Yes I was shocked and believe I have reason to be"

"Really whys that?"

"I have reason to believe that Nancy Ellison the mother of Wayne Smith is now Nancy Cooper"

"What! You're kidding me, whatever makes you think that?"

"Because listen to this, this is the criminal record of Nancy Ellison.

Nancy Ellison: Born 1946 in Bishops Stortford, Hertfordshire.

Father: Harold Ellison.

Mother: Elizabeth Ellison.

Convictions:

Arrested on May 6th, 1965 in the Kings Head Public house, Soho, London where she was working as a barmaid. She was caught being in possession of and selling Cannabis and tablets known to be uppers and downers.

She was sentenced for four years imprisonment in Holloway prison London. Was pregnant when sentenced, and gave birth to a boy whilst in prison. Nancy Ellison never revealed to the prison staff who the father of the child was. The baby was taken away by social services and given the name Wayne Smith and put into a care home because Nancy Ellison at the time was seen as being unfit to bring up a child due to drug addiction.

After she had given birth, she agreed to undergo treatment and was transferred to a secure drug rehabilitation centre where she was cured of her addiction.

She was released from prison 1967 and put on Probation for the remainder of her sentence, no further convictions".

Inspector Roberts rubbing his forehead and frowning said.

"I'm sorry I still can't see why you think that this Nancy Ellison is Nancy Cooper"

"Because of what George Armstrong revealed to me yesterday. After you had left his office yesterday to come back here, George told me something very interesting about the Coopers that I wasn't aware of. Remember I have known Nancy, Walter, John and Mary for many years and remember Rose and Sam being born"

"So what was it that George told you?"

"He told me why Walter Cooper's brother Joseph who is John Coopers father left the village years ago and has never been back"

"Right, go on"

"Apparently when Joseph and Walter Cooper were growing up they were always competing with each other to see who could be best at everything. When they started going to the village school in Takely they met Nancy Ellison, who was in their class. From the first day, Walter and Joseph both became sweet on Nancy. Nancy knew they were both sweet on her and used to play them along. This went on for years. Then when they were in their late teens she started going out with Walter for several months before she suddenly decided to go out with Joseph instead. Walter was enraged, and he and his brother had a big fight one night in the pub, after which they continually kept arguing with each other. A few months later Nancy discovered that she was pregnant and that Joseph was the father. However, Nancy didn't tell Joseph that she was pregnant, but went to see Joseph and Walter one night and told them both that she was fed up with the two of them fighting and arguing over her and that she couldn't live like that and was leaving the village to get away from the pair of them. That night she packed her bags and left the village"

"So then what happened?"

"She went to live in London and didn't tell anyone except her mother that she was pregnant. When she got to London, she got a job as a barmaid in a pub in, Soho, and started drinking heavily which she had never done before, she also started going to parties and got into taking drugs. She then started selling drugs which eventually led to her getting arrested for being in possession of and selling drugs which resulted in her getting sent to prison where she had the baby".

"Good gracious so you could be right, but how does George Armstrong know about what happened?"

"Walter told George years ago, and they have kept the story a secret"

"So why did Nancy come back to the village?"

"She came back because her mother was taken seriously ill and wanted her back to be with her. Nancy's father had died some years before in a car crash, so her mother was living on her own. Walter was the first one to see that she had come back and went straight round to see her and seeing her and her mother's plight because they were struggling financially he paid for the mother to have private health care and virtually supported both Nancy and the mother. Nancy told Walter about what had happened to her in London. Walter blamed his brother for what had happened and went and confronted him, telling him to leave the village and never come back or else. Joseph left and went to live in Devon. Soon after he left Nancy and Walter got married"

"So Joseph met and married a woman in Devon and they had John, who is the father of Rose and Sam. How come Nancy never had any more children?"

"She couldn't have any more children, something to do with the time when she was into taking drugs. But she thinks the world of Rose and Sam as well as John and Mary the same as Walter does even though he knows that John is his brother's son"

"So Nancy's son is this Wayne Smith. I wonder if Nancy knows her son is called Wayne Smith and how did he find out his mother's maiden name? What happened to Nancy's mother?"

"Nancy's mother died three years ago. I don't know if Nancy knows her son is named Wayne Smith and I don't know how this Wayne found his mother's maiden name, the same as I don't know if he knows who is father is and that Nancy is married to his father's brother"

"Good grieve! Just supposing that he does know, and having snatched Rose and Sam has found who they are"

"Exactly so what's he planning to do with them, and where is he keeping them it could be anywhere?"

"He could be planning to hold them for ransom especially if he knows that his brother is a very wealthy and successful businessman"

"Exactly, I need to talk to Walter and Nancy Cooper and find out if they have been in contact with Wayne Smith"

"Agreed do you want them brought in or are you going out to their cottage?"

"Send a car out to pick them up straight away and delivered to our office"

"I'll do that right away"

"Oh and we better have someone discretely watch their cottage day and night just in case Smith decides to pay them a visit"

"I'll get Constable Baxter and Constable Wallace to do that they are used to carrying out discrete surveillances"

Inspector Roberts picked up his phone and pressed out the numbers for the front office. Constable Baxter answered the phone, and the Inspector informed him as to what he and Constable Wallace were to do. Constable Baxter said he would inform Constable Wallace and that they would carry out the Inspectors instructions straight away.

Charley sat down at his desk and began to reread through the files of Wayne Smith and Nancy Ellison when there was a knock on his door.

"Come in" he called out.

The door opened, and a constable popped his head round the door saying.

"Excuse me sir the television and media have arrived and are outside wanting a statement"

"Very good I'll come down"

Charley stood up and left the office and went down to the ground floor with the Constable, who said.

"Inspector Munro gave me these to give to you they are copies of Wayne Smith's photo for you to give to the media"

"Excellent thank you Constable"

Charley and the Constable along with other uniformed officers went out to the front of the Police station where the BBC, ITV, Channel four news reporters were waiting along with reporters from the local and national newspapers all crowded together all waiting to hear what was going on.

"Good day to you all my name is Detective Chief Superintendent Humphreys I am the senior police officer of Bishops Stortford police station"

"Can you give us some more information about the two youngsters that have been reported missing from Bishops Stortford, are they local youngsters?"

One of the reporters asked.

"No they are not local youngsters; they had come from Devon on a visit to stay with relatives"

"We heard that their parents are presently abroad have they been informed?"

"Yes their parents are aware that they have been reported as having gone missing"

"Can you tell us the names of the relatives whom they were staying with and where they live?"

"I'm not prepared to tell you that"

"Is it true that you and your officers carried out a search for the two youngsters in and around the area of Hatfield Forest in the village of Takely?"

"Yes we carried out a search of that area of Hatfield Forest"

"Did you discover anything?"

"We found that Rose and Sam had gone into the forest for a walk. Having carried out a search we came across evidence in the depth of the forest to show that they had been abducted by a man who had been in the forest poaching Deer"

"Do you think this same man is connected with the disappearance of Joy Manders aged sixteen who went missing from Epping Forest earlier this year?"

"Yes because from the new evidence that we found we now know for certain that all three were abducted by the same man. We also have evidence to show that this same man was responsible for the abduction of other youngsters who were reported as having gone missing from other forests in and around the London area over the last five years. This is of great importance to us in helping to solve all of these missing person cases"

There were gasps from the reporters gathered around along with them all asking.

"Do you have a name for the man you are looking for?"

"Yes the man we are looking for is a Wayne Smith aged 47. He might also be using the name Wayne Ellison. We have to advise you that we believe this man to be highly dangerous and should not be tackled by members of the public. If anyone knows, this man and his whereabouts would they please contact us as soon as possible as we need to apprehend him?"

"Do you have pictures of this man?"

"Yes and we would ask you to circulate this man's photos so that he can be brought in for questioning"

Charley handed out the copies of the photos of Wayne Smith, which all the reporters hastily took. There was a lot of clickings of cameras then one of the reporters asked.

"Can you tell us about the evidence you have found to prove that this Wayne Smith is responsible for all of the abductions?"

"I'm not prepared to share that information with you yet. Once this man is apprehended then I will share that information with you. Right that's all the questions that I'm prepared to answer for now. Good day ladies and gentlemen"

"One last question if you please, do you have any idea as to what this man may have done with the youngsters he is alleged to have abducted?"

"I will hopefully find out when he has be apprehended"

Charley and the other police officers who were with him then turned and went straight back inside the police station.

Whilst all the press and TV crews hastily retreated back to their different newspapers offices and TV stations.

Charley instantly made his way back up to his office where Inspector Roberts asked.

"How was it?"

"The usual demands, at least they will publish Wayne Smith's photo which hopefully will bring a positive response from people who have seen or know him and might want to talk"

"True and when Wayne Smith sees his photo all over the media he is bound to make some moves to ensure that he is not caught"

The phone rang on Charley's desk, and he picked it up saying.

"Yes what do you want?"

"The Coopers are here sir"

"Walter and Nancy Cooper"

"Yes sir"

"Good bring them up would you?"

"Right away sir"

Charley put down the phone and said.

"Let's see if they have been keeping secrets from us"

Five minutes later Walter and Nancy Cooper were shown into Charley's office both of them had worried looks on their faces and Walter asked as he and Nancy sat down in front of Charley's desk.

"What's up Charley why have you called us in, have you found Rose and Sam?"

"No, we haven't found them yet but we do now know who snatched them" Charley replied.

"Really well that's good news have you made an arrest?"

"No, we are still looking for the suspect. The reason I have brought you in is because I need to ask you some important questions"

"I see well ask away Charley" Walter replied.

"Nancy I need to ask you before you married Walter was your maiden name Nancy Ellison?"

"Yes Charley, why do you need to ask me that?" Nancy replied fidgeting in her chair.

"Was your father Harold Ellison and your mother Elizabeth Ellison?"

"Yes but why do you need to know?"

"Yes why are you asking Nancy these questions, what has it got to do with Rose and Sam going missing?" Walter asked looking agitated.

"I will explain my reasons when Nancy has answered my questions"

"Well I hope you have a good reason for asking Nancy these questions Charley" Walter responded.

"Nancy when was the last time you saw your son?"

Nancy and Walter looked at each other then back at Charley with looks of surprise.

"What are you talking about Charley you know that Walter and I don't have any children"

"But Nancy you do have a son who was born in 1965 before you were married to Walter"

"What are you talking about, that's ridiculous"

"No Nancy it's not ridiculous in 1965 you were serving a prison sentence in Holloway prison for drug dealing. You were pregnant at the time and gave birth to a son in prison who was taken away from you and put into social care because, at that time, you were a registered drug addict and alcoholic who was seen as unfit to look after your son".

Nancy's jaw dropped, and she suddenly burst into tears. Walter jumped up and shouted.

"This is too much Charley I won't tolerate your questioning Nancy like this. How can you sit there making these statements, where's your evidence, and what has this got to do with the disappearance of Rose and Sam?"

"Sit down and calm down Walter. I'm sorry Nancy to have to bring up your past. But it is relevant to my enquiries into finding Rose and Sam. I need to find out Nancy if you have seen or heard from your son since he was taken away from you and put into care"

"So you know things about Nancy's past but you still need to tell us why it's relevant to your enquiries. People in the village don't know about Nancy's past and what she went through all those years ago and we don't want her past made public"

Walter said as he sat down and put an arm around Nancy's shoulder.

"I sorry Charley you are right I do have a son, but I haven't seen or heard of my son since the day he was taken away from me forty-seven years ago," Nancy said still crying.

"How can you be sure do you know the name that was given to your son by social services?"

"Well no, they never told me the name he had been given" Nancy replied wiping tears from her eyes with her handkerchief.

"Do either of you know of anybody by the name Wayne Smith?" Charley asked.

Walter looked at Nancy, and they both shook their heads and Walter replied.

"I can't remember ever meeting anybody with that name, do you Nancy?"

"No, I can't say that I do," Nancy said shaking her head.

"Who is Wayne Smith?" Walter asked looking puzzled.

"I have to tell you Nancy that your son was given the name Wayne Smith"

"Really, how do you know?" Walter demanded.

"Because we found that the finger prints on the barrier chains and locks at the exit that was used by the man we know snatched Rose and Sam match with those of a Wayne Smith. On checking the central files of criminal records, we found that this Wayne Smith's mother was a Nancy Ellison, who was born in Bishops Stortford in 1946 and that Nancy Ellison's father was a Harold Ellison and the mother was Elizabeth Ellison. His file also mentions that he was taken from his mother at birth and put into social care who gave him the name Wayne Smith. The file also gives the reasons why he had been taken into care. That's when we found Nancy's police record"

"Oh, my God! So you're saying that my son was given the name Wayne Smith and that he is responsible for snatching Rose and Sam". Nancy said with a look of horror on her face.

"I'm really very sorry but yes, now do you see why I had to bring you into ask you these embarrassing questions"

"Yes I understand now Charley; this is a terrible blow to find out that the son I had that was taken away from me is a criminal"

"As Nancy says this is terrible news and not easy for either of us to take in, such a shock," Walter said shaking his head.

"Has he a long criminal record?" Nancy asked.

"Sad to say Nancy that yes he has been in trouble from a very early age"

"Do you think he knows who Rose and Sam are and that they are part of our family?" Nancy asked.

"It's more than likely because if when he snatched them he found Rose's mobile phone then yes he will have seen you and Walters names and address as well as John and Mary's names and address listed on the phone"

"Do you think it's possible that he planned to snatch them?" Walter asked.

"Not that we know of" Charley replied.

"So now that you know he has snatched them are you not going to arrest him and rescue Rose and Sam?" Walter asked.

"We are still in the process of tracking him down as we don't as yet know where he lives, but hopefully we will find out very soon. We are making extensive enquiries in the hope that we will have him in custody within the next twenty four hours. His photo has been released to the media and the search for him has gone nationwide"

"Well I hope you find him and quick. Do you think it's possible that he will demand a ransom for their return Charley?"

"I don't know, we are not aware of him having made any demands as yet. That is why I needed to find out from you both if you had seen or heard from him"

"As we said we didn't know Nancy's sons name. John and Mary need to be told about your findings, which is going to be one hell of a shock to them as well especially for John when he discovers that he has a brother and that the brother he never knew existed is responsible for snatching his children" Walter replied.

"Yes I know and it's not going to be easy for me when I have to break that news to them when I see them this evening at the Chief Constables office. Hopefully by then we will have tracked him down and made an arrest. I have officers from police headquarters assisting us in our search, because we don't have sufficient manpower in Bishops Stortford, we are only a small police station as you know. But all of my available officers are on this case"

"We should join you when you go to see John and Mary, and I should be the one to tell John," Nancy said having now composed herself.

"Yes I understand that and agree it would be better coming from you. So I will pick you up later this evening on my way to the Chief Constables. I apologies once again to both of you for having to bring up Nancy's past and want to assure you both that when we do apprehend your son and he is brought to trial, we will do all we can to prevent the public from knowing that it was your son Nancy that was involved in this crime"

"I do hope so Charley because you must understand that I don't want my past being dragged out into the open for people to know about. I have always led a decent life since I was released all those years ago and cured of my addictions". Nancy said with a concerned expression.

"I know you have Nancy. Now you will have to excuse me as I need to see if my officers have any positive information to report. I will take you downstairs and get one of my officers to take you home, and I'll see you this evening" Charley replied.

"Yes of course Charley we'll let you get on with your enquires and see you later"

Charley stood up as did Walter and Nancy and Charley led them out of the office and downstairs to the reception desk and saw them off in one of the patrol cars.

Once they were gone he returned to his office where he was greeted by Inspector Roberts, who was completing his notes from the interview.

"That was a tough situation for you and the Coopers. Do you really believe that when this case comes to trial it will be possible not to make it known that it was Nancy's son that was responsible for snatching those youngsters?" The Inspector said.

"Tell me about it, I just hope so because if not you know what people are like with their gossiping. Walter and Nancy's lives will never be the same. It's bad enough for Nancy to discover that her son was responsible for the snatching of not only Rose and Sam but all those others youngsters. She has got to live with that and the fact that he is involved in all sorts of other crimes no doubt for the rest of her life"

"Yes what a thing to have to live with plus all the scandal it is going to make"

"I think there could be a lot more scandal to come out of this when we do get to question Wayne Smith. Now I had better phone the Chief Constable to let him know that we are searching for Wayne Smith and have found that he is Nancy's son"

Charley picked up his phone and dialled the Chief Constables number; the phone rang twice and then a voice answered saying.

"Chief Constable Stewart's office this is his secretary speaking who's calling?"

"Good morning Elizabeth it's Charley Humphreys I need to speak to the Chief Constable urgently"

"Good morning sir, just a second and I will put you through"

There was a pause then a male voice came on the line saying.

"Morning Charley what can I do for you?"

"Morning sir we have found out the name of the man who abducted Rose and Sam Cooper his name is Wayne Smith and he has a long record of being involved in drug dealing, selling of underage porn videos, pimping, assault as well as poaching. We also have positive proof to show that he was responsible for snatching Joy Manders six months ago as well as others from different forests in the London area. I have got the team busily trying to track him as we don't yet have an address for him"

"Really well that's a positive start. Have you had a visit from the media yet I heard the initial announcement on this morning's news?"

"Yes sir and they have copies of his photo which should help. When we found his criminal record on the computer, we found that his mother was a Nancy Ellison and that he was taken from her at birth because she was serving a sentence for drug dealing and as a drug addict she was seen unfit to look after him. When we checked her record, we found that she had been born in Bishops Stortford, and her parents lived in Takely. After Smith was born Nancy Ellison went into rehab and was cured of her addiction and later released. She has no further criminal record. However, I have found out that Nancy Ellison is the wife of Walter Cooper and that it is his brother who is the father of Wayne Smith. Who is also the father of John Cooper the father of Rose and Sam?"

"Good gracious! So you've questioned Walter and Nancy Cooper about this. So was Nancy married to Walter at that time?"

"No, Nancy was going out with Walters brother Joseph, and became pregnant and to avoid any scandal she went to live in London. That's when she got into trouble and went to prison. She has never seen her son this Wayne Smith since he was born and taken away from her and put into care. It has come as a shock to her and Walter to find out that her son is the one responsible for snatching Rose and Sam"

"I bet it has and do you think that John Cooper knows he has a brother?"

"No he doesn't know but when he does find out and what his brother has done he is going to be horrified"

"Not half this will cause a hell of a scandal for him and the rest of the family if it gets in the press. Do you suspect that Wayne Smith knows who his mother is and who Rose and Sam are and is planning to hold them up for ransom?"

"I can't be sure sir hopefully he doesn't know. Nancy and Walter want to come to the meeting tonight when John Cooper will have to be told about what we have found"

"Understandable .The quicker you can track Smith down and arrest him, the better. Do you think you will be able to find him quickly?"

"Hopefully with the media support and with the team questioning all their contacts we should get a lead on him very soon"

"Whew well keep me posted Charley this is turning into a very complex case that's for sure"

"I will do sir, speak to you later, bye"

"Bye Charley find this Smith and quick"

The line went dead, and Charley put down the phone and sighed.

"How did he take the news?" Inspector Roberts asked.

"Like all of us he's stunned. I'm going back down to see if there are any further developments. You had better send an email copy of the interview we had with Nancy and Walter to the Chief Constable"

"Right I will do then I'll come down and join you"

Charley nodded stood up and left to return to the incident room.

Chapter 6.

On the Thursday morning, Wayne and Celine wearily got up early to go round the different bedrooms to wake up all of the youngsters that were due to go in the van to the brothel in London. Once they had got them up and seen that they had all had a shower and were dressed and had been fed a meagre breakfast and given an injection to keep them docile they lined them up in the hall to wait for Vince who arrived just after half past nine having again been held up in traffic. Wayne and Vince loaded them in the van while Celine went back upstairs to begin getting the others up and into the bathroom which she did after dishing out the usual beatings and kicking. Once Wayne and Vince had finished the loading Vince had a quick mug of coffee before getting back in the van to return to London.

"Did you drop that shipment of drugs off to Terry" Wayne asked as Vince was about to leave.

"Yes mate he says he's going to phone you later, he was in a foul mood and moaning about the last lot of heroin you had sent him saying it had been mixed with something which he thought was chalk, same with the cocaine"

"What! The stupid prat I didn't put anything in with the heroin or cocaine I never do, you know that. It's all pure stuff that I send him"

"Well he's moaning so expect an earful when he phones"

"Yea ok, thanks Vince; I will see you late this evening. Mind how you go, bye"

"Bye see you later"

Once Vince had gone Wayne went and joined Celine to help her with the youngsters who were staying behind.

Finally when they had finished chasing them up for their showers and had fed them a meagre breakfast of a bowl of porridge and given out injections and tablets they returned them to their rooms and locked them up all with the exception of Celia and Joy, whom Celine pulled aside and said.

"I want you two to go to the dining room and clean it up and bring all the dirty dishes glasses and everything else in there that needs washing up into the kitchen and load it in the dishwasher. Once you have done that I want you to go round all the downstairs rooms and dust, polish and vacuum. So go on get started"

Celia and Joy looked at each other then turning and looking at Celine Joy blurted out in a trembling voice.

"Why can't Susan and the new girl come and give a hand,"

"Because today they are going to clean out all the bedrooms and change all the sheets. Jamie is going to help them as well"

"What about Adrian and Julian and that new kid?" Celia said.

"They are going to do some gardening. So stop bitching and get on with what I've told you to do, or you'll both get a beating" Celine replied giving them a harsh stare.

Celia and Joy turned and skulked off downstairs to the dining room to collect the dirty dishes from the night before.

Celine followed them down and went into the kitchen to prepare breakfast for her and Wayne. She took out some bacon, sausages, tomatoes, mushrooms and eggs and started to prepare everything when

Wayne walked in and seeing that she was getting breakfast took some bread and put it in the toaster then poured himself a mug of fresh coffee and said.

"I need to make some phone calls I'll be back presently"

"Ok, see you in a while but don't be too long" Celine replied smiling.

Wayne went into the study and sat down at his desk and unlocked one of the drawers and took out one of a number of ledgers opened it up and scanned down a number of pages before picking up the phone and dialling a number. Presently a woman answered saying.

"Mrs Croft speaking who's calling?"

"Morning Mrs Croft this is the Harold Boyd loan company I am phoning you because on checking our records we see that you are severely behind with your repayments. Can you tell me when you intend to bring your payments up to date?"

"Oh yes well I have been meaning to phone you to explain that my husband and I are really short of money at the moment, because we were behind with the rent and council tax bills and the council were demanding that we settle what we owed them. We should be able to pay you something towards what we owe you in arrears by the end of the month"

"Mrs Croft last month you said you were going to pay us some money towards the arrears you have with us, but as yet we have not received any money from you. Now you are saying we can't expect to receive any money from you until the end of this month"

"I'm very sorry but as I said we are really struggling at the moment what with trying to pay off the other loan companies and my husband being on shorter hours at work"

"Listen we have had enough of your excuses, and we are not prepared to allow you to continue not paying us. We will be sending one of our agents round this afternoon to collect the arrears. Now if you haven't got the money when our agent calls he will have to take your daughter who will have to work for us to pay off the arrears"

"No, please give us more time I'm begging you. We don't want our daughter having to work to pay off our arrears. She's only thirteen and still at school. Please we don't want her forced into prostitution to pay off what we owe you. Please, please I'm begging you" The woman cried down the phone.

"Our agent will be round this afternoon bye"

Wayne put down the phone then dialled another number and presently a male voice answered saying.

"Jenkins motorbike repairs how I may help you"

"Morning this is Harold Boyd loan Company Mr Jenkins we are phoning you because we see from our files that you are behind again with your repayments for the loan you have with our company. When do you intend to pay off your arrears?"

"Look I'm very sorry all right, but I've had a lot of expenses this month what with having to pay off suppliers so I could order new parts to fix my customers bikes. I have had to pay off the outstanding rent on my workshop as well, so I just haven't had the money to send you. But by the end of the month I should have some money in"

"You said that last month and the month before Mr Jenkins and we still haven't received any payment from you. So we will be sending one of our agents around this afternoon for the outstanding money that you owe us"

"But listen I have told you I don't have any money at the moment"

"Well unless you find what you owe us by the time our agent calls this afternoon you won't be around anymore because you will have had a tragic accident, and you know what will happen to your daughter then don't you"

"Jesus look don't do that you know I'm a single parent. If you do I won't be in a position to pay you anything and my daughter will have to go into care"

"We know that and we don't want to take away your livelihood. Look there is a way out of this for you if you are prepared to let us help you"

"What you got in mind?"

"As you say you're a single parent who has a twelve year old daughter. Now we are prepared to wipe off what you owe us and give you a nice tidy sum to help you pay off some of your other debts. However in order for us to be able to do that your daughter will have to work for us"

"I don't understand, she can't work for you she's still in school she's not old enough to go out to work"

"But she doesn't go to school at night and weekends so that's when she can work for us"

"Doing what?"

"We know of a film company Mr Jenkins where she can appear in their films"

"Film company making films, what sort of films"

"The sorts of films the film company make namely underage porn they sell very well"

"What! You want my daughter to appear in porn films. You can't expect her to do that"

"Mr Jenkins you currently owe us five thousand pounds. We are prepared give you ten thousand in cash in return that your daughter appears in those films. Now she would need to work for the next ten years in order for us to be in a position to grant you this offer. You wouldn't have to pay us any money in return and your existing loan with us would be wiped out"

"But she's only twelve years of age you can't expect her to do that"

"Now come on Mr Jenkins you know that you need the extra money, and you also know that you are in no position to pay off what you already owe us. So we think that you will be able to persuade your daughter to come and work for us"

"So in return you're prepared to give me ten thousand pounds and wipe off the five thousand I owe you. What if I refuse to do that then what?"

"Then you will have a nasty accident which will leave you out of business permanently and your daughter will be put into care because she won't have a father to look after her"

"So if I agree how soon would I receive the ten thousand and I suppose you will want me to sign an agreement"

"You could have that cash this afternoon. Our agent will bring you the cash and naturally yes you would have to sign an agreement. Your daughter would go with our agent when she returns from school and be introduced to the film company's director and start to work for them. She would be back home again by midnight with a written timetable showing which evenings and weekends she will be required to work. One of the film company's representatives would collect her every time she is required to work. Now should at any time you break the agreement then as I said before you would have a fatal accident. Do we have an agreement Mr Jenkins?"

"I don't have much choice do I"

"No you don't bye"

Wayne put down the phone and dialled another number, and a female voice answered saying.

"Jennifer Swift speaking who's calling?"

"Good morning Miss Swift this is Harold Boyd Property rental Company"

"Yes what can I do for you?"

"You currently rent one of our unfurnished apartments and at the time that you signed the agreement we also gave you a loan through our loan company in order for you to buy furniture. At the time that you signed the agreements you said that you were struggling because you couldn't find a cheap apartment and could not get a loan to furnish an apartment due to the fact that you were not working"

"Yes that's correct is there a problem I have been paying the rent and money for the loan because I managed to find work again"

"Yes our records show that yes you have been paying your rent and money towards your loan. However, you are still in arrears and as per the agreements that you signed at the time that you rented an apartment and took the loan it was made clear in both agreements that both the rent and the interest rates on the loan could go up at any time. Regretfully we have to inform you that the interest rates on your loan have had to go up to one hundred percent, and we have to double the rent on your apartment. This is due to the fact that you are still considerably in arrears with both your rent and loan repayments"

"Oh, my goodness! But I can't afford that even though I'm now working I'm struggling to live"

"Well we understand life is not easy these days Miss Swift, but we all have expenses so we have no choice"

"But I've just said I can't possibly afford to make additional payments on my rent and loan. What am I to do I will be homeless and if I become homeless then I will lose my job"

"Yes well we are sorry about that. However we do have a solution to your problem"

"You do what might that be"

"You will have to work for us on a part-time basis"

"Work for you doing what exactly"

"If you wish to stay in your apartment and be in a position to pay the increases we would need you to work in one of our night clubs as a female escort in the evenings and at weekends"

"An escort in a night club, what would I be required to do?"

"You will be paired with one of our clients and would be required to wine and dine with them and entertain them for the evening"

"Entertain them in what way?"

"Oh with whatever they need Miss Swift"

"I have heard stories about female escorts and a lot of them are prostitutes. You expecting me to do that"

"Are you do understand"

"But if I refuse what then?"

"We will have no choice but to send round one of our agents to evict you and reposes all your furniture and put you out on the street with nothing"

"You can't do that there are laws to protect me against such things"

"Look at your agreements Miss Swift and you will see that was what you signed and agreed at the time"

"Not to work as an escort I didn't "

"No, but the agreements clearly stated that if you failed to pay what was due we would have the powers to evict you and take goods to the value of what was owing. Now there is not a court in the country that you could go to and dispute that agreement. Now we don't want to cause you any hardship so why don't you just agree to our proposal. Our agent will call round later today to make all the necessary arrangements ok"

"Oh, my God! This is a terrible nightmare"

"No, you will be all right and we could ensure that you made a lot of money, probably more than what you're earning now. We have a number of different bonus schemes that our agent will inform you about when he comes to see you later. Good day to you Miss Swift"

Wayne put the phone down and was about to dial another number when Celine called out from the kitchen saying.

"Come on hurry up your breakfast is ready"

Wayne put the book back in the drawer and locked it up before getting up and going through to the kitchen where Celine was putting down their breakfasts on the table. He flicked on the television on one of the worktops and went and sat down to begin to eat. The clock on the kitchen wall showed the time as eleven fifteen.

On the television, there was a morning talk show where different celebrities had been invited in to talk about their current film, TV show, book or play they were starring in. That morning a well-known actor was talking about a film he had recently appeared in and the female interviewer who it was obvious was a keen fan of his was flirting and asking him lots of questions which he was quite happy to answer.

"Ha, look who's on the television he was in our club in, Chelmsford, the other night pissed out of his brain flirting with all his female fans in the club. He spent a fortune that night. He's known for getting pissed, but looking at him this morning with his smooth chat you wouldn't think so. He likes sniffing cocaine as well, but that never gets in the news" Wayne said pointing at the television screen with his mouth full of sausage and bacon.

"No, not him he's Mr Cool he is I can't think that he gets pissed and snorts cocaine. He's raised a lot of money for various charities" Celine replied.

"He's also a regular at our brothel he's a pervert likes young boys"

"No, really he's been to our brothel and likes young boys. Well who would have guessed I thought he was one for the girls?"

"Ha, you should see whom we get in there I have them all in my book that I keep which lists all the visitors we get. Handy that because a bit of blackmail can earn a fair sum of money especially when the clients don't want any nasty press revelations that could ruin their careers"

"Ah really, so are you blackmailing some of the clients then?"

"Yea of course they have to do what I want them to do"

Joy suddenly walked in the kitchen and said.

"Celia and I have finished the cleaning of the downstairs rooms. Oh! Look who's on the television he's great he is"

"Never mind who's on the television. I will come and inspect the work you have done, and if I find any dust anywhere you will both be in trouble understood" Celine said looking at Celia.

"Very good so what do you want us to do now?"

"Go and help the others clean the bedrooms go on hurry up"

"Right whatever" Celia replied with a sullen look.

"Don't be cheeky, or I will give you a belting now do as Celine tells you," Wayne said.

Celia turned and with a shudder she hastily left the room.

Wayne having wolfed down his breakfast stood up and said.

"I've got to make some more calls I'll be in the study"

"All right then I will chase the kids up. This afternoon can we go and play in the pool seeing as it's hot?"

"Yea why not, we can lock the kids in their rooms. See you later"

Wayne left the kitchen and Celine started clearing the table.

Upstairs Celia and Joy found Susan in Roses room where they were chatting sitting on Roses bed.

"Hi you must be the new girl, were you ok we heard you screaming last night what happened" Joy asked with a concerned look on her face.

"Hi, my name is Rose my brother Sam and I was snatched in Takely forest on Tuesday by that horrible man Wayne. I haven't seen my brother since I got here, and I'm really worried about him. When we got here we were separated, and I was given injections and pills which made me semi-conscious I couldn't speak properly or have the energy to fight back. Yesterday that horrible man Wayne took me into a room where he filmed and took photos of me naked on a large round bed. Then last night he gave me another injection and some pills which made me really woozy then he dragged me back to that room where this young lad forced me to have sex with him in all sorts of different ways while Wayne watched and another man filmed it all. It was disgusting I had never had sex before. I'm only fifteen I shall never forget what I was forced to do it was rape, and the young lad looked out of his mind he must be an addict or something. I just want to get away and go home to my parents" Rose replied as tears rolled down her face.

"We know what you have been through we were snatched by Wayne too and brought here. We have been here for ages. We are given injections and pills every day and are forced to have sex with lots of different men every day. I'm Joy Manders I was snatched from Epping Forrest in January by Wayne and this is Celia who was snatched from Windsor Great Park in London with her brother Julian in 2011"

"Oh, my God! I remember reading in the paper about you going missing they found your pony. So do any of you know where this place is?"

"No, we only know that there are lots of us imprisoned in this large house. The only time we go out of the house is when we have to work in the garden or get taken in a van to another large house where we are forced to have sex with all sorts of different men. We are expected to have sex with at least twenty men each day, and if the men complain about us we get beaten and forced to have ice cold showers or baths. The house here is surrounded by tall stone walls, and there is only one gate which is locked and has a security camera. There are other security cameras hidden all-round the outside, so it's impossible to escape" Celia said.

"Yes and I have been here since 2008 I was snatched by Wayne in Thetford forest in Norfolk. Like you and the others I have been given injections and pills ever since I got here. I don't know what they give us, but I know they make you dopey and you find you can't stop them doing to you whatever they want you to do" Susan said.

"Gosh, you have been here all this time. Is there no chance of getting away from here?"

"Listen there is no chance of escape we are watched every time we go out of the house. As Celia said if we don't do as we are told, we get beaten you should see the bruises I have got. I get beaten nearly every day either by Wayne or that horrible woman of his Celine who's Spanish I think"

"So we could all be here for ever and used continuously as sex slaves?"

"No, because after a time when Wayne and his gang have no further use for us he will sell us off. One of the girls Samantha left yesterday she was sold"

"Sold to whom "

"We don't know who she was sold to, or where she has gone too, but you can bet Wayne got a good price for her"

"So we will all end up being sold, that's horrible, it's just like in the old days when slaves were sold" Rose sobbed.

"Yes only we are sold as sex slaves" Susan replied.

"So who's in the house today and how come the bedrooms are unlocked?" Rose asked still sobbing.

"There are us girls my brother Julian, who is seven, Adrian, who is eleven he's been here two years then there's Jamie he's the one who raped you he's seventeen and has been here two years and is as you say an addict can't live without shots of heroin. Then your brother Sam, who is still locked in his room," Celia replied.

"So how many youngsters are there in this house?" Rose asked through her tears.

"There are I think sixteen or seventeen the rest have gone off in the van today like they do most days. The only reason the bedrooms are unlocked is because it's our day to strip the beds and put clean sheets on as well as clean the rooms. We get beaten if we don't do everything properly" Joy said.

"I want to see my brother why is he still locked in his room?" Roses asked.

"We don't know. Shush! Look out Celine is coming. Quick we must go, see you Rose"

As they dashed out of the room, Celine came along the corridor and seeing them run out of Roses room shouted.

"What you doing why aren't you stripping the beds. Right come here I'm going to have to beat you all you little bitches"

The girls ran into the different rooms and started to strip the beds. Celine went into one of the rooms the one Joy had run into and seeing Joy she ran over and started kicking and punching her until Joy fell on the floor and curled up crying out saying.

"Please no we were only talking to the new girl"

"You bitch I told you what you've got to do now start doing it"

Celine turned and went into the next room and seeing Susan she did the same to her before going round all the other rooms and beating whoever she found in there.

Rose hearing the beatings curled up on her bed crying saying through her tears.

"Mummy where are you please come and get me and Sam out of here I can't stand it anymore please mummy"

Downstairs, in the study Wayne, was busy talking on the phone threatening more people who owed money. Half an hour later Celine suddenly burst in the study with a look of horror on her face as she called out.

"Wayne come quick the news is on the television and your picture is being shown"

"What!" Wayne shouted.

He leapt up out of his chair and ran passed Celine pushing her aside as he went into the kitchen and glared at the television screen which was showing pictures of newspaper reporters and TV cameras with reporters all standing in front of a row of police officers outside

Bishops Stortford police station. Wayne's image came up on the screen and then a tall man in a suit said.

"Yes because from the new evidence that we discovered we now know for certain that all three were abducted by the same man. We also have proof to show that this same man was responsible for the abduction of other youngsters who were reported as having gone missing from other forests in and around the London area over the last five years. This is of great importance to us in helping to solve all of these missing person cases"

"Do you have a name for this man you are looking for?"

"Yes that's his picture his name is Wayne Smith aged 47. He might also be using the name Wayne Ellison. We would advise you that we believe this man to be highly dangerous and should not be tackled by members of the public. If anyone knows, this man and his whereabouts would they please contact us as soon as possible as we need to apprehend him?"

"Fuck it! How the fucking hell have they found out it was me?" Wayne shouted out.

Celine having followed him into the kitchen and heard the announcement said.

"You must have left some evidence behind"

"Don't be fucking stupid I never leave any clues I'm always careful"

"Well what we going to do then. They are bound to find you; people will recognise you when we go out"

The phone started ringing in the study.

"Go and lock those kids up now I'll see who that is" Wayne shouted.

Celine turned and ran out of the kitchen along the hallway and up the stairs shouting at the kids telling them to return to their rooms, while Wayne rushed into the study and picked up the phone saying.

"Hello who's that?"

"Wayne it's me Terry Parker, listen you're in big trouble and you owe me big time"

"What you mean I'm in big trouble and owe you. What you talking about I don't owe you anything"

"Look mate that last load of Heroin that you sold me is crap. You must have mixed it with something because my dealers are telling me that their customers are dropping like fucking flies and those that aren't dead are being carted off to a hospital where they will also die unless the doctors can do something. What you trying to do ruining my business you stupid bastard. I have important clients mate, and they are heavy you know what I mean. I could end up dead in the fucking Thames thanks to you. So you better pay me good time or else"

"Or else what?"

"Are you going to change this crap you sold me and pay me compensation? I have got to pay out a lot of money to keep the heavies off my back".

"Fuck off; I never mixed anything with the stuff I sold you. I never do that it's all pure. You must have mixed something with it you cheating bastard"

"No, you mixed it and you know it. I suppose it was that Brazilian that sold it to you and knowing him the fat bastard he had probable mixed something with it before he sold it you, so with you adding to it as well it's fucking lethal"

"I just told you I never mixed anything with it"

"Are you going to change it and pay me compensation or not"

"No so fuck off I got more things to worry about right now"

"Yea I heard the coppers are out for you, just seen you on the telly, and I'm not going down when they catch you. So if you're not going to play the game then

I'll talk to the cops they're bound to pay me good money for information about you and I will get witness protection. I'm not going back in the nick you'll see, but you are mate"

"Are you threatening me because if you are you're a dead man I'm telling you? I'll send some of the boys to sort you out and shut you up"

"Fucking try it mate and let's see who comes out best"

The phone line went dead, and Wayne shouted down the phone.

"Hoy! You there you sniffling bastard?" as Celine walked in and said.

"Who was that you were shouting at?"

"Terry fucking Parker he's threatening to shop us all to the cops. I'll fix him right now"

Wayne picked up the phone and dialled out a number, and a voice came on the line saying.

"Hello"

"Franky is that you its Wayne listen I need you to shut Terry Parker up for me permanently and quick?"

"Hi Wayne I just seen your picture on the telly. You don't think Terry has shopped you why would he do that?"

"No, but he's threatening to turn us all into the cops to save his own skin, and if he does we will all sink he knows too much about us all".

"What! The rotten bastard after all the years we've known him. Right well me and Tony will shut him up for you. Well go round to his place straight away and wait for him to make a move then well go after him and stop him before he gets to the cops"

"There's five grand in it for each of you ok?"

"No save the money we might all need it later if it gets to hot"

"Thanks Franky give me a bell as soon as you have done it ok"

"Will do bye"

The line went dead.

"You better hope that Franky does shut him up before he gets to the cops because Terry knows everything about all our different rackets"

"Stop panicking all right let's just wait. Franky and Tony will stop Parker from talking to the cops"

"But if they don't stop him before he gets to the coppers what we going to do?"

"Well there's no way that we can stay here. Well leave here and go to the houseboat in Southwold in Suffolk. He doesn't know about the houseboat. We can lie low there until I arrange to get us out of the country and across the channel. I have money stashed in a Swiss bank. We can hide low in Europe until the heat dies down then we can go to South America or anywhere we've both got false passports"

"They will be watching all the ports; we'll never get across the channel"

"Yes we will I'll ask Cyril to take us across on his yacht"

"What we going to do with all the brats including Rose and Sam?"

"Leave them all behind of course except well take Rose and Sam we can use them as insurance"

"Well you better hope Franky shuts Terry up. Do you want me to start packing some stuff for us?"

"Yes pack some clothes for us"

"You had better look out all the papers we need and some cash. How much have we got in the safe?"

"We've got two hundred and fifty grand plus I've got visa cards in different names and my Swiss bank account card as well as our passports in different names"

"Oh right well we should be alright for money then"

"Of course I'm like the Boy Scout prepared for anything you'll see".

"I bloody well hope so," Celine said as she left the room.

Chapter 7.

When Charley walked back into the incident room having sent Walter and Netty Cooper home and spoken to the Chief Constable, he went round and talked to all the senior detectives that were present to find out how they were each progressing with their enquiries. They all reported that they were still busy chasing up contacts but as yet no one had phoned in with any positive sightings of Wayne Smith. They had all had the usual crank callers saying they knew him and wanted to know if there was a substantial reward for giving information about him. Having questioned the callers as to what they knew they appeared to know nothing of any value.

Then at twelve thirty lunch time the phone on Detective Inspector Bryant's desk rang. The Inspector was busy ticking off the names of people he had already spoken to, to see if they knew of Wayne Smith. He picked up the phone saying.

"Detective Inspector Bryant who's calling?"

"I have important information that you need if you want to catch Wayne Smith, but I want to know how much you're prepared to pay"

"That depends on the value of the information you can give me. Do you know Wayne Smith?"

"Yea I know him I was one of his partners, but the bastards double crossed me, so I want to know what it's worth to you if I shop him"

"I see well as I said that depends on how valuable your information is"

"Listen I've just told you I was one of his partners and that I'm prepared to tell you everything about him. How much is the information worth to you?"

"Are you prepared to tell us where we can find him?"

"Fucking hell are you thick! I just told you I know all you need to know about him"

"Just one second"

Detective Inspector Bryant covered the mouthpiece of the phone and called across to Charley who was talking to one of the detective Sergeants.

"Excuse me sir I think I might have a positive lead on the line. He says that he was one of Wayne Smiths partners but because Smith has double crossed him he is prepared to tell us everything about him including where we can find him. He wants to know how much we are prepared to pay him for the information"

"Do you think he is genuine or is he another crank?" Charley replied.

"Hard to tell at this stage"

"Alright ask him how much he thinks his information is worth"

Detective Inspector Bryant uncovered the mouthpiece of the phone and said.

"How much do you think your information is worth?"

"Fucking hell! Right seeing as I know everything about him and the names and addresses of all of the people who work for him, plus all his business outlets and all his overseas contacts which will be more than you need to put him and all of his gang away for a very long time. I'll want one hundred thousand, a new identity and passport and witness protection"

"I see well you are expecting a lot especially if you have been involved in criminal activities with Smith. I need to speak to my boss again just a second"

The Inspector covered the mouth piece again and repeated to Charley what the man claimed he knew and what he wanted in return for the information. Charley having walked over to the Inspectors desk and was standing beside him said.

"Alright tell him we need to meet him and today"

The Inspector raised his eyebrows then uncovering the mouthpiece said.

"My boss says he needs to meet with you today"

"Let me speak to your boss you retard" the man replied.

"He wants to speak to you sir" The Inspector said handing the phone to Charley.

"Hello I'm Chief Superintendent Charles Humphreys I'm in charge of this investigation. Now listen If you are prepared to give me all the information that you claim to have about Wayne Smith and his organisation and it leads to his arrest as well as all of the members of his organisation then I will ensure that your demands are met"

"Right well Chief I can tell you that the information I have is genuine. I'm not another of the phony cranks wasting your time. I'm looking to get my own back on what Smith has done to me. I'm no fool I know that if I give you all that information Smith or one of his associates will want to silence me for good. That's why I need both the money, new identity and witness protection"

"I understand perfectly what you are saying and I'm prepared to negotiate with you. However if having heard all the information you are prepared to give turns out to be useless then there will be no deal is that understood"

"Loud and clear, you won't be disappointed I can assure you"

"Right well we need to meet up today. Name the place you want to meet up, and I will come and collect you. It will be safer for you to talk to me in my office"

"All right but only you and the Inspector come to meet me. If I see you have set a trap then you'll not get anything from me understood"

"Understood only the Inspector and myself will come and meet you. So where do you want to meet and at what time?"

"Right meet me in one hour's time in the car park at the Green Man pub Takely I will be in a grey Renault car in the car park. Oh and bring twenty grand in cash with you just to show good faith".

"Ok you have a deal, the Inspector and I will meet you in an hour"

"Right bye"

The phone went dead, and Charley put down the phone and let out a sigh. Everyone in the room had stopped what they were doing and had gone quiet listening to what had taken place.

"Where are we going to get twenty grand so quickly?" the Inspector asked having overheard what the man had said.

"We will have it I will phone the Chief Constable now to get authorisation. I will be back shortly" Charley replied as he turned and rushed out of the room and made his way up to his office.

The other detective Inspectors and Sergeants in the room along with the other officers gathered round Inspector Bryant wanting to know what the man had said.

Half an hour later Charley walked back into the incident room carrying a large black briefcase and called out to the Inspector.

"Are you ready Inspector Bryant, if so let's go"

Everyone turned and looked first at Charley then at the Inspector.

"I'm ready sir"

"Come on then, we haven't got all day. We will go in my car"

Inspector Bryant grabbed his jacket off the back of his chair and followed Charley out of the room, while everyone stood watching as the two of them left.

Once Charley and Inspector Bryant were on their way towards Takely in Charley's car the Inspector asked.

"So do I take it that the Chief Constable has agreed to this man's demands?"

"Yes so we had better get a result"

"Let's hope so, and you were able to get the money as well"

"Yes after the Chief Constable had spoken to the bank. Oh, you had better take these just in case there is any trouble." Charley opened the glove department and pulled out a loaded Smith and Western revolver along with a small box of bullets and passed them across to the Inspector.

The Inspector frowning took the pistol and box of bullets and put the pistol in one of the inside pockets of his jacket and the box of bullets in the side pocket of his jacket not saying anything.

"Do you know how to use that thing if needed?" Charley asked.

"Yes sir I have been trained to use firearms"

Ten minutes later Charley drove into the car park behind the Green Man pub and parked up facing the exit. The car park was empty apart from their car. Two minutes later a grey Renault car pulled in and parked up further along the car park.

"Hopefully that's the informants car" Inspector Bryant said.

"Right well go and see if it is him get him to come over; he can talk to us in my car"

"Will do"

Detective Inspector Bryant was just about to get out of the car when suddenly a pale blue Jaguar car swung into the car park at speed and came to a stop alongside the Renault.

Leaving the engine running two heavily built men each dressed in dark suits and carrying automatic pistols leaped out of the Jaguar. The one next to the Renault opened the driver's door and pulled the informant out from behind the wheel and threw him over the bonnet of the Renault and pointing his pistol at the informants head said.

"You're a dead man Parker no one squeals' on Wayne Smith and lives"

Terry Parker, who was in his mid-forties and of medium build with fair wavy hair and dressed in a pale grey suit and open necked white shirt, looked up in horror at the man pointing the pistol at his head and called out.

"Ah! Tony it's you wow! What you on about?"

"We have been watching you mate. Waiting to meet the coppers and blab to them?"

"What! Are you crazy I was going for a drink?"

"Liar shoot the bastard and let's get out of here quick".

The driver of the Jaguar said as he looked across at Charley's range rover parked up.

"I bet they're the coppers he's going to blag to that are parked over there. We'll take them out an all, we can't leave any witnesses"

"Ah, shit! Right now go" Charley said as he and the Inspector leaped out of the range rover their pistols drawn pointing at the two men.

"Police drop your weapons or we will shoot" Charley shouted.

"Fuck off copper" the driver shouted back and began firing his pistol at Charley and the Inspector.

Charley and the Inspector instantly ducked down. As the Inspector, ducked down he aimed his pistol and began firing back at the driver who suddenly let out a cry as he grabbed his chest and fell back against the Jaguar his pistol dropping from his hand as he slid down and fell flat on the ground face down.

The man pointing the pistol at Terry raised his pistol and fired back at Charley and the Inspector as he opened the passenger door of the Jaguar and pushed Terry in slamming the door. He continued firing more shots as he ran round and got in behind the wheel of the Jaguar then reversed at high speed before swinging out of the car park, crossing the road into a lane almost opposite the pub that led directly towards the forest.

Charley and Inspector Bryant hastily got back in the Range Rover and followed the Jaguar at high speed. The Inspector grabbed the radio phone off the dashboard and pressing a number a voice answered saying.

"We heard the shots anyone down"

"Yes one dead in the cark park. Get there now and take care of it we are in pursuit over"

"Will do over"

A police car siren could be heard as a patrol car that had been parked up hidden in one of the cottage gateways near the pub sped out towards the pub cark park.

At the same time as the Inspector was speaking on the radio phone Charley opened his window and placed his siren that he had plugged in on the roof, and it immediately began flashing its blue light and letting out a piercing siren.

The Inspector opened his window and pointed his pistol aiming at the Jaguars rear tyres and began firing.

The Jaguar suddenly braked sharply then swerved turning to the right and shot through the entrance gates into the forest just missing a startled gateman who leapt back out of the way. The Jaguar continued in a straight line along one of the tarmac tracks between the trees. Charley also braked sharply and followed the Jaguar through the gates and along the track in hot pursuit.

The Jaguar suddenly coming to the end of the tarmac track swiftly turned right into the open grass area and continued in a straight line alongside the trees before suddenly swerving left crossing the open area and driving into a narrow muddy track that was surrounded by thin trees and thick bushes.

Charley having caught up followed the Jaguar hot on its tail. The Inspector having fired all his shots and not managed to hit the tyres of the Jaguar withdrew his arm and opened up the small box of bullets some of which spilled onto the floor as he began to reload his pistol.

The Jaguar suddenly turned left into a narrower muddy track where the surrounding bushes scratched both sides of the car. Too late it was a dead end, Franky jammed on the brakes and the car skidded and screeched to a halt embedding itself in a clump of bushes. Terry Parker was thrown forward hitting his head on the windscreen knocking him almost unconscious.

Charley, who was close on the Jaguars tail, stopped suddenly across the entrance of the last track that the driver of the Jaguar had entered. Turning to Detective Inspector Bryant he said.

"Wait don't get out of the car, he's stuck in a dead end track, we have blocked his exit"

Franky grabbed Terry Parker by the back of his neck and pulled him back against the seat from the windscreen and pointed his pistol at Terry's neck saying.

"Right did you talk to those coppers?"

Terry shaking his head still in a daze turned and looked at the Franky and said.

"No of course not Franky what the fuck do you think you're doing, Wayne will be livid when he finds out what you've done"

"He's asked me and Tony to shut you up. What were you going to tell those coppers tell me before I blow you're fucking brains out"

"I wasn't going to tell them anything I told you I was going for a drink in the pub"

"You're lying Wayne told me that you had threatened to talk to the cops"

"Listen Franky, Wayne sold me a load of bad heroin and we had a row because he wouldn't change it and pay me compensation"

"What you mean bad heroin?"

"He must have mixed it with something bad because the guys who sell it for me told me that their clients were dying like flies".

"Wayne wouldn't sell you crap heroin, your lying".

"No I'm not he did"

"Oh yea, well to bad he's paying me five grand to shut you up so tough"

"You will never get it those coppers will kill you too like they did Tony. You're only chance is if you talk to them, as well. They have offered me good money to put Wayne away".

"Oh yea and how much they paying you then"

"One hundred grand, twenty grand up front and witness protection. Look Wayne's had it his picture is on the telly it won't be long before they find him"

"They've offered you a hundred grand and brought you twenty grand that's more than I'm due for killing you".

"Listen they'll have called for backup, so there's no way you can escape. See they're just sitting there at the end of the track waiting to see what you do"

"Fuck it! Right get out of the car I'll take my chances with you as hostage"

Franky let go of Terry, and they both got out of the car. Franky kept his pistol pointed at Terry as they both squeezed alongside the car pushing their way through the surrounding bushes. Once clear of the car Franky pushed Terry in front of him levelled his pistol on his back and said.

"Right no funny heroics or you get it first, now move"

Charley and Detective Bryant seeing the two men approach got out of the Range Rover and stood pointing their pistols at them.

"Stop right there and drop your pistol or we will shoot. There are armed officers manning all the exits so you can't get away" Charley called out.

"I want to do a deal; I know everything about Wayne Smith this git knows nothing he's scamming you. You give me the same deal that you offered him, and I will tell you everything you need to know about Wayne Smith" Franky replied.

"What do you know?" Detective Inspector Bryant called back.

"I told you I know everything you need to know. This git knows nothing"

"Ok, put your hands on your head and walk towards the car" Charley called out.

Franky pushed Terry aside and put his hands on his head still holding his pistol in one hand.

"Hey! Wait don't listen to him he's lying I've worked with Smith for years, so I know everything about him. This man has been sent by Wayne Smith to shut me up" Terry shouted.

Franky having got within ten feet of Charley, and the Inspector suddenly dropped his hands from his head and pointed the pistol straight at Charley and was about to pull the trigger. But Inspector Bryant seeing his actions fired at point blank range. Franky spun round dropping his pistol and fell face down spread-eagled out on the ground.

Inspector Bryant and Charley rushed forward. The Inspector picked up Frankie's pistol and put it in a plastic bag that he took from his pocket as he knelt down to examine the body. Charley grabbed Terry, who was shaking by his arm and pulled him towards the Range rover turned him round and spread eagled him against the side of the car frisking him for any hidden weapons. As he did so, he said.

"What's your name?"

Terry still shaking in shock replied.

"Terry Parker"

"Right so who was that smart arse?"

"His names Frank Richardson and the other one was Tony Billings they were two of Wayne Smith's henchmen who were sent to shut me up"

"So did you or do you work for Wayne Smith?"

"Yes I worked with Wayne Smith"

Charley took a pair of handcuffs from his pocket and clamped them on Terry Parkers wrists saying.

"Right well you had better start talking"

"I said I will talk but only if I get what I asked for"

Detective Inspector Bryant who having checked the man on the ground walked back, and as he opened the front door of the Range Rover and reached in and took the radio phone he said.

"He's dead sir".

"Right I see well call the patrol car and let them know where we are and get them to arrange for his body to be collected and to send a pickup truck for the

Jaguar. Tell them to get here quickly because we need to get back to the station and hear what Mr Parkers got to tell us"

"Will do" the Inspector replied as he switched on the radio phone.

"Right Mr Parker get in the car," Charley said opening the rear door and pushing Parker in onto the back seat.

"Are you going to pay me and give me protection as you said?" Parker asked.

"We will discuss that when you tell me what I need to know" Charley replied closing the rear door.

"The patrol car is on its way the other man has already been collected and the Landlord of the pub has been informed as to what the shooting was about. Someone at the pub phoned the local newspaper and a reporter is on his way to the pub to ask about the shooting". Inspector Bryant said.

"Well we don't want a reporter coming here" Charley responded as he lit a cigarette.

"We should be gone by the time the reporter has finished at the pub. Only the patrol car knows we are here. It's lucky that there was no one around here to see what happened apart from the man on the gate"

"I will speak to George Armstrong let me have the radio phone"

Inspector Bryant handed Charley the phone, and Charley phoned George, who immediately answered saying.

"Charley I just heard from Pat on the gate that you were chasing a Jaguar in through the gates is everything all right?"

"Yes George it is now. We stopped a couple of Wayne Smiths heavies. Listen one of our patrol cars is due any minute, as well as a tow truck, to collect the Jaguar and a van to collect the other one of Smiths henchmen. I will be leaving very shortly so I will speak later ok"

"Whatever you say Charley, do you need any of my men to assist?"

"No thanks George it's better that they don't come here. But I would be grateful if you could get your people to keep any members of the public away from this area until my people have cleaned up ok"

"I understand will do Charley, speak to you later bye"

The phone went dead, and the patrol car suddenly appeared its sirens and lights flashing as it raced across the open grass area towards them and pulled up alongside the Range Rover and stopped. Two uniformed officers got out and approached Charley and the Inspector. One of the officers a thick set middle aged tall Sergeant said.

"Is everything ok sir"

"Yes thank you Sergeant Alistair, the driver of the Jaguar a Franky Richardson tried to shoot us but failed. He's the one over there on the ground; he's dead. The man in the car I need to take back for questioning as he is a prime source of information about Wayne Smith"

"I see sir; well we have sorted the other one out; a tow truck and van are on their way here. We will wait here as you need to get back to the station"

"Thank you I will talk to you later as I will need your report and will have to write up mine as well"

"Very good sirs see you later"

The Inspector got in the Range Rover, and Charley switched off the siren and flashing blue light that he had put on the car roof earlier and having put them back in the car he got in and backed the car and swiftly turned it round and headed back across the grass area and along the tarmac track and out of the forest entrance waving at Pat the gateman as he went through the gates.

Once back at Stortford police station having parked up in the station car park he and Inspector Bryant escorted Terry Parker up to Charley's office and sat Parker down in front of Charley's desk. Inspector Roberts was also in the office talking on his phone when they arrived and seeing them walk in he finished his call and set the phone down saying.

"Are you two all right I heard about what happened?"

"Yes we are all ok, this is Terry Parker one of Wayne Smiths gang he is going to tell us all he knows about Wayne Smith aren't you Mr Parker"

Charley replied with a stern look on his face as he sat down behind his desk, and Inspector Bryant with a half-smile nodded a greeting at Inspector Roberts as he sat down next to Parker.

"Yes I said I would" Parker replied.

Charley took a recorder from one of his desk drawers along with a twin set of small microphones and a new cassette which he loaded into the machine and then plugged in the microphones so that one faced him, and the other faced Parker. Having switched on the recorder he said looking directly at Parker.

"Right so for the records I need your full name age and present address"

Inspector Bryant also took out from his pocket a notepad ready to take notes.

"My name is Terry Parker I'm forty five years of age and I live at number 45, High banks, Bishops Stortford in Hertfordshire".

"You have come here today to give us information about Wayne Smith aged forty seven whom we are seeking in connection with the abduction of a number of youngsters. You are also freely going to tell us about your association with Wayne Smith is that correct?"

"That is correct"

"So how long have you worked with Wayne Smith?"

"I have worked with Wayne for sixteen years and know all his rackets" Parker replied.

"Where is Wayne Smith what's his address?" Charley asked looking Parker in the eyes.

"He lives in a large house just outside of Epping called 'The Weeping Willows' which is just past the cemetery on the B182 which is off the B1393. The house is at the end of a private tree lined track surrounded by ten foot stone walls with only one entrance gate".

"What are his mobile phone number and house phone numbers?"

Parker reeled off the numbers then Charley asked.

"Is the house registered in the name of Wayne Smith?"

"No, he has registered the house using the name Harold Boyd company chairman. He has a number of businesses registered under the name Harold Boyd company Ltd. He also has overseas businesses"

"I see well tell me about the ones he has in England first. What sorts of businesses?"

"Night clubs, nail bars, massage parlours, adult shops, property letting and a loan business"

"What are the names of each of these places and where are they located?"

Parker provided the list of names of the different night clubs, nail bars, massage parlours, adult shops, and property letting offices, along with all their addresses which were located in both Essex and Hertfordshire. In Chelmsford, Harlow, Colchester,

Brentwood, Southend on sea, Stevenage, and St Albans.

"These are a front for what?"

"Prostitution, drugs and supply of underage sex videos as well as sex trafficking"

"Go on what else?"

"He has another house that he owns in the West End of London which he uses as a brothel that caters for very rich clients with weird sexual tastes"

"What you mean kinky sex?"

"Yea that as well as underage sex with both males and females"

"What age ranges?"

"Youngsters from the age of six to twenty"

"Give me the address of this house"

Parker gave the address

"You say this brothel is used by rich clients, who are the clients?"

"I only know that they are wealthy overseas clients as well as prominent British figures such as business men, politicians, Judges, senior priests from different churches, and even senior police officers"

Charley raising his eyebrows at hearing the list of clients and asked.

"Do you know the names of these clients?"

"No way, Wayne keeps lists of all the clients at his house outside Epping"

"Right ok, so tell me about his house in Epping who lives there apart from him?"

"His long term partner Celine Montrose"

"Is there anyone else living there?"

"Yes he has some youngsters living there"

"His children you mean"

"No he doesn't have any kids of his own"

"So who are these youngsters?"

"Youngsters he has either snatched or bought"

"How many youngsters are there in his house, in Epping?"

"There are sixteen in all"

"What sixteen! It must be a big house" Charley said with a look of surprise.

"Yes it's a large house but he keeps them in pairs locked up in bedrooms"

"Christ! Go on. Do you know the names of these youngsters and their ages?"

Parker gave out all the names nationalities and ages including the names of Joy Manders, Rose and Sam.

All three police officers sighed out loud at hearing the information about each of the youngsters then Charley looking angry said.

"Is he using his house in Epping as a brothel as well?"

"No the youngsters are picked up by van every day by one of his partners Vince Carter at about nine and taken to the house in London, and then they are brought back in the early hours of the following morning"

"What's the address of Vince Carter and his phone numbers?"

Parker gave the address and phone numbers then Charley said.

"So all these youngsters have been forced into prostitution by Wayne Smith?"

"Yes and they also have to appear in porn videos"

"Porn videos even the seven year olds"

"Yes all of them"

"Does he make these videos at his house in Epping?"

"Yes he has a studio there for the making of porn videos"

"Does he make the videos himself?"

"Some he does but most are made by one of his other partners Mike Elbourn who lives in London and comes over to make the videos"

"This Mike Elbourn what's his address and phone numbers?"

Parker gave the address as well as the mobile and landline phone numbers.

"Is this Mike involved in the sale of the videos and if so where does he sell them?"

"Yes he is and he sells them through the different adult shops that Wayne smith owns in Essex and Hertfordshire. As well to clients who use the Brothel in London"

"So tell me about the night clubs, nail bars, massage parlours and adult shops"

"The night clubs, nail bars and massage parlours all employ prostitutes who are in their teens and even older. They all live in the towns where those places are"

"You say some are in their teens, from what ages?"

"Varies those who work in the night clubs are from fifteen to nineteen. Those in the nail bars and massage parlours are from thirteen to nineteen. They work in the back and are available to certain clients"

"What clients?"

"Those who Wayne has referred, they have to mention that they have been referred by Wayne"

"How does Wayne find the clients?"

"All sorts of places from clients who use the night clubs, brothel in London and some who visit the adult shops"

"So do any of the youngsters from his house in Epping work in any of the nail bars, massage parlours and night clubs?"

"No only in the brothel in London"

"So those prostitutes working in the night clubs nail bars and massage parlours where are they recruited?"

"They have been forced to work as prostitutes and drug pedlars. He gets them through his loan and property letting business as well as from overseas"

Charley sighed and frowning said.

"How can he get them through his loan business and property letting business?"

"The majority of the people who have borrowed money from him through his loan business are those people who can't get loans from anywhere else because they are already in debt with banks, mortgage companies and credit companies. He loans them money and when they get to the point where they can no longer pay him and if they have children who are aged from six up to nineteen he tells the parents that he wants the kids to work for him in return for what they owe him. If they refuse or threaten to report him to the authorities, he sends some of his heavies round to smash all the furniture and fixtures up including the cars if they have one.Then if that doesn't work he beats them up as well and throws them out on the street. They become homeless and dare not say anything for fear of what he might do next"

"But there are organizations now that help people who are struggling with debt why do they go to him for money?"

"Because even with help from those organisations people still struggle and if they have kids they have more pressure on them to feed and clothe the kids as well as the kids wanting things"

"But the older teens can get work to bring in extra money"

"Yes some can but it's not enough, because he sets very high interest rates on his loans"

"Whew! So you say he also gets them through his property letting business how does he do that then?"

"Similar he rents to older teens that might have left home for many reasons; some might be students wanting a place to live. Even if they are not working he still lets them rent from him and offers them loans at cheap interest rates. However after a while he informs them that the interest rate has had to be increased as have the amount for each monthly repayment of the loan and rent. If they can't pay then they have a choice either become homeless or work for him to pay off what they earn. They either sell drugs or become prostitutes or do both. If they are still in work then when they finish theirs days' work they have to begin working for him in either the clubs, the London brothel or on the streets. Same with the students, some are even made to appear in his porn videos"

"So do you know the names of his people who run these businesses of his?"

"No not all of them but I can tell you some of them and the names and addresses of his partners"

"Go on give me the names and addresses of those who you know"

Parker reeled off a list of names as well as some of the addresses.

"So is that's all the names that you know?"

"Yes you will have to ask him he will know all of them"

"You said he has other business addresses outside of the UK?."

"Not addresses no he has contacts outside of the UK"

"Who are they and what businesses are they into?"

"People that he does deals with for drugs and sex trafficking"

"Give me their names and tell me where they are"

Parker reeled off names and lists of places which the Inspector also wrote down.

"You have given us names of people in the north and south of America as well as in Thailand, Philippines, parts of Africa and Saudi Arabia. Tell me about their dealings with Smith what exactly do they do?"

"They deal in drugs, sex trafficking, porn videos"

"Ok, so what do you know about Wayne Smiths sex trafficking set up?"

"A lot of it's done through the internet"

"How I want all the details?"

"He has set up a web page called 'Bees Domestics and Care workers Company.com' that he uses for recruiting young overseas care workers and domestics from the Philippines and Thailand. He has a recruitment agent in Manila in the Philippines as well as one in Bangkok".

"I see go on"

"What happens is the young people apply online, they have to be aged between seventeen and twenty-five. They fill out the form on the computer giving details of where they live and their education, as well as any work they have done or are doing. They also have to state whether they have ever been abroad. They have to upload a full length photo of themselves as well as a passport photo. The agent if he thinks they are what is needed will then reply back and ask them to come for an interview in Manila or Bangkok. The agent instructs them to bring four more passport photos along with a copy of their birth certificate and certificates of qualifications if they have any. The interviews are always held in hotels in the agent's rooms"

"Then what happens"

"Once they go for an interview the agent informs them that for them to work abroad they will need visas and a passport. If they don't have a passport, the agent informs them that he can get them one and also arrange for them to have a work visa to work abroad which all costs money. If the potential worker doesn't have sufficient money to pay for their passport and costs involved in processing the required paperwork, and most of them haven't. The agent tells them that they can still be considered, but they will have to repay the costs from their wages once they start work abroad. The agent gets them to sign an agreement stating that they agree to that arrangement and that the workers' wages will be paid by the employer direct to 'Bees Domestic and Care workers Company', who will then pay them. They also have to sign to say that they agree to work only for the company no less than five years. They also have to agree to work either in the UK or Saudi Arabia . If they agree to do so and sign all the documents, the agent informs them that they will be contacted as and when the agent has got all the paper work processed. They then return home and wait to be called"

"It sounds like a legitimate business"

"Yes but it's a scam"

"Why and in what way?"

"Because most of those recruited are sold off to buyers once they arrive in either the Uk or Saudi Arabia. The buyers are people who are looking to use people both males and females to become sex slaves who will either work directly for the buyer or be used by the buyer to work in a brothel. The buyer takes them either to their homes or directly to one of their brothels where they are imprisoned and never allowed out. If they don't do what is required of them then they are beaten and starved as well as being forced to take drugs in order to keep them quiet and docile. The buyers will be required to pay a minimum of at least three thousand pounds for one of the workers. The workers if they are sent to a brothel will be required to service at least twenty to thirty clients a day at around thirty to forty pounds a time. So the buyers quickly recoup their money back. The buyers resell the workers to other buyers after a time, so that they can then buy more workers".

"So all these recruits end up being sold. But how do the agents manage to process all the paperwork?"

"The agents have contacts within the different immigration departments who are rewarded financially to process the papers for the potential workers. Once the papers are processed the agent contacts Wayne to let him know that he has signed up a number of male and female workers who are eligible to work in either the UK or Saudi Arabia. Wayne has his customers in those countries that are looking for sex slaves"

"So does that apply just for Domestic workers? What about the care workers?"

"On the company web page it also says it's looking for care workers who will work with either elderly couples or elderly individuals in their homes. They are sold off in the same way as the domestic workers when they arrive in the country they are sent to"

"But when the workers arrive in either Saudi or the UK they have to be able to give the name and address of their employer that they are going to work for"

"That's right they do, and the names and addresses that they give are legitimate names and addresses. The immigration department doesn't check to see if the employer has agreed to employ that person because it's not the potential employer who goes to meet the worker at the airport it's an agent of the company who goes to meet the worker who informs the Immigration department that they have come to take the worker to the employer as that worker is contracted with the company. Immigration don't know that some of the named employers have been given a nice amount of money to say that they are the ones employing that worker. Besides there are those people who work in the immigration depart who are also given money to turn a blind eye and process the paperwork allowing the worker to enter the country that they have been sent to".

"So it's always one of the representatives of Wayne's company who meets the worker at the airport?"

"Yes who shows proof to say that he is a representative for 'Bees Domestics and Care workers Company Ltd' and is the one who will take the worker to the named employer"

"So once the worker has passed through immigration, then what happens?"

"The worker is either sold to the buyer who poses as the new employer at the airport or is taken to Wayne's house in Epping where the buyers come to pay for the worker and take them away. Sometimes Wayne keeps the workers for himself to work as a prostitute in the back of one of his clubs, massage parlours or nail bars. Once the worker is taken to where ever, they are enlightened to the fact that they are to be used as sex slaves. The duped workers are then given injections to stop them making a fuss"

"But what about the workers families back home surely they expect to hear from them?"

"True but they don't know where they have gone to because the workers are only told where they were going when they reach the airports and are met by the agent who has with him their passport and paperwork. The new workers aren't given the opportunity to phone home if they have arrived at the airport without their families. If they do come with family to the airport the families are told which country that their son or daughter is going to work in but not where or with whom they are going to work within the country that they are going to"

"But if the families don't hear from their sons or daughters they must know about the web site and where their youngsters went to meet the agents"

"Yes they would know the web site but they can't locate the agents because the agents never meet the potential workers in the same place, and the agents are always changing their mobile phones so there's no way they can phone them. There aren't any phone numbers on the web page either or a company address. Don't forget they only recruit people that come from poor families who live in remote villages whom to get on the internet have to go into the nearest town to an internet café because most of the time there's no internet connection in the villages. Even if they do get to speak to an agent to enquire about their missing son or daughter they are informed that the son or daughter no longer works for the company and that the company doesn't know where they have gone onto"

"Good God! So how long has Wayne Smith been doing this?"

"For about six years. He's made a huge amount of money from just that racket alone. He also has another racket where he gets people in from all over Europe into England"

"What's that then?"

"He pays male's to go on the internet posing as people looking for girlfriends or boyfriends from the different countries of Europe with a view to getting married. Once they find someone online they form a relationship online and after a time agree to go over to the country where they live to meet them posing as tourists. The boyfriend from England either goes across to Europe by car or flies out to the country where the boyfriend or girlfriend lives. Once there they meet up with a girlfriend or boyfriend and court them and offer them the opportunity to come back to the UK with them on a tourist visa. If they agree he then pays for any tickets and expenses needed and they come over. Once they arrive they are either taken to Wayne's house or to an apartment that Wayne has rented. They are then given injections and told that they are to be sold as sex slaves".

"Strewth! But surely the relatives of the victims must contact the authorities to report that their sons or daughters have not returned?"

"Yes they do but the boyfriends who go out from England always use false names, passports and addresses. So it becomes more difficult to trace them. Lots of people arrive every year in the Uk and then disappear"

"Whew! All right so now I need to know what part you played in his organisation, what exactly did you do?"

"I was one of his original partners I dealt with drug distribution. He would make contact with overseas drug suppliers and once the deal was set up, and the goods arrived I was responsible for selling quantities of the drugs to other dealers. I also sent supplies to the night clubs where the managers were responsible for selling them in the clubs. I did that for three years then decided I wanted to run my own business. Wayne understood and said he still wanted me as a partner in the business. I agreed to remain a partner but only on the understanding that when the shipments of drugs arrived I would buy them from Wayne and distribute them. He made money, and I made money. It worked well until he started getting greedy or stupid because the drugs that he started selling me had been messed with. Either he or his suppliers had mixed other ingredients with the drugs which made them not as effective. I was getting complaints from my buyers because their clients were complaining about the quality of the drugs sold to them. I told Wayne about this, and he laughed saying he would see to it. But he only put fewer additives in the drugs I told him if the drugs were no good my buyers would look elsewhere and business would not be as good"

"So what happened?"

"He wouldn't listen and things got worse I was getting more complaints from the dealers that I was selling too, and they didn't take kindly to the fact that they were losing customers so began to stop buying from me. I was being left with drugs that people no longer wanted. Then Wayne said he would ensure that, in the future, he would only sell me pure drugs. For several months, he did, and I was able to gain back a lot of my original buyers. Then it changed again because he started selling me crap again, only this time I was getting complaints because my buyers were telling me that their pushers were informing them that a lot of their customers were either becoming seriously sick or dying. I was being threatened by my buyers who told me that if I sold them anymore crap my life would be at risk. Wayne continued to deny having mixed other ingredients with the drugs he sold me. I demanded he pay me compensation because my buyers wanted their money back or else they would have me killed"

"So because he wouldn't give you compensation or change the drugs, and your life was at risk you decided to come and talk to us"

"That's right because if I didn't I would soon be a dead man. You saw how serious Wayne is from what happened earlier"

"Quite now tell me where did you first meet Wayne Smith and the other partners, and get the sort of money needed to start"

"I first met Wayne and the other partners in prison we got to know each other and talked about what we each wanted to do when we got out. Wayne suggested we all team up and set up different rackets. When we were all released we, needed to get some money as we had very little money at that time. So we had to borrow money from a bank and building society"

"What you talking about a bank and building society weren't going to lend you money without having proper employment"

"They will if you ask them nicely as you point guns at the heads of the managers"

"That's not borrowing that's stealing"

"Not if you pay it back with interest. This is what we did when we had made more than we had taken"

"How could you possibly do that without exposing yourselves?"

"We got someone to deliver the money in briefcases to the managers of the bank and building society that we had originally taken money from with a letter addressed to the managers saying thank you very much here's the money we took from you plus interest. The managers weren't going to say anything were they because the bank and building society had already claimed on their insurance so for them it was an extra bonus? What the managers did with the money we don't know, but there was never any publicity to say the bank and building society had received their money back. Makes you think doesn't it"

"So what's the name of the bank and building society?"

"I won't tell you that because if I'm ever short of money I know who to go and see if you know what I mean"

"So you Wayne Smith, Mike Elbourn and Vince Carter were all partners in the business. So you must have been involved in the sex trafficking side of the business as well as all the other sides?"

"Well yes originally but as I said I was responsible for drug dealing"

"Were you ever involved in the snatching of any of the youngsters?"

"No Wayne always does that"

"Did you ever have sex with any of the youngsters?"

"No way I'm not into that"

"So you made money from selling drugs and you were also involved in the armed robbery of a bank and building society as well as being a onetime partner and accomplice in Wayne Smiths organisation"

"Yes but I told you I have had enough and need to get away. I have people after me threatening to kill me because of the last shipment of drugs that Wayne sold me. Seeing as he won't help me, I have no option but to come and spill the beans to you. The hundred grand, witness protection and new identity will help me get out of the country and go and live a quiet life somewhere"

"Quiet so but first I need to find out if everything that you have told me is correct. I am grateful to you for the information you have given me. That's all the questions that I need answering from you at this moment in time I will be asking you more questions later"

Charley switched off the recorder.

"Fine so what happens now?" Parker asked looking tired.

"I have no choice but to keep you in custody here until I have organised a safe place to keep you. Inspector Roberts would you take Mr Parker down stairs and ask Sergeant Baxter to lock him up and to ensure he is given food and drink"

"Certainly sir, come with me Mr Parker"

Parker stood up and still handcuffed went with the Inspector out of the office.

Once he had gone Charley looked at Inspector Bryant, and they both burst out laughing then Charley said.

"Well what a turn up, I think we might have just struck gold. Let's see if he is telling us the truth. I need to confirm that all the addresses he has given us do exist. Would you phone down to the incident room and ask one of the Sergeants to get the addresses checked and let us know, we need that information as fast as possible"

"Right away alright if I sit at Inspector Roberts desk Sir"

"Yes help yourself are you hungry I know that I am"

"Yes and thirsty gosh look at the time its five thirty already"

"He'll so it is right I will phone down and get us some sandwiches and tea"

Charley picked up his phone and pressed out a couple of numbers and waited two minutes before there was a reply.

"Hello Chief Superintendent Humphreys what can I do for you?" a female voice asked.

"Joan is that you, could you send up an assortment of sandwiches enough for three people and tea for us all?"

"Certainly sir it won't be long, bye"

The line went dead, and Charley dialled another number and waited. A woman's voice answered almost immediately saying.

"Chief Constables office this is his secretary speaking who is calling?"

"High Elizabeth it's Charley Humphreys again I need to speak to the Chief Constable urgently"

"Oh hello sir just a moment and I will put you through"

"Hello Charley how did you get on with the informant you mentioned earlier"

"Well sir I have to tell you that I and Inspector Bryant went to meet the man Terry Parker at the arranged meeting place and no sooner had we arrived he turned up but was closely followed by two henchmen in a Jaguar who jumped out of their car and were about to shoot him. Inspector Bryant shot one of the henchmen, but the other one managed to make off with Parker. We pursued them and ended up in the forest at Takely where there was a further shooting, which resulted in the other henchman being shot also. We managed to get Parker back to the police station, and I have just finished interviewing him. He has given us very valuable information enough to put Wayne Smith and all his people away for a very long time indeed"

"Good gracious Charley were either of you or anyone else hurt in the shooting?"

"No sir fortunately, the two henchmen are dead though and the local press have got the story so don't be surprised if you get a call from the national media"

"Ump right so were there any witnesses at the scenes of the shooting?"

"Only at the meeting place but one of my officers sorted it out and everything has been cleared up at both sites. We know from Parker who the henchmen were and that they had been sent by Smith to stop him talking to us"

"I see so have you found out where Smith lives?"

"Yes sir and all the names and locations of all his businesses and criminal activities, which are in Essex and Hertfordshire"

."Excellent so you want arrest and search warrants drawn up and fast for the Essex police to carry out the raids in Essex"

"Yes sir that's one of the reasons why I'm phoning you. We need the cooperation of Essex police and central London police forces to help carry out the raids and searches. I will email you all the addresses that I need warrants for searching. The men sent in to carry out the different raids will need to be armed. I will raid his house but will need a swat team because if he is there when we arrive there could well be a shootout or stand-off with hostages"

"Really so he has places in Essex and central London, so where does he live then?"

"Would you believe just outside Epping it's a large house where he is keeping the youngsters that he has snatched as well as others that he has got through sex trafficking. We will need a trauma team as well when we raid the house and one for when they raid the address in the West end of London which is used as a brothel where some of the youngsters that are kept prisoner in his home are forced to work each day"

"I see and do you know if Rose and Sam Cooper are being held at his house?"

"Yes sir they are"

"Right email me all the addresses of the places you need raided along with this man Parkers statement, and I will talk to the Chief Constable of Essex police. I will arrange for the flying squad to carry out the raid on the address in the West end and ensure they have a trauma team with them. I will send you our swat squad and trauma team from here. Right what's the time ah six fifteen you're not going to be able to be here to meet the Coopers? Never mind they will understand when I tell them what's happening. You'll want all the raids to be carried out tonight won't you?"

"Yes sir because the sooner we get those youngsters free, the better. I'm also concerned that when Smith hears on the news that his henchmen failed to shut the informant up he might try and make a run for it or make a stand at his house"

"I agree, leave it with me I will get things organised from this end and phone you back shortly ok. Oh and well done"

"Thank me when those youngsters are safe and we have Smith banged up sir"

"Alright Charley bye"

The line went dead, and Charley looked across at Inspector Bryant, who had just put down his phone and said.

"Any news on those addresses I asked you to get confirmed?"

"Yes sir all positive. Did I hear the Chief Constable say he will send us the swat team and a trauma team?"

"Yes now I need to email him all the addresses that have to be raided along with Parkers statement, can you give me the list"

"I have already prepared the email for you with all the addresses I just need you to check it against my list to ensure I haven't missed out any before I send it to the Chief Constable"

"You're a star come on let me see. Where are those bloody sandwiches and tea I'm starving aren't you?"

Charley went over and checked the list of addresses on the Inspectors list and the ones he had put in the email.

"Spot on send"

The Inspector sent the emails then picked up his phone again and was about to phone the canteen when there was a knock on the door.

"Come in" Called out Charley.

The door opened, and a young lady carrying a tray with the sandwiches and mugs of tea walked in saying.

"Sorry for the delay sir"

"No matter thank you very much just put them on my desk would you"

The young lady put the tray down on his desk and quickly exited the room.

Charley picked up his phone and pressed a couple of numbers and after two rings it was answered by a male voice.

"Yes sir how can I help you"

"Ask Inspector Roberts to come up to my office right away would you, oh and also Inspectors Munro and Franks"

"Right away sir bye"

The line went dead.

"Right let's eat these sandwiches because I don't suppose we will get a chance to eat again until goodness knows when. We have a busy time ahead of us" Charley said.

He and the Inspector started eating the sandwiches and drinking the tea when there was a knock on his door.

"Come in" Charley called out.

The three Inspectors walked in and looked around.

"Good take a seat gentlemen I need to let you know if you haven't already heard from Inspector Roberts what we have discovered and what is planned for tonight. Hopefully by tomorrow morning we will have Wayne Smith in custody along with all the rest of his gang and have rescued all those youngsters that he has snatched"

"Wow, that's great news" Inspector Munro said smiling.

"Yes great so tell us what you have found out" Inspector Franks said also smiling.

"Right well this is what we have found out and what we plan to do, so listen very carefully".

Chapter 8.

Back at Wayne Smiths house in Epping there was a hive of activity. Celine was busy packing some cases with clothes for the pair of them along with wash kits and towels. Wayne having taken all the money out of the safe as well as the different credit cards and passports he had for him and Celine in different names put everything into a number of briefcases which he put by the desk in the study.

He then went down into the back cellar into a room which was lined with floor to ceiling wine racks on three of the walls and walked to the end of the room where to the left hand side of the wine rack he pressed a button on the wall and there came the sound of a loud click and the central section of the wine rack moved outwards on runners that were on the underside of the rack. After it had moved out four feet, it came to a stop leaving enough space for Wayne to walk into the gap where behind the rack on the wall there was a heavy steel door with a steel handle and a small panel the size of a mobile phone in the centre of the door at eye level. The panel contained buttons with numbers on it.

Wayne pressed out six numbers, and there came another loud click. He pulled the handle and the door opened to reveal an entrance into a small room that measured eight feet in length by eight feet in width. On all the walls around the room, there were steel shelves on which there were different sized metal cases and different sized wooden boxes. He went over to the left hand wall and opened one of the metal cases inside of which there was an Uzi submachine gun nestled in thick black foam. He withdrew the submachine gun, checked it before returning it to its case and putting it on the floor. He then took down a box containing ammunition and put it next to the case.

Then took down some more cases of weapons and boxes of ammunition from the shelves. Once he had finished selecting what he wanted he carried some of the cases upstairs to the study then went back and closed the steel door and the centre panel of the wine rack before carrying the remaining cases and boxes up into the study. Satisfied that he had got what he needed as well as sufficient assorted weapons should he need them he was about to go out when Celine came in saying.

"I've packed us a couple of cases each. Did you sort out everything?"

"Yea l will bring the van around. I will need you to help me load all these briefcases and cases in"

"Right ok well the cases are in the hall ready to be loaded"

They left the study and Wayne went out of the front door and walked round to the garage at the back of the house and opened up the doors and went inside where the white van he had used on Tuesday to snatch Rose and Sam stood alongside his Mercedes and Celine's Porsche. He got in the van and drove it out and round to the front of the house and parked up just as Celine opened the front door and came out carrying two large suitcases. He got out of the van and opened the rear doors. Celine passed him the cases, and he put them inside. Celine then fetched another two large cases from the hall, and he put them in the back. They both went back into the house to the study, and each took two of the four briefcases Wayne had packed and carried them out and put them in the back of the van. They then went back and began taking out the metal cases containing the different weapons Wayne had selected and loaded them into the van. Finally, they carried all the different boxes that contained magazines of ammunition for all the different weapons and loaded them in the van.

Once they were all loaded and packed away Wayne closed up the van, and they went back into the house to the kitchen where Celine poured out a couple of glasses of wine, and they sat down.

"It's a bloody shame we've got to leave here I have always liked this house," Celine said.

"Yea well that's life, we will find another house abroad. Might even get a bigger house"

"What about all the businesses we will lose all of them and the money they were making us"

"Listen we are ok we have enough money to live comfortably on we don't need them. No, it's time to relax and enjoy life. As I said we will go to Switzerland and stay there until the heat dies down which will give us time to decide and plan where we want to go"

"What about Vince and Mike you can't leave them to be caught?"

"No, I won't leave them behind they will come with us to Switzerland, and like us they can choose where and what they want to do. There's enough money in my Swiss account to give them a decent amount of money, plus they have money of their own. I should phone round all our different banks and make arrangements to draw out some large amounts of cash"

"But even if you do when are you going to collect it"

"Today of course we will take what we can with us"

"But your pictures on the television they will recognise you"

"No they won't because the photos old and besides all the accounts are in the name of Harold Boyd so they won't connect me with my real name"

"But just supposing someone does recognise you they are bound to call the cops"

"Will you stop winging come on you can come with me I will phone the banks then get shaved and showered and put on my best suit and we will go and collect the money"

"You want me to come too well I had better get dressed up, as well. Which car are we taking?"

"We will take the van of course because it's already loaded up"

"What you going to do with the brats?"

"You locked them up right"

"Yea but I thought you wanted to take Rose and Sam with us if we have to make a run for it"

"Go and get them dressed give them a shot to knock them out and we will put them in the back of the van"

"Bloody hell Wayne you don't half take risks. Come on then go and get ready while I see to the two kids"

"I've got to phone the banks first. I will be up in a minute or two"

They got up and left the kitchen and Wayne went into the study and began phoning round all the different banks where he held accounts in London to arrange to withdraw large amounts of cash. After three quarters of an hour, he had made all the calls and the banks had agreed to have the money ready for him to collect.

He went upstairs shaved and showered then went into the bedroom and opened his wardrobe took out a clean pair of underpants and socks from a drawer then picked out a light grey mohair suit along with a pale blue double cuff shirt and dark blue silk tie. He then proceeded to get dressed. Celine had already showered and had changed into an extremely expensive red and black silk summer dress. She wore a pair of expensive black leather high heeled handmade Italian shoes and had picked out a small black leather handbag that she had bought when they were in Paris the year before and was putting on her makeup and an extremely expensive perfume.

"Did you have any trouble with the banks?" Celine asked.

"No, of course not they know I'm one of their valued customers. Did you sort Rose and Sam out?"

"Yea they out cold on their beds and the other brats are all locked up in their rooms. Do you think this dress is all right?"

"Yes very sexy that should keep people from looking at me they will all be looking at you instead of me"

"Yea but fancy going in the van we could have taken the Mercedes. What will people think seeing us in expensive clothes getting out of that grubby van?"

"They can think what they like. We will park in a side street of course not in front of the bank"

"Yea ok, well I need you to help me bring Rose and Sam down stairs when you are ready"

Wayne having got dressed and put on an expensive pair of black highly polished leather shoes splashed on some aftershave, then a pair of Tom Ford sunglasses. Looked at himself in the mirror and said.

"Who's a handsome looking guy then?"

"Ha! Come on you'll do" Celine laughed.

They left the bedroom and Wayne went and got Rose and carried her downstairs and put her in the back of the van while Celine carried Sam down and passed him to Wayne, who put him in the back of the Van. Once he had locked the doors they both got in, and Wayne drove out of the gates and headed up the long private tree lined drive out onto the road where they continued then got onto the M25 heading for London.

It wasn't long before they arrived in the centre of London, and Wayne managed to park in a side street close to one of the banks he had phoned earlier. They got out and casually walked to the bank and went inside and up to the enquiries desk, where a middle-aged man of medium build, who was dressed in a dark grey suit stood behind the counter and seeing them said.

"Good day sir madam how may I help you?"

"Good day to you my name is Harold Boyd here is my bank card, business card and passport I have come to collect a consignment of money that I arranged with your manager to collect"

The man looked at the bank card and business card as well as the passport and having satisfied himself that the man in front of him matched the photo in the passport he said.

"Very good Mr Boyd just one moment while I go and check with the manager"

The man quickly turned and walked off towards one of the doors behind the counters and knocked on the door and went in. Two minutes later he returned with the manager who was carrying two large black briefcases. The manager looked at Wayne and smiling said.

"Here we are Mr Boyd we have put your money in these two briefcases which you may have with our compliments. Now I just need you to check the contents and sign the withdrawal form"

Celine, who stood next to Wayne, looked at the manager and gave him one of her sultry smiles and the manager started to blush. Wayne checked the briefcases and the withdrawal slip and then took his gold Mont Blanc pen from his inside suit pocket signed and dated it and passed it back to the manager who was still looking at Celine and said.

"Thank you that all seems to be in perfect order. Good day to you I will see you again soon bye"

"Oh yes goodbye Mr Boyd"

Celine and Wayne picked up the briefcases and casually walked out of the bank and made their way back to the van. Wayne then hid the two briefcases behind the driver's seat before they both got inside the van, and Wayne drove off in the direction of the next bank.

Within an hour and a half they had been to three different banks where they had picked up a further six briefcases and put them in the van. No one had paid much attention to Wayne as they were all too busy looking at Celine in her mini silk dress that showed off her perfectly formed long legs.

"That's it time to get back I told you we wouldn't have any problems, you were a great distraction and it worked a treat"

"Whew well I'm just glad it went all right I was scared I can tell you. So how much have we got in all those cases you've just collected?"

"Oh just over a million in all which should keep us going for a while"

"What! Fucking hell just over a million how much you got in those accounts"

"Oh there's over a million in each of the banks"

"Whew! I didn't know you had all that much money; I knew you had plenty but hell. So how much you got in the Swiss account then?"

"Twenty million may be more now with the interest"

"They say crime doesn't pay, well you've done all right. Am I glad I found you, well no that's not true; you found me when you bought me from that guy in Rio?"

"Yea I certainly got my money's worth; you have never let me down. Now think about it look at all the money I've earned from drug deals alone then there's the brothel which only caters for very rich clients. The clubs with the escorts who are prostitutes that I have forced to work for me, massage parlours, and nail bars and of course the porn videos which sell by the thousands all over the world. Not forgetting the sex trafficking business where I have sold loads of youngsters and adults"

"There's your property letting and Loan Company as well"

"Yea this is how I recruit some of the escorts and kids who appear in the porn films"

"So how much is Vince and Mike worth then, they are your partners?"

"They get twenty five percent each of the profits and I take the other fifty percent. Well I'm the brains behind it all"

"Looking at them you wouldn't think they had got a lot of money"

"That's what they want people to belief"

"But you still have all those working for you that need to be paid, then there are the overheads of all the premises, back handers to the cops to keep them from looking to close at what's going on it can't be cheap"

"No, but we make enough to buy their loyalty, not like Parker he wanted to go out on his own as a big time drug dealer. The dirty rat but he will be out of the way very soon so we won't have to worry about him"

"So with all that money you have where are we going live then?"

"Good question I haven't decided yet. We will have to get knew identities once the heat dies down which shouldn't be a problem"

"Well we have to get out of the country first"

"I told you Cyril will get us across to Holland then we go to Switzerland. Ah we are back time to get a nice come of tea Franky should be calling me soon to tell me he has dealt with Parker"

They drove in through the gates and parked in front of the house where everything seemed normal and got out of the van and went inside the house to the kitchen. Celine put the kettle on, and Wayne sat down and switched the television on. The clock on the kitchen wall showed it had just gone seven in the evening. There was a documentary showing on the television all about troubles in the Middle East; suddenly the programme switched to the news room where a news reader was sat behind a desk and behind him was Wayne's photo on the wall. The news reader said.

"We are sorry to interrupt your programme but we have just heard that a man has been detained by the Hertfordshire police in connexion with the missing youngsters Rose and Sam Cooper. The police have stated that the man they have detained is not Wayne Smith but the man has given them valuable information concerning Smith. The man whom police have not named was detained after a double shooting which resulted in two men being shot dead in the village of Takely in Essex where the two youngsters went missing on Tuesday. We will bring you more news as and when we receive it. Now back to your programme"

The documentary returned, and Wayne jumped up saying.

"Come on let's get the hell out of here. The coppers must have got Parker and shot Franky and Tony shit what a mess"

"What about those brats Rose and Sam do you still want to take them with us or leave them here?"

"Yes we are taking them with us as insurance" Wayne replied as he took out his mobile and presses out some numbers, and instantly a voice answered saying.

"Hi Wayne I've just heard the news, looks bad mate that bastard is bound to tell the coppers everything. What you got in mind?"

"Listen Vince it's everyman for himself Celine and I are going to the houseboat in Suffolk. So Contact Mike, Jack, and Phil and tell them to come to the houseboat as well as yourself, but don't tell any of the others where you are going. I'll arrange for Cyril to take us all across the channel on his yacht. I've got enough money with me plus all the false credit cards and enough weapons for all of us if it gets really dodgy"

"Sounds good to me, I'll contact Mike and the others and tell them, and then I'll make my way to the houseboat. Good luck, I'll see you later, bye"

"Good luck mate, see you later"

Wayne switched off his phone and grabbed Celine by the arm and they ran out of the kitchen and down the passage and out of the front door and immediately got in the van. Wayne started it up then reaching for the remote control on top of the dashboard he pressed one of the buttons and the gates automatically opened he dropped the remote and drove out of the gates and along the tree lined drive onto the road.

"Whew we are out of there. We will need to stop somewhere to top up with fuel but we should have enough to get us out of Essex"

"I meant to ask you earlier did you remember to change the number plates on the van?" Celine asked.

"Yea I did it yesterday"

He continued driving and once he was on the A12 heading in the direction of Suffolk he increased his speed but kept within in the speed limits heading towards Southwold. They made one stop on the way at a garage where they got fuel for the van and bought some groceries. Within two and a half hours, they arrived in Southwold, which was still full of holiday traffic, and they slowly managed to get down onto the road alongside the river Blyth were there were a number of different sized boats of different sorts moored up. Wayne drove along until he saw his houseboat named 'The sunrise' and he pulled up in front of it. There was nobody in the immediate area near the boat.

"We should be all right on the boat, no one will notice of us," Wayne said.

"Well let's hope so. We had better get the brats inside first"

"Yea well put them in one of the spare rooms"

They got out of the van, and Wayne walked along the wooden walkway on to the boat and unlocked and opened the entrance door before coming back and unlocking the back doors of the van. They both looked round to ensure that no one was around before they each lifted one of the still unconscious youngsters out of the van and hastily took them on board and laid each of them down on one of two single beds in one of the bedrooms. They closed and locked the bedroom door and went back out and continued to bring all the cases and boxes on board. Wayne put the cases containing the different weapons and boxes of ammunition in the storage areas under the seat cushions of the bunk seats in the living room area. The briefcases with the money, credit cards and passports he put in their bedroom along with their suitcases.

Once finished Celine opened a large bottle of cola and poured them each a glass, and they sat down on the sofa in the living dining area. Wayne looked at his watch and saw that it had just turned ten in the evening.

"When do you reckon those brats will wake up" he asked looking at Celine.

"They should start waking up any time now. I will prepare us some dinner and make some food for them as well"

"Right well hopefully Vince and the others will arrive soon"

"Where they going to stay there's not enough room on the boat"

"They can stay in a hotel or one of the many guest houses, they will find somewhere. I had better give Cyril a call"

"Do you really think we will be ok here?"

"Yes Parker doesn't know about the boat so he won't be able to tell the coppers where we are"

Celine finished her glass of cola got up and went to the kitchen and started unpacking the foods she had brought with them. Wayne took out his mobile and pressed his contact list and having found Cyril's number he pressed the button and it began to ring. Presently a voice answered saying.

"Hello Wayne you alright mate I heard the law are after you"

"Hi Cyril, yes that's right, Celine and I have had to leave the house because one of my ex partners Terry Parker went squealing to the police"

"Really the rotten bastard, so where are you both?"

"We near you mate we've come to the houseboat"

"Ah, you should be all right there. I'll come over and we can have a drink"

"Good because I need to ask you if you can take us across to Holland in your yacht"

"Yea if that's what you want, I will have to drop you off the coast in a dingy because I won't be able to go into any of the ports without customs coming nosing around"

"Thanks mate, so when can you come over so we can discuss the details?"

"I will be over at about eleven because I'm busy finishing off some decorating that I needed to do in one of the rooms in the Guest house is that alright mate"

"Yea we aren't going anywhere, Oh have you any vacant rooms in your guest house?"

"I have just two vacant why mate?"

"Vince, Mike and two of my henchmen are on their way up here so they need somewhere to stay"

"Well Vince and Mike can have a room each, the other two well they could share the room I'm finishing decorating if they don't mind the smell of paint"

"No problem thanks Cyril I'll see you later bye"

"Bye, see you later"

The line went dead, and Celine called from the kitchen saying.

"Did you phone Cyril?"

"Yea he says he'll take us across to Holland on the yacht. He's coming over late this evening to discuss details, and he says he can give Vince, Mike and the boys rooms to stay in"

"That's good; you know you will have to pay him good money if he's going to take us all across to Holland"

"Of course but that's all right, better that than staying here cooped up for weeks on end. Once we get to Holland I can hire or buy a car and we can drive to Switzerland"

"Well thankfully its summer time and not winter, all that snow in Switzerland," Celine said as she came in carrying a large tray on which there were two plates of ham salad along with fresh bread cutlery and a bottle of white wine and set the tray down on the table.

"This looks good I'm starving we haven't eaten since breakfast," Wayne said as he began eating his food.

There came the sound of a van pulling up on the quay next to the boat followed by two beeps of the horn.

Wayne and Celine looked at each other; then Celine stood up and looked through one of the windows that faced the quay side.

"It's Vince he's made it"

"Great get an extra plate and glass he's bound to be hungry" Wayne responded as he stood up and went through the living room and out through the door up on to the deck.

"Hi mate I made it, how's things it's peaceful and quiet round here," Vince said seeing Wayne appear on deck.

"Everything is fine mate come on in we just having some grub, expect you're hungry as well"

"Yea, not half I haven't had a chance to eat anything since early this morning" Vince replied as he followed Wayne back inside the houseboat.

"Hi Vince come and sit down and join us I'll pour you a glass of wine," Celine said as she came back from the kitchen carrying a plate of ham salad along with cutlery and an empty glass.

"Thanks Celine most welcome" Vince replied as he and Wayne sat down.

"So did you manage to let Mike and the others know to come here?" Wayne asked.

"Yea I phoned all of them they should be on their way"

"Good well I've phoned Cyril and he's coming over late this evening to discuss details of getting us all across to Holland in his yacht. You, Mike and the boys can stay at his"

"Nice one thanks mate. If we can get across to Holland, we can make for Switzerland yea?"

"That's right that's what I told Celine, we can lie low there until the heat dies down then decide where we go to. What did you do with the youngsters you had in the van this morning?"

"Left them at all the different locations. Everyone was talking about Parker doing the dirty on you, I warned them to watch out for themselves because there are bound to be police raids at all our premises and your house"

"Thanks mate, yea Parker is bound to have told the coppers the addresses of everywhere. Never mind we should be alright here he doesn't know about the houseboat"

"I better check the brats they should be waking up about now," Celine said as she walked through to the passage where the bedrooms where.

"You brought the two new youngsters with you mate?" Vince asked frowning.

"Yea as insurance, because if things get tough we can trade them"

"Whew that's a bit dodgy mate; you should have left them at the house. You're not planning to take them to Holland as well are you?"

"Why not I can sell them off to some people in Amsterdam I know they will willingly buy them and pay good money for them"

"Were you put them?"

"They are in the spare bedroom; Celine doped them up before we left to keep them quiet"

"Well she will have to keep them sedated because the last thing you want is for them to be screaming and shouting attracting the attention of people walking past"

"She will don't worry have another glass of wine"

Celine unlocked the spare bedroom and went into find that both Rose and Sam were coming round. Rose was the first to open her eyes, and with blurred vision she immediately noticed that she was in a different room to the one she had been in before she had become unconscious from the injection given to her by Celine, who was now standing in front of her shaking her shoulder saying.

"Wake up come on I need you to eat"

Sam stirring at the sound of a voice opened his eyes, and like Rose with blurred vision he realized he was no longer in the same room that he was last in. He saw Celine with her back to him shaking and talking to Rose, who was lying on a bed opposite him. He blinked and rubbed his eyes trying to comprehend what was happening. Rose seeing Sam on the bed opposite her lifted herself up and with a slurred voice called out.

"Sam, Sam is that really you, your here are you ok?"

"Rose thank goodness we are back together again"

"Keep your voices down or else I'll beat the pair of you. Just sit up straight" Celine said waving a finger at them.

"Rose where are we what's going on are you alright" Sam blurted out

Celine turned to Sam as he sat up and said.

"If you must talk, talk in whispers"

"Where are we where have you brought us to?" Rose whispered looking at Celine with an enquiring expression on her face.

"You're on a houseboat miles from where you were before. You won't be staying long because we are all going on a boat across to Holland"

"On a boat and why are we going on a boat to Holland?" Rose blurted out.

"Because we are so there, now unless you want me to give you another injection to put you unconscious you had better not shout or scream. I have prepared you both some food and when you have eaten you both need to get a shower"

"I need to go to the toilet" Sam whispered with a slurred voice.

"Come on then stand up and come with me, be quick"

Sam slowly and stiffly lifted himself off the bed and stood swaying the inside of his head spinning from the effects of all the injections he had been given. Celine took his arm and ushered him out of the small room locking the door behind her. She then led him along a narrow passage and opened the door of the small bathroom in which there was a shower enclosure and wash basin next to the toilet. She pushed Sam towards the toilet and said.

"Hurry up and do what you going to do"

Sam still half-conscious unzipped his trousers and began to pee not really paying attention to where he sprayed. The pee for the most part missed the inside of the toilet and went against the wall beside the toilet and onto the floor. Celine cuffed him round the back of his head saying.

"Look what you're doing you idiot"

"Ache" Sam called out as he zipped up his trousers and turned round.

Celine grabbed his arm and led him out back along the passage and unlocked the bedroom door and pushed him inside before relocking the door and going back towards the kitchen.

"Sam come and look out of the window; there are lots of different boats moored up, and I can see people walking along a path on the other side of the river. We might be able to attract their attention" Rose whispered in a hoarse voice as Sam came in.

"Do you think we are on the Thames somewhere?" Sam asked as he walked over to the window and looked out.

"No, it's too narrow for the Thames. It looks familiar I'm sure we have been here before with mum and dad. I'm trying to remember but my head is so mixed up"

"Mine too they kept pumping me with injections and making me take pills, so I didn't know what I was doing or what was going on. I do remember being thrown on the bed naked and lots of flashing lights, but much of everything else seems a complete blur. I remember hearing lots of different voices though. What did they do to you Rose?"

"You don't want to know they made me do the most horrible and disgusting things that I have ever experienced, it makes me sick just to think about it, so I don't want to talk about it. Like you, they kept giving me injections and tablets which made me feel powerless to do anything. Most of the time I was semi-conscious. Look at my arm it's full of bruises from the injections"

"Yes look I'm the same. I don't know what they gave us. I don't even know what day it is or what time it is my watch has gone"

"Mine has gone to. The last thing I can remember is being in the room they put me in and waking up to see some girls around my bed. They told me their names and how old they were and how long they had been kept in that house. Some had been there a long time. They told me that there were loads of youngsters imprisoned in the house. Then that woman Celine came, and she gave me another injection. I don't remember anything more until I woke up to find us together in this room"

"You met some more girls and they told you there were lots of youngsters imprisoned in the house, gosh what do they do with them all?"

"I'm not going to tell you Sam, all I will tell you is that those other youngsters are really suffering and have been through hell. If we get away from here and get to the police I shall tell them what they told me"

"We must try and escape Rose; we might have a chance seeing as we are on a boat"

"Yes you could be right. Look Sam at those two boats across there the small ones that look like fishing boats, I recognize the signs on them see the letters we are in Suffolk. We are on the river Blyth between Southwold and Walberswick. We are on the Southwold side of the river" Rose said excitedly.

Sam looked across at the two boats that Rose was pointing at and with a semi smile on his face replied.

"Yes that's where we are, we came and stayed on the caravan park near the dunes. Shush listen I can hear voices, yes it's that horrible man who's called Wayne but I don't recognise the other man's voice though"

Sam went over and put his head to the door listening then turning he said.

"Yes that's who it is, and I can hear that horrible woman Celine's voice, as well. There must just be the three of them. Look out she is coming back"

He quickly went and laid back on his bed just as a key could be heard turning in the lock. The door opened, and Celine walked in carrying a tray on which there were two small plates of sandwiches and a slice of fruit cake on each of the plates and two glasses of cola.

"Right sit up and eat these, this is all you'll get until the morning," Celine said as she set the tray down on the end of Roses bed.

"Is this all we are getting we haven't eaten since I don't know how long" Rose blurted out.

"Shut up you'll get a proper meal tomorrow but only if you keep your mouths shut" Celine replied staring hard at Rose.

Rose having sat up shook and lowered her head.

"I will be back in a while to get you both showered. You both smell terrible"

"Well we have been in the same clothes since Wayne snatched us from the forest, whenever that was" Sam whispered.

"Yes that was on Tuesday it's now Thursday evening. When you have had your showers you had better leave your clothes in the bathroom, and I will see they get washed" Celine replied as she turned and went back out and locked the door.

Once she had gone Rose, and Sam took a plate each along with a glass of the cola and sat on the edges of their beds and began wolfing down the sandwiches and cake not saying anything as they ate. Within minutes, their plates were empty, and Sam said between mouthfuls of cola.

"I'm still hungry Rose; we won't last long if that's all she is going to feed us on"

"Sam we need to try and attract the attention of people walking along on the opposite side of the river. We can't shout out or bang on the window because if Celine or Wayne hears us they will give us another injection to knock us out again"

"If we had paper and a pen or pencil we could write a note to put on the window telling people who we are. Our names must have been in the papers and on the television news by now. People will be watching to see if they see us"

"Yes they will, let's look in those drawers and cupboard there might be some paper and a pen in them," Rose said standing up and going over to a single built in wardrobe and opening the door and looking inside. Sam also got up and went over to the dressing table which had two drawers and opened the first drawer and looked inside.

"Rose look what I've found," Sam said as he held up a large pen knife.

Turning her head, Rose looked at the penknife saying.

"Great hide it under your mattress"

She then went back to looking inside the wardrobe in which there were several men's trousers and shirts on hangers and some shoes. There were two small shelves inside the wardrobe and on the second one there were some handkerchiefs and a couple of peak caps and a pair of old sunglasses which had one of the arms missing. Also on the shelf there was some loose change consisting of five, ten and fifty pence pieces as well as some copper coins. On the second shelf, she saw to her delight a couple of black Biros and an old paperback book along with three leather belts that were coiled up. She grabbed the Biros along with the coins and the paperback book and turning said.

"I've found a couple of Biros some lose change and this book we can tear the pages out and write across them Sam"

"Well done there are only men's jumpers in these drawers and a half empty bottle of aftershave. But wait hang on look a screwdriver yes that and the pen knife will do the job I have in mind"

"What do you plan to do Sam?"

"I plan to take the pane out of the window which is not glass but Perspex"

"But the window is too small for either of us to climb out of Sam, so what's the point of taking the pane out"

"Once I have removed the pane we can put our hands out and wave to people to attract their attention and hold up the signs we make. We will wait until after we have had our shower and Celine has locked us back up in here"

"Yes but will you be able to get the pane out?"

"I can try it's held in with a rubber seal so it shouldn't be too difficult to lift the pane out"

"Ok, we will try after we have had our showers, and she has locked us back up. I just hope she doesn't give us another injection to knock us out again"

There came the sound of the key in the lock, Sam quietly but quickly closed the drawer and went back on to his bed and hid the pen knife and screw driver under the bed. Rose did the same with the bits that she had taken from the wardrobe. The door opened, and Celine put her head round the door saying.

"Right you first Rose come along and get your shower"

Rose stood up smiled at Sam and went out of the room. Celine took hold of one of her arms while she locked back up the door then pulled Rose along the passage and opening the bathroom door pushed her inside saying.

"Hurry up and get undressed, leave all your clothes on the floor"

Rose took off her windcheater jacket that had scratch marks and rips in the sleeves as well as earth stains from when she and Sam had been chased in the forest. She then took off her trainers followed by her socks, jeans, shirt, bra and pants. It was then that she saw blood stains in her pants and the inside of her jeans along with bruises on her sides and legs; she suddenly began to get flashes of blurred remembrance of what had been done to her in the studio at the house.

Looking at Celine and shuddering at the memory of what had happened, she said.

"You're a woman you must know what I was forced to do it is disgusting and despicable. Have you no feelings?"

"Girl you're now living in a different world to the one you left behind. You've got to learn to do whatever you're expected to do. I know what you're feeling I went through the same as you. I was snatched like you and sold to Wayne"

"So if you went through the same as me, how can you live with that man knowing what he did to you?"

"There was no escape I had a choice I either did what was expected or he and the others would continue to feed me drugs until I became so addicted I wouldn't be able to go a day without the shots of heroin and snorts of cocaine. I didn't want to end up like that I've seen what happens to girls who become addicted after a time they become useless and so end up being given an overdose and dumped on the streets where they die. If you want to survive girl just do what they want. If you show willing you end up making good money. I was one of the first Wayne bought and knew that to survive I had to play along. I have him eating out of my hand. I've got my own Swizz bank account with enough money and I now live a very good life"

"You know the police won't stop until they find him as well as me and Sam. Then what are you going to do stay with him and face punishment or run?"

"The coppers won't catch him he's too smart Besides we are all going to Holland. Now enough of the talking and get in the shower you stink"

Rose stepped into the shower and having switched it on she took a bottle of shampoo from the shower tray and began to wash her hair, and as she did so her mind began to clear and she thought about what Celine had told her and asked herself if Celine would really stand by Wayne or would she make a run for it knowing that if she was to be caught she would be sent to prison for a long time for her involvement in the crimes he had committed. But what if they did get to Holland then what would happen to her and Sam. She continued to think about that as she took a large sponge and a bar of soap and began to wash her body.

Once finished she turned off the shower and stepped out and took the towel Celine handed and quickly dried herself then wrapped the damp towel around herself saying

"I don't stink now do I?."

"No you don't come on let's get you back to your room your brother has got to have his shower"

Celine grabbed hold of Rose by the arm and took her back to the room, and they went inside.

"Come along Sam hurry up"

Sam followed Celine out of the room, and she locked the door before taking hold of Sam's arm and dragging him into the bathroom. Sam took off all of his clothes and dropped them on the floor then stepped into the shower and began to wash himself.

Once finished and dried like Rose he wrapped the towel around him and Celine led him back to the room and went inside and drew the curtain across the window saying.

"Right I don't want to hear any sound from either of you. If I do then you will both get a beating and be given another injection to knock you out, is that understood?"

"Yes we will keep quite we promise. When are we going to Holland?" Rose replied.

"In a few days until then you will stay in this room. I will bring you breakfast in the morning"

Celine turned and left locking the door behind her.

Rose and Sam sat on their beds not saying anything, both listening to make sure that Celine had gone back to join the men. When they heard;, her voice talking to Wayne Sam reached under the bed and picked up the knife and screwdriver whispering.

"I'm going to start to try and get that pane of Perspex out"

"Do it quietly we don't want them to hear any noise. I will write the signs" Rose whispered back.

Sam went to the window opened out the largest blade of the pen knife which was very sharp and began cutting in a line along the middle of the rubber seal. The blade went through the rubber easily to the pane. Once he had cut all the way round he removed the strip of seal then took the screwdriver and managed to insert it under the lower edge of the pane and ran it along at the same time easing the pane out towards him. Within ten minutes, he had managed to lift the pane out of its frame.

While Sam had been busy removing, the pane Rose had taken the paperback book and tore out some pages and written with the Biro in large capital letters on one of the pages the word 'HELP' she had gone over and over the word until the word stood out. She had then taken another sheet of paper and again in capital letters had written out 'WE ARE' and on the next sheet wrote 'ROSE' and on the next 'AND' then on another 'SAM' and finally on the last sheet she had written 'COOPER' she had gone over and over each of the words until they all stood out.

"Look Sam see what I have written, people are bound to be able to read the words once we have caught their attention. We will have to hold up one sheet at a time " she whispered.

Sam turned and looked at the words she had written then whispered back.

"Looks good, they should be able to read them"

"How are you getting on with removing the pane is it coming lose?" Rose whispered.

"Look I've managed to remove it" he whispered back holding up the pane.

"Oh well done, let's see it we can attract some people's attention"

Rose went over to join Sam at the window. Sam managed to squeeze his arms through the open space and began waving in the hope that people walking on the other side of the river would see him.

Presently a man who was walking his dog stopped right opposite the window as his dog squatted down to pee. The man stood looking around him then his attention was drawn to Sam waving his arms. He looked at Sam and Sam seeing the man looking at him withdrew one of his arms and turned and whispered to Rose.

"Quick give me the first sheet of paper"

Rose passed him the sheet, and Sam put his arm back through the window and held up the sheet in both hands. The man stared at the sheet of paper and Sam still holding the sheet in one hand whispered to Rose as he withdrew his free arm.

"Give me the next sheet"

Rose passed him the sheet, and Sam put his arm back through and held up a sheet of paper. The man continued to stare at Sam, and as he did so a couple appeared pushing a baby in a pushchair. The woman saw Sam and turning to her husband said something. They both stopped next to the man with the dog and started talking to the man. Sam seeing he had got their attention waved frantically then withdrew one of his arms and whispered.

"Give me the sheets with our names on quickly"

Rose passed him the sheets, and Sam putting his arm back through the gap held up each of the sheets one after the other. The husband of the woman having read the names called across.

"Are you Sam Cooper if so where is your sister?"

Sam passed the sheets of paper from one hand to the other and then held up his thumb before withdrawing his arm and whispering to Rose.

"We've got their attention quick they want to see you"

Rose put her face to the opening then waved at the people. The wife of the man seeing Rose must have recognised her because she excitedly said to her husband and the man with the dog.

"It's them the two youngsters who went missing this week. They must be held prisoner on that boat"

All three stared across at Sam and Rose. Then the husband called out just loud enough for Sam to hear.

"Are you being held prisoner?"

Sam and Rose waved and then each gave the thumbs up sign.

The man gave a thumb up and called out quietly again so Sam could hear.

"We will call the police and let them know where you are. You will soon be safe"

Rose and Sam waved to them before coming away from the window.

"Wow! We did it Rose we are going to be rescued" Sam whispered excitedly smiling.

"Yes thank goodness, oh, I hope the police will arrive quickly" she smiled back.

The husband and wife and the man with the dog held a brief discussion before they all hurriedly went off together towards the town centre of Walberswick to find the police station.

Back in the living room area of the boat Wayne, Vince and Celine were sat talking and drinking the wine oblivious to what had gone on in Rose and Sam's cabin. Wayne looking at his watch said.

"Where the hell has Mike and the others got to they should have been here by now?"

"Must have got stuck in the traffic coming out of London" Vince replied.

"Yea I suppose so. Vince do us a favour go and buy some more bottles of wine" Wayne said.

"Yea go on Vince I fancy getting pissed," Celine said.

"Yea good idea why not I'll take the van and have a drive round there's got to be a supermarket or shop selling wine"

"I'll get changed out of this suit and put some casual gear on. Got to look like holiday makers" Wayne said standing up.

"Yea me too," Celine said giggling.

Vince stood up and made his way out onto the deck and went along the wooden walkway and then stepped off the boat onto the quayside got in his van and headed off in the direction of the town. The daylight was beginning to fade, and it would soon be dark. A soft summer sea breeze blew in from the mouth of the river and lights along the quayside began to switch on. On some of the other boats, the lights were already on inside the cabins where families could be seen eating their evening meal or sitting relaxing and chatting. Everywhere seemed peaceful and quiet the sound of the water of the high tide could be heard splashing against the sides of the quay and hulls of the boats along with the sounds of rigging flapping against masts of moored up yachts both on the river and parked up on trailers the other side of the path. Sea gulls swept low along the river occasionally diving down onto the water then swooping back up with small fish in their beaks. Through the open window of his van, he could smell the scent of the river and mud as well as the sea. This is better than all the noise and glaring lights of London he thought to himself as he began to whistle out a tune as he drove along. People were still coming along the quayside some taking their dogs for an evening stroll other returning to their moored up boats after having spent the day on the beach further along and either side of the opening to the river from the sea.

Back on the houseboat Wayne and Celine went into their cabin to change. Wayne was restless and kept looking at his watch as he changed out of his suit into a pair of jeans and sweatshirt.

"What you keep looking at your watch for, why don't you just relax" Celine said getting out of her dress.

"Something's not right Mike and the others should have been here by now. I just hope they haven't been caught"

"No surely not they are too smart for that they would have left as soon as Vince phoned them to tell them to come here"

"Well I just hope they haven't that's all I don't want them telling the coppers where we are"

"No they are not like that scumbag Parker they won't give us away"

"I hope your right there's too much to lose"

"They will be here you'll see now relax come on give me a cuddle, it's not like you to start fretting," Celine said with a seductive smile on her face as she stretched out in just her bra and knickers on her back on the bed.

Wayne seeing her movements smiled back and replied.

"Yea you're right let's have a cuddle before Vince gets back"

He lay down on the bed and took her up in his arms, and they had just begun kissing.

When the sound of a car pulling up sharply outside on the quay attracted their attention. Wayne looked up and listened as he heard voices.

"That's Mikes voice he's arrived thank goodness. Come on quick"

They both leapt off the bed. Wayne dashed out of the room while Celine pulled on a pair of jeans and T-shirt.

Wayne went along the passage and through the living area and had just got onto the deck as Mike and the two heavies from his loan company walked along the wooden walkway towards the boat.

"You three took your time; I thought you might have been caught," Wayne said.

"No mate, don't laugh we got lost, but we are here now. Where's Vince?" Mike said.

"He arrived ages ago he's gone to get some booze, he should be back soon"

Mike and the two heavies Jack and Phil stepped onto the boat, and they all followed Wayne inside the boat and went into the living area just as Celine appeared.

"Hi Celine we got lost"

"Dozy buggers sit down I will get some more glasses. Have you had anything to eat?" Celine said smiling.

"Yea thanks we stopped off and ate on the way here" Mike replied.

"So Wayne that Terry shopped us the bastard," Phil said.

"Yea and you heard what happened to Franky and Tony" Wayne replied.

"Yea it's all over the radio, poor buggers. So what's the plan Vince said something about us all going to Switzerland" Mike said.

"That's the plan I phoned an old pal of mine who's got a large yacht moored up on the river. He's agreed to take us all across to Holland. He's coming over later to discuss the details" Wayne replied.

"Cool, but it could be a bit dodgy the port authorities will be looking out for us," Mike said.

"He will drop us off in a dingy just off the coast, we can make our way in and once ashore we can hire or buy some cars and make for Switzerland. We have plenty of money with us and I've got lots of different credit cards we can use that are in different names"

"We will have to make more than one trip in a dingy because we won't all get in the one," Phil said.

"No we will all get in the one large dingy, there will be eight of us going"

"Eight of us who are the other two, there's only six of us?" Mike asked.

"I brought the two new brats with us Rose and Sam as insurance. I can either hold them for ransom or sell them for a good price to a guy I know in Amsterdam"

"Bloody hell you're taking a risk bringing those two with us. Better to leave them like we did with all the others" Mike replied.

"Yea it's a big risk Wayne as Mike says better to leave them," Jack said.

"No I have my reasons for taking them"

Just then the sound of a van pulling up could be heard through the windows.

"Ah, good Vince is back," Wayne said looking through one of the windows.

They all turned to look through the windows and saw Vince coming along the wooden walkway onto the deck carrying a number of carrier bags. Wayne got up and walked to the door and opening it said.

"Hi Vince, the others, have arrived. What did you manage to get?"

"Yea I see Mike's car. I managed to get us a load of beers, Whiskey, bottles of wine and some snacks" Vince replied as he came in through the door.

"Hi Vince you all right mate" Mike asked.

"Yea fine mate, it's quiet along the river. We shouldn't get any trouble here"

Wayne took the bags and took out all the contents and put them on the coffee table.

"Wayne has just been telling us about his plans for all of us to go on his pal's yacht across to Holland," Mike said.

"Yea it sounds good. Did he tell you we will be staying at his pal's house for a few days?" Vince replied as he sat down and opened a bottle of whiskey.

"No, he hadn't told us that yet. He told us he plans to take those two new kids with him" Jack said.

"Yea daft idea, but he thinks it will be ok, so that's what we will do" Vince replied.

"So when's this pal of yours due to get here?" Phil asked.

"He should be here around eleven tonight. He's ok I have known him for years, he won't let us down" Wayne said pouring out some whiskey.

"Ok, so tell us what you got planned for when we get to Switzerland?" Jack said.

"Wayne began to relay out his plans.

Chapter 9.

While back at Bishops Stortford police station Charley having earlier informed Inspectors Franks, and Munro about what he and Inspector Bryant had found out from Terry Parker went on to explain what he had got planned and what he needed each of the Inspectors to do. He then told them to make the necessary preparations. Inspectors Franks, Munro and Bryant left the office to return to the incident room to make the necessary preparations leaving Charley and Inspector Roberts in the office.

"This is going to be a huge operation involving a lot of officers if all those places of Smiths are to be raided at the same time" The Inspector said after the others had left the office.

"Yes it will but as I said at the briefing the Chief Constable is arranging with the Essex police to carry out the raids on all the Essex locations, and we will have our own Hertfordshire police raiding the Hertfordshire locations. All those that are arrested are to be taken to our headquarters in Welwyn Garden City. The same as with all the youngsters that get rescued. You and I will raid Smith's house with one of the Swat teams along with a team from the trauma section who will take care of the youngsters that we find there".

The phone on Charley's desk rang, and he instantly picked it up saying.

"Chief Superintendent Humphreys".

"Chief Constable Stewart here have you briefed your team yet Charley?"

"Yes sir and we are already just awaiting your signal to go"

"Good and the Swat and trauma teams have they arrived and been briefed?"

"Yes sir"

"Right well everything is set up. I have spoken to the Chief Constable of Essex police and informed him of what we have planned. He has just got back to me to say that all his officers from the different police stations in the different locations have been briefed and are ready to go. I have spoken to the London Flying Squad and they are also ready to make the raid on the London house that Smith is using as a brothel"

"Excellent sir so what time do you plan for all the raids to be carried out?"

"All the locations are to be raided at the same time. This is to be at eleven o' clock this evening. It's now ten o' clock. I take it you can be at Smiths house by then?"

"Yes sir I will be there. All my team are ready and understand that we have a long nights work ahead of us"

"Yes it's going to be a long night and tomorrow is going to be busy too. I have spoken to Rose and Sam Coopers parents, and they are naturally extremely worried. Walter and Nancy Cooper were at the meeting also, and John and Mary Cooper were informed about the fact that you had discovered that Wayne Smith is the son of Nancy Cooper. John Cooper was naturally shocked to learn that his brother whom he had never heard of or seen was the one responsible for all the snatchings of youngsters including his own children. He has spoken to his father who was terribly upset at hearing the news and was insistent that he is brought from Devon to our headquarters to be here to be with his family. Devon police agreed to fly him up, and he arrived an hour ago. Needless to say, it was not an easy time for the Coopers especially for Walter and Nancy to see him after all these years. However, he does not hold anything against Nancy and seems to be the most understanding man. It looks like the Cooper family might at last settled their differences and become united once again. So like all of us they are just hoping that you rescue Rose and Sam"

"Whew it couldn't have been easy for any of them. I wish I could have been there to help"

"I understand but we are all awaiting for you to find and bring back Rose and Sam to safety. All the Coopers have all gone and booked into a hotel and to get something to eat and wait to hear from us"

"Very good sir well as I said we are all ready at this end, so I shall leave now and go and raid Smiths house and will see you later"

"Ok well good luck Charley and take care, see you later bye"

"Bye sir"

Charley put down the phone and let out a long sigh then turning and looking at Inspector Roberts said.

"Come on let's go I will tell you what the Chief has just told me when we are in the car. We are due to hit Smiths house at eleven o' clock"

"Right I'm ready" Inspector Roberts replied grabbing his jacket off his chair.

He and Charley left the office and rushed down the stairs to the incident room and went in and found everyone who was going to be involved were all gathered together chatting.

"Right pay attention everyone we have had instructions from the Chief Constable to proceed. So those of you due to come with me let's get going. Inspector Bryant, Munro and Franks as I said at the briefing you are to return to headquarters to await those who are to be arrested and to carry out the interviews. The remainder of the team I need you to stay here and to see if anyone else comes forward with any further information about Smith and his outfit. I expect that after the news has been announced that Smith has been arrested there are more than likely to be victims who will be prepared to talk about what he has done to them. We are due to raid Smith's house at eleven o' clock. You all know what's expected so let's do it. Good luck everyone"

The swat and trauma teams along with the inspectors followed Charley out of the room and made their way out of the building to the police car park and got into either their own cars or like the trauma team into one of the mini buses and the swat team in another mini bus that had blacked out windows. Charley got in his Range rover with Inspector Roberts. Charley led the way out of the car park, and they all set off some heading for headquarters while Charley along with the swat and trauma team headed for Smiths house in Epping.

On arriving in Epping Charley along with the two mini, buses drove through the town and turned off into the road where Wayne Smiths house was located. Charley and the two teams pulled up on the road at the top of the tree lined private drive that led to Smiths house at ten forty five P.M. The swat team in their minibus then turned into the drive and slowly went down the drive followed by Charley and the trauma team. Three quarters of the way down everyone stopped and the swat team all but the driver got out and continued on foot to the gates of the house. On reaching the gates, the Inspector leading the swat team an Inspector Hollis seeing the video camera mounted on top of one of the gate posts signalled one of the team to deal with it, and signalled another member to deal with the lock on the gate. Both men went about their task and within less than a minute the camera was out of action, and the gates opened.

Inspector Hollis lead the team through the gates, and they split up into three teams of four. One team went round the left hand side of the house leaving two men ready to go through the two side windows and two to go through two of the rear windows. The other team of four did the same for the right hand side of the house, while the Inspector and his four man team made for the front door. On reaching the door, the Inspector waited for confirmation in his earphone that all teams were ready and in a position. Once confirmed he said into his microphone "Go". Everyone switched on the spot lights on their helmets. Those in front of windows using steel batons smashed the glass before entering the house. Two of the Inspectors team using a steel battering ram smashed open the front door, and they all charged into the hall. One man went into the room on his left another went into the room on his right, and the Inspector and the remaining swat officer continued down the hall. The Inspector went into the study where he was met by one of the other members who had smashed his way through the side window of the study.

Once satisfied that there was no one downstairs the Inspector followed by the other eleven men charged upstairs and split up and began searching through all the rooms where they came across those youngsters who had been locked up and left in their rooms since Wayne and Celine had left them since early that morning.

All the youngsters were both shocked and at the same time relieved at seeing the armed police officers burst into their rooms. Inspector Hollis radioed through to Charley to report what they had found. Charley followed by the swat mini bus and the trauma team drove down the drive and through the gates and parked up outside the front door. They all got out and went into the house and switched on the lights in each of the downstairs rooms.

Inspector Hollis and his men having gathered the youngsters brought them all downstairs and into the living room where they sat down on the sofas and chairs. Charley along with Inspector Roberts and the trauma team went into the living room and looked around at the youngsters and immediately they could see that they were all in a bad way. Charley said.

"Good evening my name is Chief Superintendent Humphreys you have nothing more to worry about you are all safe now. I expect you are all hungry so some of my officers will prepare you all something to eat and will need to talk to you as we need to know your names where you came from and what you have been through since you have been imprisoned here. You will then be taken to our headquarters where we will contact your families and make arrangements for them to come and see you and hopefully you will be able to return to your homes".

The trauma team which consisted of both male and female police officers who were in casual civilian clothing all went over and sat down and began to talk to and comfort the youngsters. Charley looked at Inspector Hollis and said.

"Bring your men and follow me"

Inspector Hollis along with his team and Inspector Roberts followed Charley out and into the study where they all gathered round.

"I didn't see Rose and Sam in amongst the youngsters. Have you searched all the rooms Inspector?"

"We have searched all the rooms on all three floors. We haven't searched the cellars as yet. We only found the youngsters that are now in with the trauma team"

"Right go and search the cellars and check to see if there is an attic. If there is then search that, as well . Inspector Roberts you and I need to start looking for any of Smiths business papers. We will start with his desk. But first I need to phone the Chief Constable to let him know that Rose and Sam aren't here"

Inspector Hollis and his team left the study and Inspector Roberts went over to the desk and tried to open the drawers and finding them locked he took out a pen knife from his pocket and began to force the locks. Charley took out his mobile and pressed out the numbers for the Chief Constable phone and waited for a response within half a minute the chief answered saying.

"What news Charley?"

"We have raided Smith's house sir but there's no sign of Smith or Rose and Sam. We have found two young lads aged about seven or eight as well as a teenage boy aged about seventeen who seems to be in a very bad way under the influence of drugs. There are three young girls aged about fifteen or sixteen. The trauma team is with them so we should have their names and where they came from very shortly. All the youngsters look in a bad way due to lack of food and it is obvious from looking at them that they have all been subjected to beatings and the impact of drugs"

"Oh dear oh dear that's not good news. We are getting reports in from the other raids, and the teams have said that they have made a number of arrests and have also found both youngsters in their teens as well as some young adults who have been imprisoned in the backs of the various night clubs and other premises of Smith's but like you no signs of Rose and Sam. I'm still waiting to hear from the flying squad. Oh! Just a moment Charley I'm getting a message" There was a pause then the Chief came back on saying.

"Charley we have received a call from the Suffolk police at Southwold a young couple and a man walking his dog have reported seeing two youngsters who are on a house boat on the river there waving from the window and holding up sheets of paper with their names on claiming that they are Rose and Sam. The husband of the wife called out to the youngsters and asked if they were really Rose and Sam and they put their thumbs up. The wife of the man recognised them from their pictures on the television and papers and says that she is sure that they are indeed Rose and Sam"

"Really right I will take the swat team and make my way to Southwold. I will also phone Jack Cotton I need his forensic team down here at Smiths house to collect evidence"

"Do that Charley I will speak to the Southwold police and let them know you are on your way to Southwold. I will phone you back once I have more details from them. Good luck, speak to you soon, bye"

The line went dead, and Charley said to Inspector Roberts.

"Leave that we need to head for Southwold in Suffolk Rose and Sam has been reported seen on a houseboat on the river there. I will phone Jack Cotton he needs to be here to collect all the evidence"

"Southwold in Suffolk, goodness, ok. We had better wait until Inspector Hollis has finished his search first, just in case" Roberts replied.

"Yes ok"

Charley opened his mobile and pressed out some numbers then waited before a voice answered saying.

"Jack Cotton here"

"Jack get your team over to Epping to Wayne Smith's house the place is full of forensic evidence, fingerprints and all the usual. I need you to go through and look for any business papers Smith might have left behind and any other useful evidence he may have left and gather it all up to bring to headquarters"

"Ok sir, my team are already and have been expecting your call. I have the address, so we are on our way. I will also get some officers to seal the premises we don't want the public or media swarming all over the place once the news gets out"

"Good on you Jack I will let the trauma team know you are on your way"

"Ok good luck sees you later at headquarters, bye"

"Bye Jack"

Charley switched off his phone then said.

"We need to let the trauma team and swat team know what's happening"

Charley followed by Inspector Roberts left the study and went back to the living room where Charley waved to a female Inspector indicating for her to follow him. The woman got up and followed Charley and Inspector Roberts out into the hall.

"We are on our way to Southwold in Suffolk we have just heard that Rose and Sam are being held on a houseboat there. My guess is Smith is there with them. My forensic team are on their way here so wait until they arrive before going to headquarters. Some officers are also on their way to seal off the premises to prevent anybody from the public or media getting in here"

"Very good sir we will wait here. We have the names of all the youngsters here and where they have come from. We have found Joy Manders she is in a bad way like the others. Already we are beginning to learn what these youngsters have gone through, and it's horrendous. It's going to take a long time and a lot of treatment and care before they will be ok to return back to their normal lives. Sadly for some I doubt if they will ever be able to return to a normal life especially the teenage lad Jamie Simonds, who is seventeen and has been here for two years. He is now a heroin and cocaine addict and his mental state is in a very bad way as you can imagine"

"My goodness yes I suspected this is what we would find. Smith has a lot to answer to and when we get him he will be very lucky if he ever comes out of prison again"

"Well I hope you get him and the rest of his outfit. I want to see him as I have a lot of questions I want to put to him"

"We will get him don't you worry and like you I have a lot of questions that I need him to answer. Now I must go I will see you later at headquarters. Thank you Inspector"

"Sees you later, good luck"

Inspector Hollis appeared followed by his team and said.

"We have searched the cellars and attic but no signs of anybody else. There is a lot of evidence both in the cellar and attic that forensics will have a field day with. Oh and we have found a secret room in one of the cellar rooms that are used as a wine cellar. One of my lads managed to break the seal and inside the room we have found a number of different weapons, all of which will be illegal including a powerful crossbow"

"Great good work. Well we need to leave here and go to Southwold in Suffolk. The Chief Constable has received a phone call from Southwold police informing him that Rose and Sam are being held on a houseboat there. So you can bet that's where we will find Smith"

"Right well we will follow you. Come on lads, you heard the Chief lets' go" Inspector Hollis said.

Charley and Inspector Roberts along with Inspector Hollis and his team made their way back along the hall and out of the front door and got into their vehicles. Charley led the way through the gates and along the tree lined drive back up onto the road where he turned back heading for the main road that would connect to the A12 main road going towards Suffolk.

Charley's mobile rang and recognising the Chief Constables number he answered saying.

"Hello sir, we are on our way to Southwold. Do you know the name of the boat and whereabouts it is located"

"Yes Charley the boat is called 'The Sunrise' and it's on the Southwold side of the river Blyth. I have spoken to Chief Inspector Wallis at Southwold police station, and he has already sent two of his detectives to look for the boat. They have located it and report that there are two vans and a blue BMW car parked up on the quayside in front of the boat. Wallis has sealed off the area and managed to discretely evacuate people off the boats in the immediate area to the houseboat without the occupants of the houseboat being aware. He will meet you at the entrance of the river at the harbour. He has a number of armed officers who will position themselves on the Walberswick side of the river directly opposite the boat. You and your team are to follow the Chief Inspector, who will lead you to the boat on the Southwold side of the river. He will erect spotlights on the Walberswick side of the river so that when you are ready the team that side will switch them on lighting up the boat".

"Excellent well let's just hope that if Smith is on the boat he and whoever is with him don't decide to get off the boat before we arrive"

"Well if they do, they shouldn't suspect anything because Wallis and his men will not be seen they will just watch to see where he goes. Whoever is on the boat won't be able to get far without being stopped".

"Very good sir, it's now just after midnight I reckon we should be there by just after 2 a.m. Hopefully whoever is on board may well have fallen asleep by the time we get there"

"Let's hope so. What news from Smiths house"

Charley related what had been found in the cellar and what the Inspector of the trauma team had told him. He went on to inform him that Jack Cotton of the forensics team was on his way to the house along with other officers to seal the house.

The Chief Constable hearing the news said he would phone him back as soon as he received more news from the Southwold police. He then hung up, and Charley explained to Inspector Roberts what the Chief Constable had just told him.

"Better let Inspector Hollis know I will speak to him on the radio"

Charley nodded and yawned it was going to be a long night again, and his brain was busy thinking through all that had happened over the last week. It was turning out to be one of the busiest and most dramatic weeks of his whole police career.

Chapter 10.

Back on the houseboat Wayne had explained to Mike, Jack and Phil what his plans were for when they finally got to Switzerland. He had assured them that they had no needs to worry about money as there was plenty for all of them. They all seemed satisfied with the plans and to know that financially they would be all right.

Celine made some snacks, and they all sat round drinking and eating and began to reminisce about how they had all originally met up and begun working together. Then Wayne asked.

"How come you lot have never fancied taking one of the women that we have traded. Like I took a fancy to Celine and having bought her, she has proved to be the most reliable companion?"

They all began laughing, and Vince said.

"Well that's an interesting question as for me well I have never gone short, some of those young girls I have transported about were quiet willing to let me do with them whatever I wanted. Mind you seeing as they were so full different drugs it wasn't hard. I reckon Jack and Phil never went short either"

"Yea I've had plenty, you be surprised how some of them young women react when I've gone round to the apartments that we have rented out to them to inform them that the rent is going up a hundred percent as well as the interest on the loans they have taken out with us. They beg and plead and are only too willing to do anything to help reduce what they owe. Then when I tell them they have got to work for us as escorts to pay off what's outstanding their high and mighty attitudes change, and I can do anything I want with them. I bet you've had some interesting moments Mike making all those porn videos?" Jack said laughing.

",Not half especially the young girls when they make their first video, and I have to show them what's expected of them. It helps when they have been given the injections and tablets to make them totally relaxed so much so that they will do anything and not really be aware of what they are doing. Most of the time I have had to give them a demonstration and after having made a number of videos and spent time servicing our clients they are like putty in my hands and will do anything I want them to do. Look at that Jamie character I remember when we first got him to make his first video and paired him with Samantha his eyes nearly popped out of his head seeing her naked laying down in front of him and being told he could do whatever he wanted with her. She had been given injections and pills which had the effect of making her so laid back not caring about what was going to happen. But Jamie couldn't have ever had sex with a girl before and didn't know what to do. But once he saw and realised that she was his for the taking, well he just got on with it. The more injections and pills he had, the more rampant he became he was a real stud and would last for hours. The more girls I gave him, the happier he was. Even with the young boys he didn't seem to care he would do whatever I wanted him to do. He's past it now though because the injections and pills have messed up his brain completely"

"I always envied your being able to make all them videos and to be able to have any of the girls that you filmed it must have been great," Phil said with an evil smile on his face.

"Oh, it was especially when I had three or four girls all together making videos. A mass orgy it was"

"Yea your videos always sell well, we've made us a fortune from them Mike," Wayne said.

"I only ever made one video, and you paired me off with a spottily faced youngster who must have only been about fourteen who didn't have a clue what to do I had to show him what was needed, and then when he got the hang of it he was like a thing possessed I couldn't get his grubby hands off me remember Mike," Celine said.

"I remember I was laughing all the time, then Wayne came into the studio and seeing you said enough was enough he didn't want you to make any more videos because he had other plans for you, and we know what they were that's why you're here now" Mike replied.

"I wasn't going to let everybody see what I had chosen to be mine" Laughed Wayne.

They all laughed, and Wayne poured out more whiskey all-round then said.

"What's the time ah it's gone eleven thirty Cyril should be here soon then we can find out when he plans to take us on the yacht"

"I will need plenty of sea sickness pills I hate being on a boat at sea," Phil said.

"It should be all right the weathers great at the moment so the sea should be calm enough" Mike responded.

"It's the thought of going in a rubber dingy that's what will make me want to throw up" Phil replied.

"Nah it's a big dingy with an outboard engine we will be all right, we can land on one of the beaches at night no one will take much notice seeing us come ashore they will just think we have been out on the thing for the day out" Wayne said.

"But what about coast guards they have radar and things so they are bound to pick up a yacht off the coast and a dingy coming ashore" Jack said.

"Loads of people use small boats going up and down the coast so why should they suspect anything unusual. He's not going into any of the ports because once he's off loaded us he will turn round and come back here" Vince said.

"Vince is right look at this place there are lots of yachts and boats moored up that go out to sea for a day's sailing, and some go across to Holland, Belgium and France all the time," Wayne said.

"That's right they do so we will be all right you will see" Mike replied.

There came a sudden knock on the door of the houseboat, and everyone looked towards the door.

"Hopefully that's Cyril" Wayne whispered.

Vince pulled out a large automatic pistol from under his jacket and whispered.

"Take a look Wayne I will cover you"

Wayne quietly stood up and went over to the door, and there came two more knocks on the door and a voice from outside whispered.

"Quick open the door it's me Cyril"

Wayne cautiously opened the door a fraction and Vince stood up pointing his pistol towards the door. The others sat silent also continuing to look towards the door.

Seeing Cyril standing outside Wayne smiled at him saying.

"Fucking hell Cyril we never heard you come on board, come on in"

"Sorry mate, I walked here; everything all right is it?"

Vince put away his pistol as Wayne opened the door wider to let Cyril in. The others relaxed once more, and all began to smile.

"Yeah, everything is fine, you remember Celine, Vince and Mike," Wayne said as Cyril stepped into the living area smiling and looking around at the small group gathered round the coffee table.

"Yes, gosh, it's ages since I have seen you all. I don't recognize those two guys"

"Ah yes well you won't have met them before, the big guy sitting next to Mike is Phil and the tall guy next to Celine is Jack, they run my loan and property rental side of the business"

"Good to meet you" Cyril replied as he came over and sat down the other side of Mike.

"What would you like to drink Cyril?" Wayne asked.

"Oh straight whiskey will be fine thanks"

Vince poured out a large tumbler full with whiskey and passed it to Cyril saying.

"You've changed since I last saw you, you have filled out mate, and business must be good"

"Yea it is Vince, I have got two more guest house in the town and I changed my yacht to a bigger one that also has two powerful twin engines. It cost me a fortune but it's proving to be very useful"

"You still bring in drugs and diamonds then?" Wayne asked.

"Yeah, I now one of the biggest drug dealers in Suffolk. I have a large number of buyers, and as for the diamonds I'm bringing loads in from Antwerp in Holland and selling them to some of the top dealers in London"

"Well business must be good especially as you now have two more guest houses and a new powerful yacht," Mike said smiling.

"So what's to do Wayne you said that you have had to close all your business down and that the law are looking for you?"

"Yeah that's right as I told you on the phone one of our ex partners whom you will remember Terry Parker decided to sell us out the bastard"

"Yeah so you said, and you lost two of your heavies who tried to stop him blagging to the cops. I saw your picture on the television and in the papers and heard about the shootings. That's' rough. So you say you all plan to go to Switzerland, are you going to start up again in Europe?"

"I haven't decided yet, we might all retire and go and live in the Caribbean or somewhere else. But for now our main aim is to get to Switzerland and chill out there until the heat dies down, then we will see" Wayne replied.

"Are you all going to be all right for money when you get to Switzerland?"

Wayne and everyone laughed, and then Wayne replied saying.

"Hark at Cyril, are we going to be all right for money. Listen mate we have more than enough money in Swiss bank accounts, why you need some?"

"No mate I'm loaded. I was just wondering if when you get to Europe you fancy doing some business with me. Remember years ago we did some good business together?"

"Yeah, we remember, we did have some good times, and then we seemed to be busy setting up our own rackets. What had you in mind then?"

"I still have my trafficking business which is doing all right. I bring both girls and boys in from Europe smuggling them in on my yacht. Once here I take them and put them in one of my guest houses where buyers come to buy them. It's ideal when the holiday seasons over because Southwold and Walberswick are very quiet out of season"

"Ah so you still in that racket as well then. I could have sold you all my stock?" Wayne laughed.

"You could have and I would have bought them off you, bit late now".

"Yeah but I have still got two left that I could sell you if you're interested?"

"You have where you got them then?"

"They are here on the boat locked up in the spare bedroom"

"Really what are they and how old are they?"

"A young boy aged eleven and his sister aged fifteen"

"Not the ones that the cops are looking for are they?"

"Yeah I was planning to take them with us to sell to a guy I know in Amsterdam"

"They will be too hot for me to sell mate, but yeah sell them to your contact in Amsterdam. Are they any good?"

"Oh yeah, the girl was fresh meat when I snatched her, she was still a virgin wasn't she Mike. Then we made her make some videos. The boy is fresh never been had, I only made an introduction video of him"

"Wow! Pity that they are too hot for me to buy, but they will bring you a good price, especially the girl if she has a good figure and looks"

"Oh yeah, she's a good looker and has a cute body on her. The boys cute too has that innocence about him you know what I mean"

"Yeah I know what you mean; they always fetch a good price"

"So you would like us to get involved with you trafficking. What would you want us to do?"

"I was thinking that once you get to Switzerland and the heat dies down you could snatch some Swiss girls and boys and bring them across into either one of the small French ports or Belgium ports where I could bring the yacht in and smuggle them on board to bring back here. On the other hand we could sell them across Europe I have contacts all over Europe who we could sell to"

"What do you reckon guys does that appeal to you?"

"Why not I'm up for it" Vince replied smiling.

"I could still continue with the videos," Mike said.

"What about you Jack, Phil" Wayne asked.

"Yeah, why not, we could help with the snatching" Jack replied.

"Yeah, I'm up for that" Phil replied also smiling.

"What would you want me to do?" Celine asked with a frown.

"Same as what you do now because we would need somewhere big enough to store them until we transport them to wherever. So yeah they have to be kept under control and fed, and you are good at doing that"

"Ok, I could do that I suppose, but I thought you wanted to have a break from all of that?"

"I do and we will have time to relax until the heat is off our backs. But you know we will soon get bored, so while we are all taking a long earned break we could also be planning how we can organize things. Cyril here can come over to Switzerland, and we can sit down and get things together, isn't that right Cyril?"

"I go along with that, I reckon we will do well and could open up a whole new set up all across Europe. You could even start your Asian set up again under a new name if you wanted to as well"

"That's very true Cyril and we could even look at different parts of Africa, especially as you have your yacht. There are the pirates from Somali that we could trade with"

"Hey yeah, now that's a thought because there is always a demand for fresh black girls and boys, and with all those refugees out there who knows" Cyril said smiling.

"I think this calls for another drink, let's drink to a whole new set up. They may have closed us down in England, but we have the rest of the world to do business" Wayne responded.

Vince filled all everyone's glasses with whiskey then they all raised their glasses, and Cyril said.

"Here's to a new partnership, may we all make even more money"

They all knocked back the whiskey then putting the glasses down Vince refilled them from a new bottle and said.

"So Cyril tell us what you got in mind for getting us across to Holland"

While Wayne and the others were all chatting and steadily get drunk Rose and Sam switched off the light in their room and stood listening in the dark at the door to the conversations. Then Sam whispered to Rose.

"Did you hear that they are talking about the things they have done to the other youngsters that are prisoners in the house where we were. It's disgusting the things that they are all boasting about. Did you hear what Wayne is planning to do with us when his friend Cyril takes them and us across to Holland? He says he will sell us to someone he knows in Amsterdam".

"Yes come away Sam I don't want to hear any more of their conversations, they are all sick perverts. I can guess what that friend of Wayne's in Amsterdam will want us for and it's sickening"

"Yes and they plan to go to Switzerland and start all over again in partnership with that man Cyril. I hope those people we signalled went to the police to tell them that they had seen us" Sam whispered in reply.

Rose turned away from the door and went over and got in her bed and shivering replied.

"I hope they did Sam because unless the police come tonight we are going to be in serious trouble, in the morning, when Celine discovers you have taken the pane out of the window which is making It cold in here now. That's why I've got into bed to keep warm. You should do the same. We need to try and sleep, but I can't"

"Yes I'm going to but first I want to have another look out of the window"

Sam went over to the window and drew back some of the curtain and peered out across the river. To his surprise he saw that the lights all the way along the path besides the river that had been lit up earlier had been switched off. He also noticed that the lights on the larger yachts, cruisers and other boats moored up on that side of the river had also been switched off, and everywhere seemed to be exceptionally quiet. He put his head out of the window and looked both ways along the river and could see that the only light appeared to be coming from the moon which he could see high above him to the right.

Having adjusted his eyes to the darkness his attention was drawn to his left where on the opposite side of the river he suddenly saw a number of figures moving stealthily in single file along the path. Some were carrying what looked to be large spot lights on tall tripod stands others were laying out lengths of cable back to a large generator. Then he saw more figures appear directly opposite him from behind a fisherman's wooden hut. They were all dressed in dark overalls and thick over vests and steel helmets with visors. All of them were carrying rifles and the man leading them was carrying a megaphone. They spread out in a single straight line and lay down with their rifles all pointing at the house boat. Sam's eyes lit up in amazement as he realized who they were. Quickly he came away from the window closing the curtain and went over to Roses bed whispered.

"Rose, Rose are you awake,"

"Yes Sam of course I'm still awake why?"

"Come and look out of the window you won't believe who is out there opposite the boat"

"What are you on about, who is out there?"

"Come and see quickly"

Rose lifted herself out of bed clutching her towel around her as she followed Sam to the window. Sam drew back the curtain a little way and pointed across to the other side of the river and whispered.

"Look can you see them there are armed policemen directly opposite us and they have got spotlights"

Rose sleepily rubbed her eyes and looked out of the window to where Sam was pointing. At first she didn't see anything then she saw movement. She stared hard for a few seconds trying to comprehend if what she saw was real. Then seeing the reality she grabbed Sam's arm and pulled him away from the window at the same time whispering.

"Oh! My goodness Sam it's the police and they are armed. We are going to be rescued. I wonder if there are policemen lined up on the other side of the boat".

"I expect so I wonder when they will make a move."

"Quick Sam take that chair and wedge it against the door handle. We must stop Wayne and any of his lot getting in here when the police do attack.I know that they will try and grab us to hold us as hostages" Rose whispered.

Sam felt around in the dark for the only chair which was a wooden hardback chair and nearly tripped over it before he picked it up and carried it to the door and quietly and carefully wedged it under the handle.

"Perhaps we should put that set of drawers against the door as well Rose" he whispered.

"It will be to heavy they might hear us trying to move it"

"Come on Rose let's try and lift it. Better safe than sorry because if they do break in here they will as you say use us as hostages"

They fumbled their way in the dark over to the set of drawers; Sam stood one side and Rose the other. They tied their towels tightly then Sam whispered.

"Ok ready lift"

They both began to lift and heavy as it was they managed to begin to move it.

"Quietly Sam don't make any noise"

They struggled to get it across to the door and set it down as quietly as they could in front of the chair wedging it firmly. They both sighed with relief and stood catching their breath, and then Rose whispered.

"Quick let's take the duvets off our beds and lay on the floor and remember to keep your head down because if those policemen start shooting I don't want my head blown off"

Sam nervously giggled and replied.

"Me neither, not after all we have been through"

They went over to their beds and pulled the duvets off each wrapping their duvet around them then laid down flat on the floor waiting and listening for any sounds from either side of the boat as well as inside. But the only sounds that they could hear were of Wayne and his group still laughing and chatting loudly obliviously to what was going on both outside the boat and what Rose and Sam had prepared.

"Are you ok Sam?"

"Yes are you?"

"I'm fine. I just hope they attack soon and we get out of here fast"

"Yes the sooner the better"

Charley and his team having driven with speed arrived in Southwold and made for the harbour where they found that the approach road had been cleared of cars and sealed off with a barrier across the road. Standing to one side of the barrier there were four armed police officers as well as a tall, thick set middle aged man who was dressed in a dark windcheater jacket over which he had a thick bullet proof jacket and a pistol holster around his waist. Charley pulled up at the barrier and opened his window and the man came over and leaning in through the open window said.

"Hello you must be Chief Superintendent Humphreys and Inspector Roberts. Welcome to Southwold I'm Chief Inspector Wallis of Southwold police"

"That's me, and yes this is Inspector Roberts, pleased to meet you, my Chief Constable informed me that you have located the boat where Rose and Sam cooper are being held prisoner and that you will have got some of your armed officers in a position opposite the boat. Have there been any signs of movement on the boat?"

"That's right I have some of my armed officers opposite the boat who have rigged up spot lights ready to be switched on. All the lights along both sections of the river for a quarter of a mile have been switched off. We have managed to evacuate people off their boats that are close to the houseboat. I have two of my men very close to the boat watching to see if anyone on board comes out. They have informed me that they can see five men and one woman in the living area of the boat who are all sitting around a coffee table heavily drinking and chatting. They have identified one of the men as Wayne Smith. He recognised him from seeing his picture on the television and in the newspapers".

"Good and are there any signs of the two youngsters?"

"Yes my Inspector on the other side of the river not long ago reported seeing them both looking out of the window of their cabin. He believes that they have spotted my men and are waiting to see what we are going to do"

"Right well as you can see I have brought our swat team who are ready and eager to go in so if you're ready we will follow you"

Charley and Inspector Roberts got out of the car, and Charley waved to Inspector Hollis for him and his swat team to follow them. The swat team disembarked from the minibus and lined up. Charley went round to the back of his car and opened the boot and took out two bullet proof vests one he handed to Inspector Roberts saying.

"We had better wear these we can't afford to take chances. Oh and you better have one of these"

Charley took out two Smith and Wesson revolvers from a metal case and handed one to the Inspector saying.

"They are loaded I did it earlier"

"Thanks let's hope we don't need to use them"

"I agree I hate having to use them, come on let's go and get Smith"

They both put on their bullet proof jackets and pocketed the pistols as they and the swat team followed Chief Inspector Wallis, who had begun to walk briskly down the road leaving the four armed police officers manning the barrier. At the end of the short road, Chief Inspector Wallis turned onto a hardcore track that went alongside the river. The only sounds to be heard were the lapping of the water on the river and rigging slapping against masts. They continued to walk along in the dark until they got within five yards of the boat then Inspector Wallis stopped and pointing with his hand at a houseboat whispered.

"That's the boat, as you can see there are still lights on. Best if your swat team go ahead and line up alongside the front of the boat and make ready, once in place, we will go forward, and I will signal Inspector Peacock on the other side of the river to switch on the spot lights. He has a loud hailer and will call out for those on board to come out. My two officers who are at the front of the boat will switch on two handheld spotlights that they have with them which will flood light the top deck"

"Right ok, let's get on with it" Charley whispered back.

He turned and signalled for Hollis and his team to move into place. Hollis and his men very quietly moved forward and lined themselves up directly alongside the boat where they squatted down and pulled down their night goggles before aiming their weapons directly at the windows of the cabin that was lit up inside.

Chief Inspector Wallis took his radio phone and pressed a button twice which was the signal for the policemen on the other side of the river to switch on the spotlights. There came a sudden blaze of lights from across the river which lit up the boat. The two officers at the front end of the boat switched on the two powerful lights they had with them, and the top deck lit up. A man's voice from the other side of the river called out through the loud hailer.

"ALL OF YOU ON BOARD THE SUNRISE HOUSEBOAT THIS IS THE POLICE COME OUT WITH YOUR HANDS UP. YOU ARE

COMPLETELY SURROUNDED BY ARMED POLICE OFFICERS"

On hearing the loudhailer announcement and seeing the sudden flash of lights come on lighting up all one side of the boat, Wayne yelled out.

"Shit! Quick there's loaded weapons under your seats help yourselves".

Vince didn't wait he drew out his heavy automatic pistol from the shoulder holster under his jacket and dived to the floor and started crawling for the passageway towards the bedrooms. Wayne, Jack, Phil, Mike, Cyril and Celine also dived to the floor. The men lifted up the seats on the bunk seats they had been sitting on and reached in and grabbed at the weapons that Wayne had put there earlier. Having each got one of the weapons they hastily crawled in different directions across the floor. Wayne and Celine headed for the kitchen, and the others made for cover behind anything they could find.

Mike was the first to fire using an Uzi submachine gun he sprayed a row of shots through the window nearest him, two of the swat team fell backwards against the side of one of the vans and slid down landing in crumpled heaps on the ground.

Jack smashed the window nearest him which faced across the river with the butt of a sawn off pump action shotgun he then pointed it through the broken window and began blasting away.

Phil also with an Uzi began firing spraying shots in a line that went through the sides of the boat and windows directly in front of him.

Cyril had taken cover cowering down flat on the floor under a table. He had taken a pistol but could not concentrate on firing due to all the noise of the shooting around him, which scared him.

Vince having crawled to Wayne and Celine's bedroom and still flat on the floor pushed open the door where he saw a man holding a revolver in one hand and a powerful spotlight in his other hand squatting down on the deck through the window directly in front of him. Instantly he fired off a couple of shots at the man. The bullets missed the man and smashed into the lamp sending it spinning out of his hand. The man fired back, and a bullet tore the side of Vince's right arm. Vince let out a loud yell dropping his pistol at the same time.

Instantly the rest of the swat team, all opened fire bullets, sprayed through the windows and across the room and tore up everything in sight. Phil was struck in the head by one of the bullets and died instantly. A bullet grazed the top of Jacks shoulder and he instantly dropped the shotgun and fell face down on the floor not daring to move. Mikes Uzi was shot out of his hands and like Jack he threw himself down flat on the floor not daring to try and recuperate the fallen weapon.

The table under which Cyril was hiding had its legs torn off making it collapse down on top of him almost knocking him out. He lay stunned and petrified not daring to move.

Wayne and Celine having crawled into the kitchen lay on the floor. Wayne looked up through the window which faced out onto the rear deck and saw three men standing in line near the rear of the boat. He raised the Uzi he had in his hand and was about to fire through the window when Celine pushed his hand down shouting.

"No! Don't they will kill us both?"

"What the fuck you doing you stupid fucking cow, do you want to spend the next twenty years in prison" he shouted back pushing her hand away.

He pointed the Uzi at the window and squeezed the trigger a hail of bullets ripped through the Perspex sending fragments flying everywhere. Charley, Inspector Roberts and Chief Inspector Wallis, who were the ones near to the rear of the boat all dived to the ground as the bullets whipped through the air. Charley fired back blindly as he did so, and one of his bullets went through the window and hit Celine in her back as she laid spread out on the floor. She let out a loud scream. Wayne ducked down lowering his Weapon and as he turned to look at Celine another volley of shots came through the window one of which hit him across the knuckle of the hand he was holding the Uzi in. His finger instantly pulled the trigger, and the bullets sprayed all around the inside of the kitchen smashing everything in sight. He dropped the weapon grabbing his hand and at the same time yelled out.

"Alright, alright stop fucking shooting, you fucking got my woman"

The shooting stopped and Inspector Hollis and six of his swat team followed by Charley, Inspector Roberts and Chief Inspector Wallis, who had all picked themselves up rushed along the wooden walkway on to the boat and burst through the door and into the living area their weapons at the ready. The room was full of smoke and dust and a strong smell of cordite from the shooting.

They all stood looking for a few seconds at the state of the room with its torn up upholstery, furniture, smashed bottles, glasses, plates and windows. Before turning their attention back to the wounded men and the dead Phil.

Two of the swat team rushed forward kicking aside the weapons that had been dropped and handcuffed Mike, and Jack. One of the team went to the kitchen, and one of the others went along the passage where he found Vince propped against the wall clutching the wound in his arm.

"Where are the two youngsters?" The swat man said kicking aside Vince's pistol;

"In there"

Vince replied grimacing pointing to the spare bedroom door with his uninjured hand.

The swat man took a pair of handcuffs off his belt and clamped them on Vince's wrists before turning to the bedroom door and trying to open it.

"Who's there" A terrified Sam called out lifting his head from under his duvet.

"Police its ok you are in no danger now open the door"

"Proof it you could be one of the bad people" Rose blurted out also lifting her head.

"My name is Constable Harding I'm a police officer with the swat team we have caught all the bad people you are safe now. We need to get you off this boat to take you to your parents John and Mary, who are waiting for you at our headquarters along with your great uncle Walter and great aunt Nancy. Your grandfather Joseph is there too"

"It must be the police" Sam said shaking his ears still ringing from the sound of all the shooting"

"Just a minute we need to unblock the door we barricaded ourselves in" Rose replied her voice shaky.

"Ok, take your time, you are safe now" The policeman replied.

Back in the kitchen the other swat officer seeing Wayne sat holding his injured hand and staring at Celine, who wasn't moving handcuffed him and said.

"Come on get up and move yourself out of here now"

"What about my woman she's hurt" Wayne replied looking up and glaring at the officer.

"I will attend to her, now move"

Wayne picked himself up and staggered out into the living area holding his injured hand. Inspector Hollis took hold of his arm. Wayne looked around the room at all the policemen gathered then at the damage that had been made and his pals dead, injured and handcuffed. He shook his head in disbelieve.

Charley stepped forward and staring Wayne in the eyes said.

"Wayne Smith you are nicked"

Cyril emerged from under the wrecked table shaking, and one of the swat team grabbed the pistol from his hand before handcuffing him.

At the same moment, Rose and Sam appeared with the swat Constable who seeing and recognising Charley both rushed forward and clung to him. Rose said bursting into tears.

"Thank goodness it's so good to see you. I knew you would come for us, thank you so much"

"Yes thank you," Sam said also bursting into tears.

"There, there you're safe now there is no need to cry. Come on we are going to take you to see your mum and dad. Where are your clothes?"

"The woman Celine made us leave them in the bathroom she said she was going to wash them" Rose sobbed.

"Inspector Roberts would you take Rose and Sam and find their clothes and see they get dressed then take them and put them in my car"

"Certainly, come along Rose, Sam"

He stepped forward and took hold of one of Rose and Sam's hands and gently pulled them away from Charley saying as he led them out of the room back along the passage.

"Now let's go and find your clothes and get you dressed. You don't want to stay here any longer. We will go and sit in the car and wait for my boss"

"Is chief superintendent Humphrey's your boss then?" Sam asked.

"Yes he is"

"He's our friend, are you going to be our friend too?" Sam asked looking at the Inspector tears still running down his face.

"Yes of course, any friend of my boss is a friend of mine"

"The policeman said our granddad was with our parents and great uncle Walter and aunt Nancy. My granddad hasn't seen or spoken to Walter and Nancy for ages so are they talking together now?" Rose said as they got to the bathroom.

"Yes they are and your granddad has come all the way from Devon just to be with the family"

"Oh great that's good news isn't it Sam"

"Yes but I expect we are going to be in big trouble for disobeying mum and dad and going into the forest?"

"No, you won't get told off; they will only be too happy to see that you're safe and well" Inspector Roberts said smiling.

"Thank goodness for that. We are never going into the forest again on our own are we Rose?"

"No, never" Rose replied.

"That's good now get dressed. I will wait outside the bathroom for you" Inspector Roberts said.

Rose and Sam went into the bathroom and closed the door.

Back in the living area Mike, Jack, Cyril along with Vince all stood in line with their heads down not wanting to look at either Wayne or the police officers.

The swat officer who had handcuffed Wayne came from the kitchen and said.

"The woman is dead"

"Fucking bastards, tell these fuckers nothing guys" Wayne blurted out.

"Shut up Smith. Sergeant get this lot out of here we need to get them to the hospital first to get them patched up before we take them to headquarters" Charley said turning to one of the swat Sergeants.

"Right move yourselves" the Sergeant said nodding to Charley.

. "How about your two officers that were shot Inspector Hollis" Charley asked.

"They are going to be alright they were only bruised thanks to their bullet proof jackets"

"Thank goodness for that. Any other officers injured?"

"No sir thankfully"

"Right ok, well take them to the local hospital. I will join you there in a short while"

Hollis and his swat team led Wayne and his accomplices out and off the boat and back to the mini bus.

Inspector Roberts reappeared with Rose and Sam, who were now dressed and quickly led them off the boat and along the quayside up to Charley's car.

Once they had all gone leaving just Charley and Chief Inspector Wallis in the living room area of the boat Chief Inspector Wallis got on his radio to Inspector Peacock and instructed his team to pack up and come across to the boat. The two officers who had been at the back of the boat came inside, and one of them said.

"What would you like us to do?"

"We need to search around to find whatever Smith has got hidden here" Charley replied.

Without saying anything they all began to search around the rooms and found the remainder of the weapons and boxes of ammunition along with all the briefcases of money as well as the false passports, visa cards which they stacked up in the middle of the living room area floor.

"I expect you will want to take all of this with you Chief Superintendent?" The Chief Inspector asked.

"Yes could your men load everything into the back of my car?"

"Certainly officers Watson and Sprigs you heard The Chief Superintendent quickly get these things moved"

The two officers nodded and began to carry the bags out. Charley then said to Wallis.

"Can you see to it that the dead man and the dead woman's body are removed their bodies need to be sent to the mortuary at Bishops Stortford hospital for examination? This boat needs to be removed from the river and taken to somewhere secure so that a forensic team can examine it for evidence"

"I will get onto that straight away and see that the bodies are removed and transported to the hospital at Bishops Stortford. As for the boat I will talk to the harbourmaster and have it removed from the river and taken to the car park at my police station. We have enough space there and the forensics team can then examine it. The same with the two vans and the BMW parked outside on the quay side"

"Excellent, thank you, and thanks to you and your officers you have all been most efficient and helpful. I'm sorry to have burdened you with this task"

"Not at all it's the first time we've experienced a major incident like this in Southwold. I'm pleased at the way everything went and proud of how well my officers performed"

"Me too it's a shame that the woman was killed along with that man they would have given us important information no doubt"

"Yes but we should be thankful that none of our officers were killed or seriously wounded and that we managed to get Rose and Sam. I recognised one of the other men his name is Cyril Jones. He owns three guest houses in Southwold and also owns a very large powerful motor yacht which he has moored up further back along the river. I have been trying unsuccessfully to catch him for years"

"Really what do you suspect he is into?"

"We have been watching him as I said for a number of years because we have suspicions that he has been using his boat for smuggling drugs and diamonds. We have repeatedly searched his boat and guest houses, but have never found anything. I bet Smith has had dealings with him getting him to smuggle drugs in from Holland or Belgium, and I wouldn't be surprised if Smith was going to use him to get across the channel"

"Interesting yes that would explain why Smith has brought all that money and false passports along with credit cards. He was hoping to get out of the country and I bet he planned to take Rose and Sam with him"

"Well don't worry I will question Cyril Jones and let you know what I find out?"

"Thanks and once I have questioned Smith and his cronies then between us you might well be able to bring substantial charges against this Jones's character, as well".

"I hope so because I suspect he must be into a lot of nasty things for him to have been able to afford to buy two more guest houses and the large yacht that he owns"

Right I had better get going as I need to go first to the hospital to collect Smith and his accomplices then continue to headquarters. I will wait to hear from you within the next few days"

"You will indeed now leave everything at this end with me I will speak to you soon. Good luck and bye"

"Good luck to you too, and thanks again for everything. Speak soon, bye"

They shook hands and went out and off the boat where Chief Inspector Wallis's team were assembled waiting instructions. Charley walked over to his car which Inspector Roberts had brought and parked up. The two officers had finished loading all the briefcases along with all of Smiths weapons and boxes of ammunition. Rose and Sam were sat in the back of the car talking to Inspector Roberts. Charley got in behind the wheel and turned to look at Rose and Sam and asked.

"Are you ok?"

"Yes we are now, but we are very tired and want to sleep," Rose said.

"Understandable so yes get some sleep we have a long journey. I will wake you when we get to headquarters where John and Mary are waiting for you"

"Thank you Charley and John goodnight" Rose replied as she and Sam cuddled up and closed their eyes.

Charley smiled and looked at Inspector Roberts then started the car and turned it round and drove back along the quay to the main road and seeing a sign pointing to the town's hospital he turned and drove in its direction.

"So they have a new friend then Inspector"

"Yes it would appear so" The Inspector replied smiling.

On arriving and parking up outside the Casualty department next to the swat minibus that had arrived earlier Charley turned to Inspector Roberts and said with a smile.

"You had better wait here John with your new friends. I will go and see if they have patched up Smith and his cronies"

"Very good sir" The Inspector replied smiling back.

Charley got out and went into the casualty department where he was met by Inspector Hollis, who said.

"The Doctors and nurses are still patching them up they shouldn't be long. I spoke to one of the Doctors who said that they weren't that seriously injured and wouldn't need to be detained"

"That's good the quicker we can get them to headquarters the better"

"Did you sort things out with Chief Inspector Wallis?"

"Yes and we found loads of valuable evidence in the boat which I have loaded in the back of my car. He is going to send the two dead bodies to Bishops Stortford Morgue for examination. Were you able to find out the names of the others with Smith including those dead? I suspect the woman was Celine, Smith's woman"

"Yes your right her name is Celine Montrose, and the man is a Phillip Griffin, who was one of Smith's heavies. The others are a Mike Elbourn, Vince Carter and Jack Wainwright"

"Very good well done. Has Smith or any of the others said anything of use?"

"No, they are not saying anything, which comes as no surprise. They must be well pissed off knowing that we have caught them and that they haven't managed to get away"

"Well they must have been planning to go somewhere because we found a large quantity of money as well as false credit cards and passports. Oh and the other man who wasn't injured has been taken to the local police station. Chief Inspector Wallis informed me that the man who is Cyril Jones lives in Southwold and that he has been trying to catch him for years as he suspects he is into drug smuggling. He owns a very large and powerful motor yacht and we suspect Smith was going get Jones to take him and his lot across the North Sea to Holland or Belgium"

"Well the only place they will going is prison"

"Yes and with all the evidence we have on them it will be for a very long stretch"

The curtains on the treatment bays opened and Wayne along with the others came out their wounds having been treated and dressed. They were escorted with members of the swat team and were still handcuffed. They all had grim looks on their faces, but none of them was saying anything. People who were sat waiting to be treated looked in amazement at seeing them and the armed officers and watched as they were led out of the department and loaded back inside the minibus.

The Doctor in charge came over to Charley and the Inspector and said.

"We have patched them up and they are fit to travel. They have been given pain killers which might make them drowsy but they should be fit to be questioned in a couple of hours"

"Thank you Doctor, we must go now, bye" Charley replied.

"Bye" The Doctor said and turned and went back to the reception desk to see who was next in need of being treated.

Charley and the Inspector hastily left the department. Charley got back in his car and the Inspector back in the minibus, and they drove out of the hospital grounds.

Once out of Southwold and heading back towards Hertfordshire Charley switched on his mobile and pressed out a number and the phone rang for a couple of seconds before a voice answered saying.

"Hello Charley what's the latest have you got Smith and are the two youngsters safe?"

Charley answered the Chief Constable giving him a full report of what had happened and when he had finished the Chief Constable said.

"Well done Charley. Now once you get back here we will lock Smith and his lot up and you and Inspector Roberts need to get something to eat and then rest. I have rooms here where you can sleep without being disturbed. Smith can wait until later to be questioned. The Coopers have come back here so I will let them know that you have Rose and Sam, which will be great relieve to them. They can take them with them to their hotel. We will need to talk to Rose and Sam after they have had good night's sleep"

"Very good thank you sir both Inspector Roberts and I are exhausted so a good sleep should help us before we question Smith and his cronies. Is there any news about the other raids?"

"Yes Charley lots of good news. The raid on Smiths Brothel in London was a major success, and we have made a number of arrests there, not only those working there, but also some of the clients. Wait until you see the list of clients you will be amazed at who has been arrested, but that can wait until later. The media are going to love this when the news is released. I look forward to seeing you soon, bye for now"

"Bye sir"

Charley switched off his phone and said.

"Well I think you might soon become Chief Inspector Roberts"

But the Inspector didn't hear him he like Rose and Sam had already fallen fast asleep.

Charley yawned and smiled to himself relieved to know that he had achieved what he had said he would do.

Chapter 11.

As Inspector Roberts pulled into the car park at Hertfordshire police headquarters, he glanced at his watch and saw that it was six thirty in the morning. He and Charley had shared the driving up from Southwold. He had slept for the first half of the long journey then Charley had pulled over and woken him up, and they swapped places, so that Charley could get some sleep. Rose and Sam had slept for the whole of the journey.

He found the car park to be full of police minibuses along with assorted cars. He drove round and managed to find and squeeze into one of the few vacant spaces. Then he nudged Charley, who woke up with a start saying.

"What's up?"

"We have arrived"

"Right. Ok," Charley replied as he sat up and rubbing his eyes looked around him.

Inspector Hollis and his swat team followed Inspector Roberts into the car park. The driver backed up directly in front of the rear entrance door to the police station. They all got out and briskly took the prisoners inside and upstairs to the first floor to the reception desk behind which there was a burly Sergeant stood talking to a constable also behind the desk. The Sergeant seeing Inspector Hollis stopped talking to the constable and said.

"Good morning sir, welcome back"

"Good morning Sergeant we have brought in four prisoners that need locking up straight away"

"Have they been formally charged sir?"

"Resisting arrest, being in possession of lethal firearms and attempting to kill members of my swat team will do for now Sergeant until after they have been interviewed by Chief Superintendent Humphreys which won't be until later this morning"

"Very good sir. Constable would you fill out the charge sheets please"

The constable produced a wad of sheets from a drawer under the desk and said.

"Could I have the name of the first one, please sir?"

"Wayne Smith aged 47 of The Willows, Epping, Essex"

"Very good and the next one"

Inspector Hollis reeled off Vince's name then turning to Vince asked.

"How old are you and what's your address?"

"Fuck off I'm not telling you" Vince replied looking half asleep.

"I see ok,; Constable here are the names of the others, forget the ages and addresses for now it's obvious that they aren't going to talk yet" Inspector Hollis replied.

"Ok, take them through and get them locked up. Constable Riley is the night duty cell officer. The cells have been filling up rapidly all night" The Sergeant said.

"I expect so. Thank you constable, Sergeant"

Inspector Hollis along with his team and the prisoners left the reception desk and went through the door that led into a short corridor that led to the cells at the back of the building. They then went through a light grey solid steel door and were met by Constable Riley who seeing Inspector Hollis said.

"Hello sir how many prisoners do you have?"

"Four constable"

"Very good follow me please sir"

The Constable took a bunch of keys down from a hook on the wall, picked up a clipboard from his small desk then walked along a passage way that also had light grey solid steel doors on either side. Half way along he stopped and opened the door on the left and said.

"What name for this one?"

"Wayne Smith"

The Constable wrote the name on the top of the first page on his clipboard and again at the bottom of the page which had a sticky label. He peeled off the label and stuck it on the front of the door. One of Hollis's men removed the handcuffs from Wayne's wrists and then pushed him through the door into the cell. The Constable then locked the door and moved on to the next cell and went through the same process again and continued doing so until all four were locked up.

When completed Hollis and his team left and returned back along the corridor to the reception area where they went through the door to the right which led to another corridor. They walked half way along before entering the swat office. There they took off their gear and put it away in steel lockers along with their weapons. Once finished and sat down the Inspector said.

"Well done everyone now we need to write up our reports and send them up to The Chief Constables office before we all go home ok"

They all nodded in agreement and then took the appropriate forms from their desks and began to write.

Charley along with Inspector Roberts woke up Rose and Sam, and they all got out of the car. They stretched and yawned. Rose and Sam looked around the car park, and Rose asked.

"Have we arrived at your headquarters Charley?"

"Yes at last we are here, we need to take you to see the Chief Constable"

"I'm hungry," Rose said rubbing her eyes.

"Me too," Sam said.

"I expect you are, we will see that you are well fed" Charley replied.

Charley took hold of one of Roses hands and Inspector Roberts took hold of one of Sam's hands, and they walked across the car park and into the building and over to a lift. Charley pressed a button on the wall and the lift doors opened and they all went inside. Charley then pressed the button for the top floor and the lift went up.

On arriving at the fourth floor, they got out, and Charley led them to the Chief Constables secretaries' office. He knocked on the door and went in to find Elizabeth sat at her desk busily word processing reports. Looking up and seeing Charley, Inspector Roberts, Rose and Sam she smiled and stood up saying.

"Ah, at last you're here sirs it's so good to see you, and this must be Rose and Sam. I will let the Chief know you have arrived"

"No need Elizabeth I heard them coming in. Good to see you Chief Superintendent, Inspector Roberts. Rose and Sam I am especially pleased to see you both safe and sound. Elizabeth would you phone down to the canteen and ask them to send up the food I ordered earlier. Oh and phone the Coopers hotel to let John and Mary Cooper know that Rose and Sam have arrived and arrange for them and the rest of the family to be brought here as I know they will want to come over right away."

"Will do Sir" Elizabeth replied picking up the phone on her desk.

"Now Chief Superintendent, Inspector, Rose and Sam come along into my office and sit down".

Chief Constable Stewart said smiling as he walked into the room from his office.

Charley, Inspector Roberts, Rose and Sam followed the Chief into his spacious office where he led them over to a long table that had chairs all around it. He indicated for them to sit down, and they all pulled out a chair each and sat down.

"Knowing that you must all be hungry I requested our canteen staff to prepare some food for you all which should be here shortly. Did you manage to get any sleep on the way here?"

"Yes sir Inspector Roberts and I took it in turns to drive here so that we could each take a nap. Rose and Sam have slept all the way here" Charley replied.

"Good well once your family gets here Rose and Sam you will be free to go with them. I know that they have booked rooms for you in the hotel that they are staying in. Later today you will be visited by one of our female officers who will need to talk to you because we need you to tell her about what happened to you from the time that you went into Takely Forest. I know it won't be easy, but you have nothing to fear because you are not in any trouble with either your family or us. Both they and ourselves know that you have not done anything wrong"

"It was all my fault for suggesting that Sam and I go for a walk in the forest. I am very sorry for causing everybody so much trouble. We will never go there again without one of our family" Rose said as she began to cry.

"There, there don't cry, as I said you are not to blame, and we are not cross with you. Everything is going to be all right" The Chief Constable said smiling.

There came a knock on the door, and Elizabeth popped her head round saying.

"The food has arrived and the Coopers are on their way sir"

"Thank you Elizabeth ask them to bring the food in would you"

Elizabeth opened the door wider, and four ladies dressed in aprons came in carrying large trays on which there was an assortment of foods along with bottles of soft drinks, as well as a thermos of coffee. They walked over to the table smiling and set out the food along with plates, glasses, cups, saucers, and cutlery in front of everybody including the Chief Constable. When they had finished they promptly left.

"Excellent come now let's eat" The Chief Constable said picking up his knife and fork.

Rose and Sam's eyes opened wide at seeing their plates were full of bacon, eggs, tomatoes, mushrooms and fried eggs. Rose stopped crying, and like Sam began to wolf down the food.

They all ate heartily in silence and once they had finished the Chief Constable stood up and went over to his office door and opening it he beckoned to the four canteen ladies who were stood in Elizabeth's office to come back in and clear the table. They promptly came in cleared and wiped the table before leaving.

As they were leaving Elizabeth appeared and said to the Chief Constable.

"The Coopers are here sir"

"Ah good show them in would you Elizabeth"

John and Mary Cooper along with Walter, Nancy and Joseph came into the room. Rose and Sam immediately jumped up and ran over to their mum and dad who smiling hugged them both. John Cooper, a tall, thick set man with neat short light brown hair and grey eyes said.

"It's so good to see you both, thank goodness you are safe"

Mary Cooper, who was of medium height slim with shoulder length fair hair and blue eyes, then said.

Page 268

"Yes thank goodness, we have been so worried, but you are here now and there is no need to get upset we are not cross with either of you"

Walter and Nancy also rushed over and hugged Rose and Sam. Nancy was crying with relief at seeing them both and Walter too had tears in his eyes.

Joseph Cooper, a tall medium, built man with dark brown hair that was going grey stood to one side looking on in embarrassment. Before coming over and hugging the two children with tears in his eyes and saying.

"I am so sorry for what you have been through, please forgive me"

Rose and Sam looked at Joseph both with tears running down their faces and Rose suddenly said.

"Granddad why are you sorry it's not your fault, don't be upset"

Joseph hugging them looked away towards the Chief Constable who looking back shook his head holding a finger to his lips to indicate that the two children had not been told that it was his first son who was responsible for what they had been through. Joseph nodded back in recognition.

Charley and Inspector Roberts who having stood up came over, and John Cooper took hold of Charley's hand shaking it saying.

"Charley we can never thank you enough for all your hard work in bringing Rose and Sam back to us safely. We will always be in your debt"

Charley looking embarrassed replied.

"No John you don't owe me anything, I said I would find them, and I did. That's all part of my job"

"Well I can't thank you enough we are all so grateful to you"

Mary came over and shaking Charley's hand said.

"John's right we owe you so much. Thank you from the bottom of my heart"

"I'm relieved to see that as a family you are all reunited. You must also thank my senior Inspector here Inspector John Roberts who has worked very hard also" Charley replied.

John Cooper shook hands with Inspector Roberts saying.

"Thank you too for all you efforts we as a family are most grateful to you"

Finally when everyone had finished thanking Charley, Inspector Roberts and the Chief Constable the Chief Constable said.

"We are all delighted to know that we have been successful in getting Rose and Sam back to you safely. We still have a lot of work to do as we will be busy interviewing those people who we have caught in order to bring them to trial"

"You need to get some rest you all look exhausted. We will be staying here in Welwyn garden city for the next few days before going to Walter and Nancy's. I expect you will need to talk to Rose and Sam, as well. So we will go now; you know where we are staying, so please call us when you need us" John Cooper said.

"Thank you, and yes, we will need to talk to Rose and Sam. I have arranged for one of my female officers who is very experienced in these situations to come to the hotel where you are staying later today to talk to them both" The Chief Constable replied.

Then taking John to one side he whispered.

"They will both need to have a medical examination as well, and may well need to have counselling because of what they have been through. I hope you understand what I am saying"

John Cooper's eyes widened then nodding he whispered back.

"Do you have reason to think that they may have been sexually abused, is that what you are saying?"

"We don't know for sure at this stage, but we have to check, and if they have then they will need to receive professional counselling which we can arrange because the trauma is bound to come out" The Chief Constable whispered back.

"Good gracious I hope they haven't I understand what you are saying. We will have to wait and see" John Cooper whispered back.

"Is everything all right" Mary Cooper asked seeing her husband and the Chief Constable whispering together.

"Yes dear I will explain to you later. Right we need to go, come along Rose and Sam" John Cooper replied looking grim faced.

"Thank you so much Charley and John and you to Chief Constable Stewart, we will see you very soon" Rose Said.

"Yes thank you very, very much, bye," Sam said.

The Cooper family then all left the room and Elizabeth took them down in the lift.

Once they had gone Chief Constable Stewart closed his office door, raising his eyebrows and sighing then beckoned for Charley and Inspector Roberts to come over and sit back down at the table.

They all sat down, and Chief Constable Stewart said.

"Charley, John I won't keep you because I know we are all tired and need to get some proper sleep. It has been a busy and traumatic week for all of us. None more so than for the Cooper family. However, I wish to thank you both for the splendid work that you have carried out so far on this case. Thanks to the information that you got from that man Terry Parker we have managed to carry out raids on all of the premises that we know Wayne Smith owned. Apart from the arrests that you made which thankfully has resulted in getting Wayne Smith and his partners. I can tell you that we have arrested over twenty others who worked for Smith in his various establishments. That doesn't include those whom we found hidden in those establishments and arrested. They included both young women and men who are foreign nationals from the Philippines, Thailand, China, North Africa, Romania, and Poland. All of them in a very bad way and it would appear that they have all been bought or brought into this country with false papers and passports and forced into prostitution. The Home Office will be informed and further enquiries will have to be made as to what is to become of them"

"Excuse me interrupting but what of the young girls and boys that were being held prisoner in Smiths house?"

"Yes they have all been brought from the house by the trauma team and have been put into a secure children's shelter. They are all in a very bad state mentally and physically and are going to need a considerable amount of psychological counselling and medical treatment before they are ready to return to their parents"

"Yes they looked in a very poor state when we saw them at Smith's house"

"Yes and they are not the only ones, we discovered more youngsters imprisoned in the backs of Smith's night clubs, massage parlours, nail bars all aged between thirteen and seventeen. They have also been taken to a secure child's home for treatment"

"Strewth! What about at the house in London that Smith was using as a brothel?" Inspector Roberts asked.

"You may well ask Inspector, when the Flying Squad raided the place they found both young girls and boys aged between six to seventeen along with both young adult women and men. They were all working against their will as prostitutes. The staffs running the place have all been arrested. A number of clients' were caught and arrested included two company directors from large, well-known companies in London. Four businessmen from Saudi Arabia, two Pakistani business men who have a taxi business in London, a member of the house of Lords namely Lord Collision, as well a TV and Film actor who you are bound to of heard of namely Peter Williamson"

"Bloody hell really!" Charley said.

"Yes really, he was found naked in bed with a young boy of seven who was in a semi state of consciousness"

"How disgusting the perverted bastard. Little did we know when we started this enquiry that it would lead us to the smashing of what appears to be a major crime outfit" Charley said with a loud sigh.

"I agree and the media are going to have a field day when we break the news. Smith and all his lot are going away for a very long time you can be sure of that. Oh and when they raided the adult shops they found stacks of underage porn videos including one that young Rose was forced to make. I haven't told John and Mary about that yet. That poor child's mind must be in turmoil, but so far she has managed to keep a brave face, but you can bet that young girl is going to need a lot of counselling"

"Oh, my goodness! That bastard Smith has a great deal to answer for. Such a tragedy, the poor girl. She never said anything to us on the way here did she John about what she and Sam had gone through" Charley said looking ashen.

"No, neither of them said anything, they are keeping it to themselves. What a humiliation for them" Inspector Roberts replied with a look of shock.

"Yes and before we have finished with this case you can bet that there will be a great deal more traumatic stories to emerge. However, we first need to get some sleep. Come I will show you to your rooms, I have made arrangements for the two of you to sleep here we have rooms for such events as you know. I will see that you are woken just before lunch time. I will be back in the office by then. Then when you have had a chance to shower and shave and have had some lunch I know you will want to interview Smith and his cronies. They can sit tight in their cells for now"

"Thank you sir that will be fine with us won't it John," Charley said.

"Yes I'm looking forward to interviewing Smith and his partners" the Inspector replied as they all stood up.

"My deepest thanks go to you both and of course to everyone who has managed to bring down Smith and his sordid empire" the Chief Constable said as they all walked out of the office.

"Not at all we're both pleased to know that we have been successful in doing our job. This is turning out to be the biggest case that we have ever had to take on" Charley replied.

The outcome.

Following all the interviews with all those arrested they were all charged with a number of different offences. They each had their own legal representatives who tried to protect their clients against some of the charges made in the hope that they would receive lighter sentences.

All of the youngsters who had been found were also interviewed by police officers who were experienced in dealing with child sexual abuse cases. They were also interviewed by social workers, psychologists, and Psychiatrists, and in a number of cases had to undergo medical examinations.

The adult victims that were also found which included both males and females some of whom had been brought into England on false papers and passports all underwent interviews with the police, social workers, Psychologists, and Psychiatrists and home office staff.

Six weeks later the case was brought to court by which time all the evidence had been gathered and all the interviews had been completed.

The court case took a further four weeks for the court to try all those who had been arrested and charged. Needless to say, the media attended the court eager to hear the full story and every day the papers and television channels reported on who and what had happened.

While the courts were busy hearing the evidence against the accused there was also an ongoing enquiry and investigation to trace back all the paperwork that had passed through the UK immigration and passport control offices both in the UK and the British

Immigration departments abroad. All the paperwork for those who had been brought into the country with a false visa, passports and papers had to be traced and checked which took considerable time and manpower.

The results of which were that a number of immigration staff both in the UK and abroad were found to have flouted the law and received substantial bribes to turn a blind eye to those coming in with false documents. Those who were found to have done so were arrested and charged.

Thanks to the cooperation of a number of overseas foreign immigration offices investigations were also carried out within the different departments which found that a number of immigration officers had also flouted the law and received bribes to turn a blind eye to those applications. Again those found to have done so were also arrested and charged by their own police forces.

Due to the publicity of the court hearings there were questions raised in the houses of parliament by a number of opposition MPs who wanted to know what the present government was doing to stop human trafficking in the country. The Prime Minister said in reply that he and his government were doing everything that they could to crack down on human trafficking, not just cases of those trafficked for sexual abuse, but also those who were being trafficked for slave labour. He announced that a new Crime Agency had been set up to deal with all areas of major crime including human trafficking and that they were having considerable success in the fight against major crime. He went on to mention that there were a number of charities now involved in supporting victims of human trafficking in the country and that they were all doing very difficult work.

Once the court had heard all the cases of those who had been arrested and charged and found to be guilty of a variety of different offences, the Judge passed out the following sentences.

Wayne Smith aged 47: Was sentenced to a maximum of 29 years on charges which included kidnapping and holding against their will young children. Pimping, running premises for the use of prostitution, Drug smuggling and selling illegal hard drugs, forcing children and adults to engage in prostitution under threat to themselves or family, the making of and sanctioning the sale of underage porn videos, bringing male and female overseas nationals into the country under false pretences with the intent of either selling them for sexual abuse or forcing them to work for him as prostitutes , forcing adults and children into receiving harmful drugs, the possession of illegal firearms and ammunition with the intent to use against others, resisting arrest and shooting at police officers with intent to kill, the carrying out of an armed robbery on a bank and building society. He was put on the child sex offender register for life.

Vincent Carter aged 46: Was sentenced to a maximum of 20 years on charges of pimping, drug smuggling and selling illegal hard drugs, forcing adults and children to engage in prostitution, the holding in imprisonment against their will young children in captivity, the sales of underage porn videos. Being in possession of illegal firearms and ammunition. Resisting arrest and shooting at police officers with the intent to kill, the taking part in an armed robbery of a bank and building society. He was put on the child sex offender register for life.

Michael Elbourn aged 43: Was sentenced to a maximum of 20 years on charges of pimping, drug smuggling, selling illegal hard drugs, forcing children and adults to engage in prostitution, the holding in imprisonment against their will young children. The making and selling of underage porn videos, the forcing of children to engage in sexual activities for the purpose of filming them, being in possession of illegal firearms and ammunition. Resisting arrest and shooting at police officers with intent to kill, the taking part in an armed robbery of a bank and building society. He was put on the child sex offender register for life.

Jack Wainwright aged 36: Was sentenced to a maximum of 18 years on charges of pimping, drug smuggling, selling illegal hard drugs, forcing adults and children to engage in prostitution, the holding in imprisonment against their will young children in captivity, the sales of underage porn videos. Physical and mental assault of children and adults, blackmail of adults with threats of violence. Being in the possession of illegal firearms, and ammunition. Resisting arrest and shooting at police officers with intent to kill. He was put on the child sex offender register for life.

Cyril Jones aged 42: Was sentenced to a maximum of 20 years on charges of pimping, smuggling both children and adults in England from Europe against their consent, imprisoning both children and adults, forcing both children and adults to indulge in prostitution against their consent, forcing both children and adults to indulge in lethal illegal drugs, drug smuggling, the sale of illegal hard drugs, the smuggling and sale of diamonds, being in possession of an illegal firearm and ammunition, resisting arrest. He was put on the child sex offender register for life.

Carlos Mendos aged 47: Who was stopped at Heathrow airport with Samantha Brooks, whom he was trying to get out of the country against her will using a false passport for her along with false immigration papers, was sentenced to 18 years on charges of human trafficking ten children aged seven to sixteen. Having sex with children aged seven to sixteen. Drug smuggling and the sale of illegal hard drugs. He was put on the child sex offender list for life. Once he had completed his sentence he was to be deported back to Brazil where he would face further charges in his own country for sexual offences with children as well as owning and running illegal brothels that forced children into prostitution. He was banned from ever returning to the UK.

Terry Parker aged 47: Was given witness protection but never managed to leave the country he was shot and killed one evening by an unknown assassin when he went for a walk from the safe house that he had been put in while his new identity was being processed. The police have yet to arrest anyone for his killing.

Lord Collision aged 56: Was stripped of his title and sentenced to 10 years on charges of having sex with both male and female children aged between six and fourteen. He was put on the child sex offender register for life.

Peter Williamson aged 35: Film and TV Personality. Was sentenced to 10 years on charges of having sex with both males and female children aged between six and fifteen. He was put on child sex offender register for life. He was later stabbed to death by a fellow inmate shortly after beginning his sentence.

All those also found using the brothel were sentenced to between 8 to 10 years and were put on the sex offender register. Those who had come on business from abroad were to be deported and not be allowed back into the country again once they had completed their sentences.

The staff who were involved in running Wayne Smith's brothel, night clubs, massage parlours, nail bars, adult shops, being part of his property rental and loan company were also given prison sentences for being accomplices in his sordid businesses.

The victims.

The children and adults, who had been found and had been forced into captivity and prostitution where they were sexually abused, numerously assaulted both mentally and psychically and forced to take drugs, all needed medical attention and psychiatric counselling. None of them has yet got over their ordeal. Those from within the UK have returned to their families.

The majority of those who had been trafficked from abroad were returned to their families in their own countries where they underwent further shame within their own community. Some are known to have been snatched by other trafficking gangs who sold them to pimps who have forced them to return to prostitution in other countries.

For Rose and Sam Cooper they have had to undergo a medical examination and psychiatric counselling. Rose had a complete nervous breakdown and is still receiving counselling and has not been able to return to school. She has become withdrawn not daring to leave her home and is being taught by private tutors in her own home. Sam has returned to his school and is excelling in his studies and has said that when he grows up he wants to become a police officer and work with the National Crimes Agency to combat major crimes including human trafficking and slavery.

Joseph Cooper on hearing the results of the court hearings and what his son Wayne Smith had grown up to become had a complete nervous breakdown which resulted in his having a massive heart attack from which he died.

Walter and Nancy Cooper have moved from their peaceful home in Essex and have gone to live closer to John and Mary Cooper to help support them with Rose. They are both working and raising funds to support those charity organisations that help victims of human trafficking.

John and Mary are continuing to run their business as well as ensuring that both Rose and Sam are given all the support that they need. They have vowed to donate twenty five percent of their profits towards supporting those charity organisations that help victims of human trafficking.

Rewards.

Chief Superintendent Charles Humphreys has joined the National Crimes Agency. He received the Queens Commendation medal as well as an MBE for his work in bringing down Wayne Smith's criminal empire.

Inspector John Roberts was promoted to Chief Inspector and also received the Queens Commendation medal. He has also joined the National Crimes Agency.

Inspectors Munro, Bryant, Franks were also promoted to the rank of Chief Inspector and are still based at police headquarters in Hertfordshire.

Chief Constable Stewart was given a knighthood and has taken early retirement from the police force and is devoting his time to supporting and raising funds for one of the charities involved in supporting victims of human trafficking.

Here are some statistics about human trafficking in the United Kingdom.

UK Human Trafficking Centre (UKHTC) Statistics. In 2013 UKHTC report found.
. 2,255 Potential victims of human trafficking were identified in the UK in 2012.
. 549 (24%) of these were children.
Gender of victims.
Of the 549 potential victims known to UKHTC in 2012.
. 310 were female.
. 208 were male.
. 31 gender unknown.
Age of victims.
Of the 549 potential victims known to UKHTC.
. 70 (13%) were aged up to nine years old.
. 113 (21%) were aged between 10 and 15 years.
. 142 (26%) were aged between 16 and 17 years.
. 96 (17%) were children when the exploitation commenced but has since become adults.
. 128 (23%) were recorded as a child with no further information relating to their age provided.
Types of exploitation.
Of the 549 potential child victims known to the UKHTC in 2012 the types of exploitation were
. Unknown (174, 32%)
. Sexually exploited (152, 28%)
. Criminal exploitation (132, 24%) of those who were believed to have been criminally exploited, the most prevalent subtypes were cannabis cultivation. (56, 42%) and benefit exploitation (55, 41%)
. Multiple exploitation types (37, 7%)
. Domestic Servitude (35, 6%)
. Labour exploitation (18, 3%)
. Organ harvesting (1, 1%)

Country of origin.
Of the 549 potential child victims known to the UKHTC in 2012 the most prevalent countries of origin were
. Vietnam (103, 19%)
. Nigeria (78, 14%)
. Slovakia (43, 9%)
. Romania (39, 7%)
. UK (38, 7%)
Source: Serious Organised Crime Agency. (SOCA) and UK Human Trafficking Centre (UKHTC) 2013.

NSPCC Statistics.
The NSPCC's Child Trafficking Advise Centre (CTAC).
Is a specialist service providing information and advice to any professional working with children or young people who may have been trafficked into the UK. The statistics below are from the services provided by CTAC between November 2007 and October 2012.
. Between November 2007 and October 2012 CTAC dealt with 785 cases.
Gender of victims
Of the 785 cases CTAC dealt with between November 2007 and October 2012.
. 427 were girls
. 327 were boys.
.31 children where gender was not disclosed (cases where CTAC gave advice without knowing the details of the child)
Types of exploitation
Between November 2007 and October 2012 CTAC dealt with
. 176 cases of children trafficked for sexual exploitation

. 160 cases of children trafficked for criminal activity
. 71 cases of children trafficked for domestic servitude
. 71 cases of children trafficked for benefit fraud
. 49 cases of children trafficked for labour exploitation
Country of origin
Of the 785 cases CTAC dealt with between November 2007 and October 2012
. 40% were from Asia
. 34 % were from Africa
. 23% were from Europe
. 1% from South America
. 1% from Caribbean
1% from Mediterranean

The UK National Referral Mechanism (NRM) received 1,186 referrals of potential victims of trafficking in 2012
. 372 (31%) of these were minors*
*The NRM defines "Minors" as children and young people aged 17 years or under at the time of the first claimed exploitation.

Gender of victims
Of the 372 referrals about potential child victims received by the UK National Referral Mechanism (NRM) in 2012

. 99 were trafficked for labour exploitation (24 females, 75 males)
. 79 were non-UK nationals trafficked for sexual exploitation (74 females, 5 males)
. 44 were trafficked for domestic servitude (34 female, 10 male)

. 22 were UK nationals trafficked for sexual exploitation (21 females, 1 male)
. 1 was trafficked for organ harvesting (female)
.127 were trafficked for unknown reasons (57 females, 70 males)

Country of origin
Of the 372 referrals about potential victims who were minors received by the UK National Referral Mechanism (NRM) in 2012, the top 5 counties of origin were
.96 from Vietnam
.67 from Nigeria
.25 from Albania
.22 from UK
.20 from China
Source: Serious Organised Crime Agency (SOCA) and United Kingdom Human Trafficking Centre (UKHTC) (2012)
United Kingdom National Referral Mechanism provisional statistics 2012.

List of some of the organisations involved in supporting victims of human trafficking in the UK.

The Human Trafficking Foundation
The Salvation Army
The Poppy project
CALLA
NSPCC
Dr Barnado's
Care UK
The Children's Society
City Hearts
Children and Families Across Borders
BAWSO (Black Association of Women Step Out)
Counter Human Trafficking Bureau
EaVes
ECPAT UK
Equality Now
The gangmasters licensing agency
Gloucestershire Domestic Violence Support and Advocy Project
Helen Bamber Foundation
HERA
Hope for Justice
Housing for women
International Justice Mission UK
The International Organisation for Migration
Jigsaw 4u International
Jubilee Campaign
Just Enough UK
Love146
The Medaille Trust
The Northern Ireland Law Centre
Odanadi UK

Purple Teardrop Campaign
STOP THE TRAFFIK
UNCHOSEN
UNSEEN
Victim Support
The West Midlands Regional Anti Trafficking Network
The William Wilberforce Trust

All of the above can be contacted on the internet.

I wish to apologies to those organisations that I have not included this is not deliberate it is because I am not aware that you exist.

I would ask that all of you who have a concern about horrors of human trafficking. Please do get involved in giving your support and or donations to all those organisations who are working hard to combat Human Trafficking.

Richard Neave, Author.

My other forthcoming books to look out for.

"The price of Art".

When six friends, who all share similar interests in the history of art, architecture, and antiques, decide to go and explore an old boarded up country mansion that belongs to a rich and powerful member of the titled British gentry. Little are they to know that their discoveries in the mansion are to change their lives forever.

This is a story about obsession, greed, betrayal, murder and double-cross, which asks the question, what is the price of art.

"Life in the Shadows"

In May 1940 Adam Jones along with other members of the British Expedition Force, made his escape from the beaches of Dunkirk in France back to England. However he wasn't to know that he would soon be returning to Nazi occupied France, only this time he would be going back as an agent of the SOE. (Special Operations Executive).

Although Adam Jones is a fictional character his story is based on the truths that describe how agents were recruited, trained and used by the SOE during WW2, and the dangers they experienced living a life in the shadows.

Follow Adam Jones hair raising wartime exploits in France and Belgium.

"Return to the Shadows".

Follow Adam Jones as once more he returns to Nazi occupied France. Where he is expected to gather important information that will help towards the invasion and liberation of France and Europe, but whom can he trust when his enemies are not just the Nazis but some of those from within as well as closer to home. This is a story full of twists, turns and betrayals.

www.ingramcontent.com/pod-product-compliance
Lightning Source LLC
Chambersburg PA
CBHW030959260626
47169CB00002B/618